The Neighborhood

Dominic Fino

Published by Dominic Fino, 2024.

THE NEIGHBORHOOD

First edition. September 18, 2024.

Copyright © 2024 Dominic Fino.

ISBN: 979-8227772527

Written by Dominic Fino.

Also by Dominic Fino

Paul Marco Thrillers
Lights Out
Nothing to lose
Death Hawaiian Style
Vendetta Vegas Style

Standalone
The Neighborhood

Table of Contents

Acknowledgement

I am grateful to my loving wife Linda, who read my manuscript several times and gave me advice and encouragement to push forward. She is not only my writing companion but also my life partner.

Chapter 1

The sun was beginning to dip below the horizon, casting long shadows across the narrow streets of Little Italy. The scent of fresh bread lingered in the air, mingling with the rich aroma of garlic and basil from nearby trattorias. It was a familiar comfort, one that Frank Solveti and Gino Colombo had grown up with. But tonight, that comfort was shattered by news that spread like wildfire through the tight-knit community.

Frank and Gino grew up on the vibrant streets of Baltimore's Little Italy, a place where every corner held memories, and every face was familiar. From a young age, they attended St. Leo's Church, where they served as altar boys, learning discipline and faith from the stern but kind-hearted priests. They were educated by nuns in grade school, who enforced strict rules but always seemed to care, and later by Jesuit priests in high school, who challenged them to think critically and broaden their horizons. This upbringing forged a deep, long-standing relationship with the Catholic Church that would stay with them throughout their lives.

The two friends spent their free hours working as busboys in the local restaurants, carrying trays piled high with pasta dishes and learning the rhythms of their bustling neighborhood. It was a place where the aroma of garlic and tomatoes simmered in the air, where old men argued over espresso at café tables, and where the traditions of the old country blended seamlessly with American life.

Organized sports never held much appeal for Frank and Gino. Instead, they found joy in the simplicity of games like stickball and curbball played in the narrow streets of Little Italy. The rules were made up on the spot, and the games often stretched into the evening, with the sounds of laughter and shouts echoing off the brick buildings. There were no coaches, no referees, and no adults to tell them what they were doing wrong—just the freedom to play, argue, and make up their own rules as they went. Those streets were their playground, and every game was a battle for bragging rights that would last until the next afternoon.

Their friendship was as solid as the cobblestones under their feet. Together, they navigated the joys and challenges of growing up in a tight-knit community where everyone knew everyone else, and the past was never far from the present. Life in Little Italy was far from easy, but it was good. There was a sense of security in knowing that your neighbors had your back, that you could always count on a friendly face at the corner bakery, or hear a familiar voice calling you by name from an open window above.

In a neighborhood where traditions ran deep and family ties were strong, Frank and Gino were more than best friends—they were brothers, bound by shared experiences, laughter, and a loyalty that only the streets of Little Italy could forge.

After graduating high school, they both enlisted in the Army and were sent to Vietnam, where they each served two tours of duty. Frank was in the infantry, while Gino was in a helicopter aviation unit. Their tours were like so many others—marked by death and destruction that no one should have seen at such a young age. Despite the trauma and the constant threat of death, they survived.

When they were discharged, they returned to an ungrateful country that went out of its way to despise rather than welcome them. Like many returning veterans, they found it difficult to relate to others.

Over the years, they managed to find gainful employment and settled back into their small community, where everyone knew everyone. Families in Little Italy were close-knit and looked out for each other. As a child, it was impossible to do something wrong without the entire neighborhood knowing the details within hours.

Frank worked at a small bakery around the corner from his house. The family that ran the bakery had lived and worked in the small shop for over 70 years. Carlo Vicaro, now in his seventies, ran the bakery. He had worked there six days per week all his life. His sons and wife, who used to help in the bakery, had all passed away, leaving only Frank to help keep the business alive. Vicaro's supplied all the bread for the eight restaurants in Little Italy and produced pastries and cakes for every conceivable celebration. Although there was always more work than time, Carlo and Frank managed to keep things running smoothly and never missed a delivery.

Gino was gainfully employed at a small garage down the street, where they mostly worked on cars and trucks. The garage, simply named Rossi Garage, was owned by Pasquale Rossi. Pasquale and his son, Mark, had worked there for many years. When Gino returned home from the service, they brought him on. Gino was in charge of engine rebuilds and brakes, but he could handle just about anything Mr. Pasquale needed.

Gino was also instrumental in bringing in a few fleet trucks from neighboring businesses, which kept the garage busy year-round. Mr. Pasquale, a much better mechanic than a businessman, took Gino's advice to branch out and attract more business. Now, they had more work than they could handle, and Mr. Pasquale was already considering hiring another man to help out.

For years, the world simply passed by the small community, which survived on family members taking over the homes of the older folks as they passed away. Unfortunately, as many younger people attended college and experienced life outside the small community, they chose not to return. As the younger generation moved away to seek better opportunities, the older generation lost the much-needed support to keep family homes and businesses alive.

The houses in Little Italy were, in Baltimore terms, called row homes—today, they're known as townhouses. These homes were all connected to one another on each block, and they were three stories and very narrow. The first floor was the living area, with a kitchen, living room, and one or two bedrooms. The entire house was long and narrow. Most homes had been converted so that the owner occupied the first floor, while the second and third floors were converted into apartments. There was no front yard; the house bounded the sidewalk directly to the street. There was a small yard at the back of the house, usually containing a garden for fruits and vegetables, and almost always a small fig tree. The yard was bounded by a small alley for emergency vehicles and trash truck access.

As the years passed, the neighborhood felt less like a place to raise a family and continue traditions. Frank and Gino saw this happening and knew it was different from when they grew up. They often talked about it as they watched the old men play bocce ball by the old morgue at the end of town. Both Frank and Gino were married, in their fifties, and are now divorced. They were both loners and liked it that way, much of their disposition shaped by long-suppressed PTSD, though neither would admit it or seek help.

Luckily, neither had children from their failed marriages, so they simply lived and worked to live. Their ex-wives had moved away years ago, and there was no communication with them. Once, Gino asked Frank if he felt lonely. Frank said, "I like being alone. I don't like to be around people and look forward to the peace and quiet I have at home." Gino listened and thought to himself, *I know exactly what you mean.*

Both Frank and Gino had cars but rarely used them since everything was within walking distance. When they were discharged from the Army, they bought their cars and kept them in rented garages at the end of town. Frank had a 1971 Ford Mustang with 42,000 original miles, and Gino had a 1972 Chevy Impala with 34,000 original miles. Both cars had been in storage for many years, and they had not been registered or insured. The two men simply hated to part with their precious vehicles and knew they were worth much more now than when they had bought them.

A few times a week, Frank and Gino would have lunch together at the bocce court. The old men would play, and the two old friends would cheer for a good game. Father Francesco Alonzo from St. Leo's Church was by far the best player in the neighborhood. Father Alonzo, originally from Sicily and well into his 80s, kept the game free of foul language, as he also refereed. He had probably baptized most of the people living in the community, and he knew everyone from birth to death. As a one-man operation in the rectory, he also conducted mass and confessions.

Many rumors had circulated about Father Alonzo when he first became parish priest. Some say he was forced to leave Sicily because he murdered two thugs who tried to rob the church. None of this could ever be proven, but it was a reputation that followed him, likely to his last position in the Archdiocese.

After work at Rossi Garage, Gino would walk a few blocks toward his house and stop by the corner bar for a cold beer. The bar was small and run by an elderly couple who had been in business for as long as Gino could remember. They also served good food, prepared in the back by Mrs. Mary DeLuca, while her husband Joey tended the bar and kept the place clear of empty plates and glasses.

The DeLuca's knew to pour Gino a draft National Bohemian beer as soon as he walked through the front door and took a seat at the bar. Gino did this five days a week, like clockwork. In about an hour, his friend Frank would join him, and together they would watch a sporting event on the big screen TV and order something to eat. Neither Frank nor Gino was any good at cooking and never spent time learning, especially with so many outstanding places to eat in Little Italy.

During the fall, there was the Italian Festival and parades through the narrow streets of town, drawing hundreds of visitors to the area and boosting restaurant sales. Many locals would go to the roofs of their homes for a bird's-eye view of the activities below. It was customary for families to gather on the rooftops to enjoy the parade and have a cookout. The streets below would be packed with visitors sampling food and drinks from the many vendors. Carnival games and numerous vendors selling handcrafted items, including T-shirts, added to the festive atmosphere.

Over the years, the small Italian community was slowly surrounded by project homes on three sides, a failed attempt by the local government to provide low-cost housing. The remaining part of town bordered the Inner Harbor, a thriving area for tourists. In earlier years, it had been a shipyard where steelworkers repaired and built ships. However, as jobs left America for overseas competition, the Inner Harbor fell into decay until its resurrection in the late '70s.

Many of the blue-collar workers in Baltimore were soon left unemployed as one factory after another shut down and moved operations overseas. The huge steel plants closed, as did automakers Westinghouse and General Electric. Even the breweries that once thrived in the area all shut their doors. It was so bad that even the long-established Baltimore Colts NFL team packed up and left town, heading to Indianapolis. Soon thereafter, the Baltimore Bullets basketball team and the Baltimore Clippers hockey team also left.

Baltimore has long been a city in decline, with more residents leaving each year. Numerous attempts were made to revive the city's economy, but they all eventually failed. Baltimore, once a blue-collar town, lacked the skilled workforce needed to fill the new types of jobs required by businesses. Many unemployed, unskilled workers were left struggling to adapt to the changing environment. City leaders, often corrupt, did little to address the evolving needs of the business world, allowing the city's problems to fester while the tax base dwindled. There was never enough money to invest in growth, and the city remained in a state of stagnation, decaying with each new administration.

The police and fire departments, desperate for recruits, were forced to lower their acceptance standards. As older, more experienced first responders retired and moved away, a void in the ranks grew with each passing year. The lower standards for recruits inevitably led to a decline in the quality of the new hires, which became painfully evident each time a corrupt member of the force was exposed. The entire city was becoming a cautionary tale of what not to do, reaching a point of no return where no administration or policy seemed capable of saving it from itself. Voters became more focused on advancing their individual causes rather than prioritizing the city's collective prosperity. Crime and lawlessness became the new norm.

Each night, the local news led with the number of shootings and deaths that had occurred overnight, eerily reminiscent of how the Vietnam War was reported to the public in the 1960s, with body counts serving as the measure of progress. For most remaining residents of Baltimore, the constant reports of crime and violence became numbing. The police department, overwhelmed and understaffed, struggled just to keep up with the paperwork on pending cases. It became common for officers to simply show up and take a report after a crime was committed, as they had no means to prevent it. The police had effectively turned into a crime-reporting agency rather than a crime-prevention one.

In Little Italy, the population of older residents dwindled, with few replacements. To survive, many homeowners were forced to rent out their upper rooms to the many Spanish and Mexican immigrants now flooding Baltimore. As a sanctuary city, Baltimore became a magnet for undocumented immigrants, who filled the ranks in the many kitchens around town as cooks and waitstaff. They also took on low-level labor jobs, such as busboys, cleaning crews, and parking attendants. Without these workers, the city might have ceased to exist years ago.

For years, the projects were drug- and crime-infested, to the point that the city abandoned any attempt to bring them under control. Even the police refused to go into the area without backup or protective gear. The government failed to provide assistance, leaving it up to the residents to defend themselves as best they could. This crime soon spilled over into Little Italy, and many residents were forced to install heavy metal gates on their doors and windows.

Frank and Gino had noticed the slow changes creeping into their community and realized it wouldn't be long before they were forced out, with a new wave of immigrants taking over. Little Italy was on the brink of losing its identity, and nothing seemed able to reverse the trend.

The crime became a regular topic of conversation at the bar as Frank and Gino drank their beer and talked about the day's events. It wasn't long before the young kids who played in the streets of Little Italy and were on a first-name basis with every resident became targets of the gangs. Muggings, purse snatchings, and home invasions became commonplace as the gangs became more brazen and willing to commit more violent crimes.

It was common to hear police sirens at night—so common that they barely paid attention anymore, as the sirens usually passed by Little Italy on their way to other parts of Baltimore. But tonight, the sirens were on Fawn Street, right in the heart of Little Italy. The flashing red and blue lights from the police cars bounced off the houses on both sides of the street. This wasn't the usual police presence.

Gino looked out his bedroom window and saw the police cars blocking the intersection at the end of the street. He quickly dressed and went outside to investigate.

By the time Gino reached the pavement, others were already standing on their porch steps and gathering in the street, watching the commotion at the corner. Frank, who lived a few houses down from Gino, also grew curious. He walked past the onlookers and made his way to Gino's house. The two met at the corner, realizing that something serious was unfolding. More police cars and an ambulance arrived, with officers and paramedics heading into Vicaro's bakery.

"I hope Carlo's okay," Gino said, worry etched in his voice. "Maybe he had a heart attack."

"Heart attack? No way," Frank replied. "Why would there be so many cops for a heart attack? Something else is going on."

As more people gathered in the street, everyone speculated about what might be happening at Vicaro's. Rumors flew, but no one had any real information.

That night, the neighborhood's usual comfort was shattered by the grim news that spread like wildfire through the community. Old Man Carlo, the kindly baker who had been a fixture in Little Italy for as long as anyone could remember, had been found dead in his bakery. The details were gruesome, whispered in hushed tones by those brave enough to speak about it. That morning, his body had been discovered, slumped over the counter, his face frozen in terror. The police had come, but their presence was fleeting, their investigation half-hearted.

Frank and Gino stood at the edge of the crowd outside Carlo's Bakery, their faces set in grim lines. They had seen death before—too much of it, in fact. Vietnam had left them with scars, both visible and hidden. But this was different. This was home. This was personal.

"They're not going to do anything, are they?" Gino muttered, his eyes narrowing as he watched the last of the police cars drive away.

"Not a damn thing," Frank replied, his voice low and hard. "They don't care about us. They never have."

Gino nodded; his jaw clenched in anger. "So, what do we do?"

Frank's gaze drifted to the bakery, where shards of broken glass glinted in the fading light. He felt the weight of the decision pressing down on him—the same weight he had felt countless times in the jungles of Vietnam.

"We do what we have to," Frank said finally. "We take care of it ourselves."

Gino agreed. "I'm with you. But first, we need to take care of Carlo. He didn't deserve to go out like this."

"Of course," Frank said. "First, we take care of Carlo. Then we figure out our next move."

"As far as I know, Carlo didn't have any living relatives," Gino said. "We should probably make the arrangements for his funeral and burial. I can talk to Father Alonzo later today and see if he has any suggestions on how to handle this."

"I think Carlo had a brother in Sicily," Frank replied. "But I'm not sure if he's still alive. I'll look through his desk later and see if I can find out if there's any surviving family. Carlo always did business in cash. He wasn't an American citizen, didn't even have a driver's license. He worked strictly for cash and paid in cash. Even his suppliers delivered goods to the bakery, and they were paid immediately in cash. There are no business records to speak of. That means he probably kept a stash of cash in his apartment upstairs. I'll check on that as soon as the cops and forensics are out of there."

"And then what?" Gino asked.

"Then I need to start making the dough for tomorrow's bread deliveries," Frank said. "All the restaurants depend on Carlo for their bread and rolls. They have no other way to get them on such short notice."

"That's a lot to handle by yourself," Gino said, concerned.

"I don't know if I can do it, but I have to try," Frank replied. "Too many people depended on Carlo. I'd hate to let them down. I'll close the storefront and just focus on making the bread. Sal, the delivery boy, can help, but he mainly delivers the bread and collects payments from the restaurants."

"Yeah, I know Salvatore. He's a good kid," Gino said. "Carlo gave him a break after he got into trouble with the law. He trusted him with all the deliveries and the cash payments."

"Okay," Frank said, nodding. "You meet with Father Alonzo and work out the funeral arrangements. I'll check if Carlo has any family left in Sicily, and I'll handle the cash in the apartment. After that, I'll get started on the dough. Let's meet later tonight to coordinate our plans."

"Sounds good," Gino agreed. "We'll take care of Carlo first, and then we'll figure out who's responsible for this mess."

Chapter 2

Gino met with Father Alonzo at the rectory just as the priest was preparing to say Mass. Gino explained that he and Frank wanted to take care of Carlo's funeral and find a final resting place for his remains. Father Alonzo was more than willing to assist with the arrangements. He offered to schedule the mass and place the obituary in the newspaper. The Della Noche Funeral Home would handle viewing and transporting the body to the cemetery. There were a few open grave plots at Holy Redeemer Cemetery off Belair Road that would be acceptable. Gino was impressed with Father Alonzo's willingness to help. He then asked, "Do you know if Carlo had any living relatives that need to be notified?"

Father Alonzo sat back in his chair pondering how to respond. He then said, "Gino, few people know that Carlo and I came from the same small town in Sicily. In fact, our families were close neighbors. Carlo has a brother named Aldo who still lives in Sicily, and I am in contact with him every Christmas. I will notify him of Carlo's passing. However, I cannot guarantee he will take the news lightly. You see, Carlo's brother is a big man in the Cosa Nostra. He may decide to take matters into his own hands. He has many contacts in New York, and the blood ties run deep."

Gino listened intently to Father Alonzo and replied, "Father, Frank and I are going to make things right regarding Carlo. When you speak to his brother Aldo, you tell him we have this under control. However, if he wants to offer some help in our pursuit of justice, we will welcome it with open arms."

Father Alonzo wasn't surprised by Gino's response. He said, "Gino, I understand the nature of street justice. It's very common in Palermo, my hometown. As a man of the cloth and your spiritual advisor, I cannot condone your future actions. However, that said, I will not do anything to hinder you and Frank from protecting the community from the people responsible for Carlo's death. Are we clear?"

"Absolutely, Father. Our conversation today ended with planning Carlo's funeral and burial arrangements."

Frank searched Carlo's apartment and found the metal box with cash under the floorboards of his bedroom. There was just over $15,000 in the box in various denominations. Frank left the box in its secure hiding place and continued searching for any signs of living relatives. As he was going through Carlo's desk, Gino entered the room and told him about the conversation with Father Alonzo.

"That's great news, Gino. It sounds like Father Alonzo is going to be a big help with the arrangements, and that's a huge load off our shoulders. But I'm a bit concerned about the help we might receive from Carlo's brother."

"Why is that, Frank? We may need some extra muscle when we figure out who's ultimately responsible for Carlo's murder."

"Yes, I understand. But I don't want outsiders coming in until we've done our due diligence. I want to make sure we find out who did this, who ordered it, and take them all down so they know not to come back to our neighborhood."

Gino said, "Okay, Frank. I get it. I'm with you all the way on this. But first things first—you better get to work on the bread orders, and I have to get over to the garage or the old man will be pissed at me for being late."

Frank went into the bakery and met Sal at the storefront. Sal was in charge of cleaning up and getting the broken glass replaced. Frank went into the bakery and started the routine ritual of dough-making.

Frank had done this so many times that he could go through the motions like a machine:

- Active dry yeast
- Granulated sugar
- Warm water
- Bread flour
- Olive oil
- Salt
- 400-degree oven, bake for 20 to 25 minutes or until golden brown

As Frank was putting the first round of loaves into the oven, Sal came in and asked if he could help. Frank said, "Sal, I appreciate the offer, but you'll have enough to do once the bread is finished cooling."

Sal replied, "Frank, you're never going to be able to keep up with all this by yourself. At best, it's a two-man job. I have a possible solution for you if you're interested?"

"Sure, what's your idea?"

"My sister lives down the street and rents the top apartment to a Mexican family. They are very nice people, but not exactly in the country legally. The husband was a baker in Mexico and is looking for work. He has no papers or bank accounts. He just does odd jobs in the neighborhood for cash."

"Say no more, Sal. Have this guy come see me as soon as you can. If he's a baker as you said, I can pay him cash with no questions asked."

Sal went to his sister's house and climbed the stairs to the third-floor apartment. He knocked on the door and was greeted by a woman in her mid-forties named Maria. "Hello, Sal. Are you here to collect the rent? We already paid your sister this morning."

"No, no. I'm here to see your husband, Diego. Is he here?"

"Yes, of course. Come in, and I'll get him."

Diego, a small man about five feet six inches tall with a stocky build, appeared and said, "Maria said you wanted to see me."

"Yes, I have a job offer for you."

Sal explained the situation at Carlo's bakery and how Frank desperately needed help. He knew about Diego's situation and was willing to pay him cash each week if he was good enough at baking.

Diego looked at his wife, almost coming to tears. Maria was already wiping tears from her eyes as she said, "God bless you, Sal. You've made us both very happy. We were very saddened by the loss of Mr. Carlo. He was a very nice man and always treated us with respect."

Diego said, "Yes, thank you, my friend. When do you want me to start?"

Sal replied, "Right now. We have a lot of bread to make, and Frank is all by himself trying to be Superman."

Maria and Diego exchanged puzzled looks. Diego said, "Who is this Superman you speak of?"

"Never mind. Grab your stuff, and I'll introduce you to Frank."

Father Alonzo attended the evening viewing of Carlo at Della Noche's funeral home. The place was packed, with a line of mourners outside waiting to get in. It was a tragic scene, and everyone was sorry to see such a good man murdered.

The next morning at 10 a.m., Father Alonzo conducted Mass for Carlo at St. Leo's. The small church was packed, with the doors kept open so those lining the streets outside could hear the sermon. It seemed the entire neighborhood was in attendance. All the shops and restaurants closed for the occasion out of respect for one of their beloved parishioners.

After the Mass, the cars lined up to follow the hearse to Holy Redeemer Cemetery. It was about a forty minute drive, and the police had to provide traffic control to ensure the procession could navigate the city streets. Bystanders looked on as the procession made its way through the downtown area.

At the cemetery, Father Alonzo made his final comments and blessed the coffin as it was lowered into the ground. As the crowd dispersed, a police detective approached Father Alonzo.

"Excuse me, Father. My name is Detective Matthew. I've been assigned to the Carlo case and would like a word with you about these proceedings."

"Sure, Detective. Walk with me, and we can talk. What do you need to know?"

"Well, we're looking at this homicide as a possible gang hit on a merchant who refused to pay protection money. So far, we're not getting much cooperation from the residents of Little Italy, and I'm here to ask for your help."

"And how do you think I can help you?"

"Well, Father, you hear things—things outside the confessional, of course—that might give us some leads to follow."

Father Alonzo was well attuned to the detective's probing. He replied, "If I hear anything that might help bring the men who committed this horrible act to justice, I will gladly tell you. However, our small community is still in mourning. Most folks are simply concerned that the city's crime is infiltrating their peaceful existence. My parishioners are not going to cooperate with the police. After all, we haven't had much luck cooperating with the Baltimore police department. It seems you come in after the violence has occurred and make a report, but we never hear anything about closure. Do you understand what I'm saying to you, Detective? We're not holding our breath as you go about what you call investigating. However, if you'd like to leave your card, I'll be glad to pass on any information I hear about—outside the confessional, of course."

"Father, I'm trying to prevent any retaliation from within your community. We know Carlo was well-liked, as proven by this turnout. I'm simply trying to keep the bloodshed from spreading to other parts of the city. As you're well aware, we already have a city in crisis, and the police are very much understaffed. Any help you can provide would be greatly appreciated."

"I sympathize with your task, Detective. I also do not wish to see escalated bloodshed in our city. I pray for peace every single day and ask God to help us all through these troubled times."

Gino went home, changed into his work clothes, and headed over to Rossi Garage. Pasquale was already hard at work, his hands deep in the engine of an old truck. As Gino walked in, Pasquale looked up and nodded approvingly.

"You and Frank did a good job with Carlo's sendoff," Pasquale said, wiping the grease from his hands with a rag. "I thought Father Alonzo was outstanding in his sermon. A fitting farewell. But now, we've got to get back to fixing these cars and trucks."

Gino nodded, appreciating the older man's words. "Yeah, Father Alonzo really captured what Carlo meant to all of us."

Pasquale continued, "I hear Frank is going to try to keep the bakery going so the restaurants don't suffer. That's a good thing. We need more people like you and Frank to help keep this community together. But I can't help thinking... why was Carlo targeted in the first place? My gut tells me it has something to do with all these gangs that have sprung up around here in the past couple of years. I just hope I'm wrong."

Gino's expression grew serious. "I'm worried about that too, Pasquale. The way these gangs are expanding, it's hard not to think they had a hand in what happened to Carlo. But until we know for sure, we're just guessing. We have to wait and see if there's really something to be concerned about or if this was a one-time thing."

Pasquale sighed, his brow furrowed with concern. "I hope it's just a one-off, but we can't ignore what's happening around us. The community isn't what it used to be, and we're all feeling it. People are scared to walk their own streets, and that's not the Little Italy I know."

Gino nodded again, knowing all too well what Pasquale meant. He glanced around the garage, where the walls were lined with old tools and yellowing photographs of a time when the neighborhood felt safer, more secure. "We'll do what we have to do, Pasquale. If things get worse, Frank and I will be ready. Carlo didn't deserve what happened to him, and we won't let his death be in vain."

Pasquale smiled, though his eyes were still clouded with worry. "Good. We need men who are willing to stand up, who won't let this place fall apart. Just promise me you'll be careful, Gino. The last thing we need is to lose another one of our own."

"I promise," Gino replied, gripping Pasquale's shoulder firmly. "We'll take it one day at a time."

With that, they turned back to the job at hand, the familiar sounds of the garage filling the air—tools clinking, engines revving, and the steady hum of men determined to hold on to what they loved.

Sal introduced Diego to Frank. Frank said, "Sal tells me you were a baker in Mexico. I need help now that Carlo is gone, and I can't do it alone. Right now, I'm concentrating on supplying the local restaurants with bread and rolls. I've suspended all pastry and cake making for the time being, but this can't go on forever. The community depends on us to supply pastries and cakes for all occasions. Do you have any experience with cake making and pastries?"

"Oh yes, Mr. Frank. I've done all these things for many years. I'm sure I can help you if you let me know the preferred recipes for such delights."

"Okay. Here's what we need to do. I want you to come in at midnight and make the bread dough. Sal will tell you how many loaves we need each day, and you'll adjust the amount of dough accordingly. I'll come in at 5 a.m. to start forming and baking the bread and rolls. Sal comes in around 11 a.m. to pick up the orders and deliver them to the restaurants. The restaurants pay Sal in cash, and he brings the cash back to the bakery, where we keep it in the small safe in the corner. Diego, I'll give you a key to the shop so you can come in at midnight and get started. I'll also give you the combination to the safe so, if we get a delivery from our suppliers, you can pay for them with cash. At the end of each week, I'll pay you cash for the hours you worked. Do we have a deal? Oh, and just call me Frank."

Diego said, "I understand what you expect of me and will not disappoint you. Right now, I want to help you finish these batches of bread, and then I'll return at midnight to start the new batch of dough."

Frank was impressed with Diego. He told him that since he was willing to go above and beyond on his first day, he would advance him $200 so his wife could buy groceries for the house.

Diego was so appreciative of Frank's generosity that he gave him a hug, saying, "Thank you, Frank. You can depend on me. I only need to see your bread dough recipe in order to duplicate the process to your liking. In fact,

I'd like to study your recipe book for pastries and cakes as well. The sooner I'm comfortable with your processes, the sooner we can offer a full menu to the community."

Father Alonzo called Gino and asked that he and Frank come by the rectory for a chat around 7 p.m. As Gino and Frank were having their daily meet and greet at DeLuca's bar, Gino mentioned that Father Alonzo wanted them to stop by for a chat. Frank said, "What do you think this is all about? Do you think he's going to try and talk us out of pursuing justice for Carlo?"

"No, not at all. I suspect he's contacted Carlo's brother and wants to pass on some information. We'll find out soon enough. Let's finish these beers and see what the padre has on his mind."

As Gino and Frank approached the rectory, they were immediately greeted by Father Alonzo. "Come in, boys, and have a seat. I have some information for you about Carlo."

Father Alonzo updated the boys on a conversation he had at the cemetery with Detective Matthew, who had been assigned to the Carlo murder case. The detective was trying to head off any retaliation from within the community. "What that tells me, boys, is that you need to be extra careful when gathering information about who hurt Carlo. The police may be watching and looking for anyone trying to stir the pot."

Gino and Frank listened carefully to Father Alonzo's advice, making a mental note of the "be extra careful" portion. Then, Father Alonzo said, "I spoke to Carlo's brother, and he is livid. He wanted to jump on a plane and find those who killed his brother. I convinced him that we have folks gathering intel on the people who may be responsible, and I promised to keep him informed."

As Father Alonzo stood up, signaling the end of the meeting, he said, "I cannot condone what you two are doing. However, I understand your dedication to Carlo. Just be careful about whom you speak to and with whom you share information. To be successful in this effort, you must use your head. Think things through. Make a plan and stick to it, unless you need to improvise to meet unforeseen circumstances. I will pray for your success."

Gino and Frank left the rectory and walked to Gino's house, where the two had a beer and discussed how they would gather information. They needed a starting point but had none. They had no leads to follow and were entirely unaware of which gang was involved, if any.

Just then, Sal knocked on the door and was invited into the conversation. Sal wanted to know what, if anything, Gino and Frank were planning. He wanted to know because he wanted in. "I know you two are planning to avenge Carlo's murder. I want to see the bad guys punished for what they did. So, I want in. I can be a big help in gathering intelligence without raising suspicion about my purpose. You must let me in on this."

Gino looked at Frank, then back at Sal, and said, "You want in? You're in. Now, how can you help us figure out who is responsible for this mess?"

Sal looked Gino in the eyes and said, "I have contacts among the younger folks in and around Little Italy. I hear things that you'll never hear. I know how to keep my eyes and ears open, as well as my mouth shut. Give me a few days, and I'll have something to share. Right now, few people are talking about what happened to Carlo. But I assure you, someone will be bragging about it soon enough. When they do, I'll let you know, and we can take that person for a trip to the county and extract the information."

Frank smiled and said, "Sal, you may have just made our day. You do what you do best, and then we'll meet to discuss a plan of action. I think you're right—someone will be bragging soon enough, and that's all we need to get the ball rolling."

Chapter 3

Frank woke up at 4 a.m., got dressed, and headed over to the bakery. When he arrived, he saw Diego hard at work, shaping loaves of dough. He also noticed several trays stacked up and ready for the oven. Frank was both impressed and surprised.

"Good morning, Diego. I see you've outdone yourself—not only making the dough but also preparing the loaves."

"Yes, I've been busy, but it's really not that hard once you get into the swing of things. I haven't had my hands in bread dough in a long time, and it felt good to watch the dough rise again. I couldn't help myself and started the forming process."

Frank said, "Just keep track of your hours, my friend. After I get the first batch out of the oven and have a taste, we'll know if you did well! By the way, did we have any deliveries today?"

"Yes. A man came around 3:30 and dropped off sacks of flour and yeast. He also had canisters of salt, sugar, and olive oil. I put everything in the back and paid the man $420 cash. He said some of the prices had gone up, so the usual $400 wasn't enough. I hope I did the right thing, Frank."

"Don't worry about it, Diego. You did fine. Over the past several months, the price of everything has increased. I'll tell Sal to pass the price increase on to the restaurants when he makes today's deliveries. They won't like it, but it is what it is. We'll never get rich making bread, but it keeps the lights on. Our big moneymaker is in the pastries and cakes."

Diego said, "I understand. I also had a look at the receipt book for pastries and cakes while I waited for the dough to rise. I see no reason why we can't start making cakes next week when we have enough supplies. The pastries will probably have to wait another week or so. Again, we'll need a lot of supplies to get those made."

Frank said, "Okay, Diego. I'll put the order in for more supplies, and we can then proceed with the cake making. I'm sure the folks in the community will welcome that service once again. You've done well. Why not take off, and I'll see you tomorrow."

"Okay, Frank. If you need me later today, just call me at my house. I can be here in ten minutes if necessary."

Frank was very impressed with Diego's work ethic. After the first batch of bread came out of the oven, he sliced open a loaf and tasted it. Not surprisingly, it was perfect. Diego was truly a skilled baker when it came to making bread.

At 11 a.m. on the dot, Sal showed up with the panel van they used for deliveries. He loaded several trays of bread and boxes of rolls. When he finished loading the van, he said, "It looks like you and Diego did very well. I'm sure the customers will appreciate the no break in service."

"Well, they may not like the price increase. Diego had to pay an extra $20 for the order today, and we need to make that up from the customers."

"Not a big deal. Everyone knows prices are going up for everything, so it won't be a surprise. Of course, they could always make their own bread and rolls if they don't like it! Right?"

Frank laughed and said, "You're correct. Now get out of here so I can clean up this place for tomorrow's orders. By the way, we'll be making cakes again next week, so let the restaurants know we're taking orders for cakes once again."

"Will do, boss."

After making the deliveries for the day, Sal came back to the bakery and handed over the envelopes of cash he received as payment. He said, "Frank, no one had a problem with the slight price increase, and they were all happy to hear you'll be making cakes again next week."

"That's good news, Sal. Just put the cash in the safe, then come back so we can chat."

Once the cash was in the safe, Sal came to the bakery side of the shop and said, "What's on your mind, Frank?"

"I was wondering if you've heard any rumblings regarding the hit on Carlo."

"I've got a few feelers out right now and expect to have something more concrete in a day or two. So far, it appears that a small gang operating off Greenmount Avenue may be our starting point. They might not be the ones directly involved in the hit on Carlo, but they could be convinced to tell us who is. These gangs are always trying to take over each other's territory. So when they get a chance to have a rival gang taken out by someone else, they welcome the opportunity. That way, they avoid a gang war and let others do the dirty work of eliminating their competition. Like I said, I'll know more in a day or two. What we need to do is figure out how to get to them and make them open up about who was behind Carlo's hit."

Frank said, "That's good information, Sal. Stay on it, and when you feel you have enough, we'll sit down with Gino and make a plan. In the meantime, Gino is securing several weapons that we may need. He's already in possession of three .22s long-barrel semi-automatics. After hours at the garage, he's been using the machine lathe to thread the barrels to accept a silencer. When he's done with that, he'll work on creating the silencers. These are weapons for close combat. In other words, they're up close and personal—very quiet but deadly in the right hands."

Sal said, "Sounds like Gino knows his way around gunsmithing!"

"Sal, there's a lot you don't know about me and Gino. When it comes to taking the fight to the enemy, we will prevail. It may be messy, but it will definitely be effective."

Over the next few days, Frank and Gino worked quietly behind the scenes. Frank kept the bakery running smoothly with Diego's help, while Gino started gathering intel on the local gangs. He contacted old acquaintances, people who owed him favors, and those who had their ears to the ground. It wasn't long before they started piecing together a picture of what had happened to Carlo.

One evening, after closing the bakery, Frank and Gino met in the back room. The dim light cast long shadows on the walls, and the smell of fresh bread lingered in the air.

"I've got something," Gino said, lowering his voice. "Word on the street is that a new gang's trying to muscle in on our turf. They call themselves the Red Vipers. They've been shaking down businesses for protection money, and Carlo was their latest target."

Frank's jaw tightened. "Did Carlo refuse to pay?"

"Yeah, that's what I'm hearing. They sent a couple of their guys to lean on him, but Carlo told them to shove it. A few days later, he's dead."

Frank cursed under his breath. "We can't let this stand, Gino. If we don't send a message now, more people are going to die."

"I'm with you, Frank. But we need to be careful. These guys aren't just small-time punks—they're connected, and they've got firepower. We'll need to plan this out, hit them where it hurts."

Frank nodded. "We'll do it the right way. First, we'll find out where they're holed up and who's in charge. Then, we'll make our move."

"Agreed," Gino said, cracking his knuckles. "Let's show these bastards what happens when they mess with the wrong neighborhood."

On Friday, Gino made his usual stop at DeLuca's after work. As he was finishing his first beer, Sal entered and said, "We need to talk. I have some information, but I'll wait until Frank gets here."

"Sure thing, Sal. Have a beer; Frank should be here shortly."

The two men drank their beer and watched the Orioles game on the TV at the end of the bar. Sal said, "The Birds look pretty good this year."

Gino replied, "Yeah, they have the defense, and they can hit, but their pitching sucks. They'll never advance in the league unless they get better pitching."

"Maybe so, Gino. But at least they're above 500 and people are starting to come back to the stands to watch them play. I know the merchants around the stadium are doing much better this year. This town could sure use a winning team to boost the downtown area."

Frank entered the bar and said, "I see we're leading 5 to 2. I'll bet you both a beer they end up losing this game when they bring in the bullpen pitching."

Gino said, "Frank, Sal has something to discuss with us. Have a seat, and we can get started."

Frank said, "Okay. Let me grab a beer, and we can go sit at a table."

As the three sat at the last table in the back of the bar, Gino said, "Okay, Sal, what do you have?"

Sal said, "Gino, you were right about the gang calling themselves the Red Vipers. They're housed on Greenmount Avenue, and I have the address. This gang is making their move into the area to sell drugs and offer protection to local merchants. My informant also said they're not the ones who hit Carlo. However, they work for a much bigger Mexican drug lord operating in Maryland and New Jersey. Apparently, this guy running the show started in New York but was eventually pushed out by the cops. He moved his operation to New Jersey and did very well. He did so well that he decided to expand operations to Maryland. His plan is to take over all the big city drug trafficking operations. The protection rackets are a means to have a steady cash flow to finance the drug trade."

Gino and Frank listened intently. Gino finally said, "Jesus, this is much bigger than I thought. We're going to need to make sure we go about this very carefully. If we screw it up, the bad guys could overrun us in one major attack."

Frank looked at Gino and said, "You hit the nail on the head, Gino. We must inflict pain on the enemy while not letting them know where or from whom the attack is coming. In other words, we need to make our attack look like it came from anywhere but here."

Sal listened to the two men go back and forth and finally said, "How the hell do you expect to pull off an attack and not make it look like it came from here?"

Gino said, "Don't worry, Sal. We simply make our attack on the Red Vipers hard and final. We extract their information and leave no witnesses. We also take whatever drugs and money they have stored to make it appear to be a rival gang operation."

Frank said, "Sal, I know you wanted in, and this is going to get messy fast. You can pull out if you think this isn't your cup of tea."

"No. No way. I'm in; I just don't have a clear picture of how all this will work."

Gino said, "Here's what we'll do. Sal, I want you to come to the garage tonight after we close. I'll give you the keys to one of the customers' trucks or cars. You then go to the Greenmount address and take a few pictures of the house's front and back. You'll do this for the next three nights, and I'll supply you with a different vehicle each night. All we need is a good way to get into the house.

Once we have this information, we'll take a vehicle to the location. You'll drive and drop me and Frank off close to the house. Then you'll park the vehicle and wait. Frank and I will go into the house, take care of business, and return to the vehicle. Then you'll drive us back to the garage. Can you do that?"

"Yes, but you don't want me to go in with you? What if you're outnumbered?"

Frank said, "We'll initially be outnumbered for sure. But we know how to make this work in our favor. While you're in the vehicle waiting for us to return, if you see anything that looks out of the ordinary, just blow the horn, and we'll make a quick exit."

"Okay. I understand. I'll see you tonight, Gino." Sal left the bar, and Frank said, "I think he'll be okay. He's just inexperienced. How are you coming with the weapons?"

Gino said, "I'm ready. I test-fired the .22s last night, and they're good to go. I believe we should also provide some incendiary assistance to cover our tracks. I'll work on that once I get back to the garage."

Frank said, "Sounds good. Just keep it simple and light, so we can stay flexible. We need to get in and out quickly, leaving no trace of ever being there. Rubber gloves will be needed, and we'll need face coverings because you can bet there are security cameras in the area. We need to make sure we load the magazines while wearing gloves, since we will not be picking up our brass. We don't want any trace of our fingerprints anywhere. On the night of the attack, it would be a good idea to put modified plates on the vehicle we use. No sense in making the cops' job easier than it should be."

"Roger that, Frank."

Over the next few nights, preparations for the attack on the Red Vipers were in place. Sal did a good job of gathering photos of the house to be raided, and Frank and Gino decided on the best way to make entry into the house with the least exposure. They also agreed to launch the attack early in the morning, around 3 a.m. If everything went according to plan, the job would be complete, and Frank would be back at the bakery by 5 a.m.

After the initial success with bread and cakes, Frank decided it was time to diversify and bring back the bakery's once-renowned selection of pastries. Diego was more than up for the challenge.

"Diego, I've put in the order for extra supplies," Frank said one morning as they were wrapping up the day's bread production. "I want to start offering pastries again next week. The community has been asking about them, and I think it's time."

Diego's eyes lit up. "That's great news, Frank. I've already been working on a few new recipes. I know the customers have been missing the old favorites, but I thought I'd try adding a few new items to the menu as well."

Frank smiled, appreciating Diego's enthusiasm. "You've got the green light to experiment. Just make sure we've got enough of the classics to keep the regulars happy."

Over the next few days, Diego meticulously planned the revival of the bakery's pastry section. He started by organizing the workspace, ensuring that everything was in its proper place and that all the necessary ingredients were on hand. His first order of business was to bring back the bakery's signature cannoli—a sweet, creamy filling inside a perfectly crisp shell. It had been a customer favorite for years, and Diego knew it would be a hit once again.

But Diego didn't stop there. He began experimenting with new flavors and combinations, drawing on his years of experience and his love for the craft. He created a lemon ricotta cake that was light, fluffy, and bursting with citrusy flavor, as well as a decadent chocolate torte that was rich enough to satisfy even the most discerning sweet tooth.

In the early mornings, while the bread was still rising, Diego could be found in the back of the bakery, whipping up batches of pastry dough, carefully layering butter and flour to create the perfect flaky texture. The scent of fresh pastries soon began to waft through the air, filling the shop with a warm, inviting aroma that drew customers in from the street.

As the pastries came out of the oven, golden brown and piping hot, Diego worked quickly to prepare the display cases. He carefully arranged the cannoli, éclairs, and tarts, making sure each one looked as good as it tasted. He also added a selection of breakfast pastries—croissants, danishes, and sticky buns—that would give the early morning crowd something to look forward to.

The cakes were the final touch. Diego took pride in his cake decorating skills, spending hours piping intricate designs and adding finishing touches. The display case soon became a showcase of his artistry, with tiered cakes adorned with delicate flowers, chocolate ganache dripping elegantly down the sides, and fruit-topped creations that looked almost too beautiful to eat.

As word spread that the bakery was back in full swing, orders began pouring in. Local restaurants wanted to feature Diego's cakes on their dessert menus, and customers were once again lining up to get their hands on the bakery's famous pastries. Frank could hardly keep up with the demand, and he was grateful for Diego's tireless efforts.

One afternoon, as Diego was putting the finishing touches on a wedding cake, Frank walked into the kitchen and watched him work for a moment. "You've really outdone yourself, Diego," Frank said, admiration in his voice. "The place hasn't been this busy in years."

Diego looked up and smiled. "It feels good to be back in the swing of things. I missed this—the creativity, the satisfaction of seeing people enjoy what I've made."

Frank nodded. "And they're enjoying it, that's for sure. We've got more orders coming in than we can handle. I'm thinking we might need to hire some extra hands if this keeps up."

Diego wiped his hands on his apron and took a step back to admire the cake he had just finished. "I'm all for it. The more we can do, the better. This bakery has always been a cornerstone of the community, and I want to make sure it stays that way. In addition, when I worked at the bakery in Mexico, my wife would help me. If you like, I can ask her to join us in this growing business."

Frank said, "I had no idea, Diego. Yes, let's bring her on and add her to the payroll. This is an excellent idea, my friend. Besides, with your wife's help, we may be able to enjoy a day off once in a while. Talk to your wife, and she can work full or part time, whichever suits her, but let's get her started immediately. She can also help Sal work the front counter providing more customers with less time waiting in line."

With Diego's skill and dedication, the bakery was thriving once again. The smell of freshly baked pastries and cakes filled the air, and the display cases were always full, offering a tempting array of treats to anyone who walked through the door. The community, once worried that the bakery might not survive, was now buzzing with excitement, knowing that their beloved bakery was back and better than ever.

The community was pretty much back to normal, and life in Little Italy was once again a place where kids were playing stickball in the streets and restaurants were operating at full capacity.

Gino, known for his meticulous planning, understood the importance of leaving no trace, especially when dealing with a well-connected gang like the Red Vipers. The idea of an incendiary device was crucial—not only to cover their tracks but also to send a strong message.

After returning to the garage, Gino began working on a simple yet effective incendiary mixture. He needed something reliable, easy to deploy, and capable of causing significant damage while remaining undetectable until it was too late.

He decided on a homemade napalm mixture. The components were straightforward: gasoline, the main fuel source—easily accessible and highly flammable; Styrofoam to thicken the gasoline into a gel-like substance that would stick to surfaces and burn longer; and motor oil to increase burn time and produce dense black smoke, making it harder to extinguish. Finally, he added magnesium strips, gathered from shavings off magnesium alloy wheels, to ensure a sustained, intense burn.

Gino shredded the Styrofoam into small pieces and slowly mixed them into a container of gasoline. As the Styrofoam dissolved, the mixture thickened into a sticky, gel-like substance. He then added a small amount of motor oil to enhance its burning properties. Gino chose small glass bottles to contain the incendiary mixture, knowing they would shatter on impact and spread the napalm-like substance. He filled the tops of the bottles with kerosene-soaked rags, which could be lit just before deployment to ensure the mixture would ignite on impact. He prepared six bottles and packed them into a padded backpack.

That evening, as Frank and Gino sat in the back room of the bakery, Gino laid out his plan. "Here's what I've come up with," he said, placing the materials on the table. "This is a homemade napalm mixture. It'll stick to anything it touches and burn hot enough to destroy evidence. The magnesium will ensure it ignites and keeps burning, even if someone tries to put it out."

Frank inspected the bottles and nodded approvingly. "This'll do the trick. Just remember, we need to be quick. We hit them hard, set these off, and get out before anyone knows what happened."

Gino smiled, confident in their plan. "Trust me, Frank. By the time we're done, there won't be anything left for them to find."

The incendiary mixture, simple yet devastating, was designed for maximum impact with minimal traceability—perfectly suited to Frank and Gino's need for a swift, effective operation.

Chapter 4

The house on Greenmount Avenue was a stand-alone, two-story structure with a basement. A single guard stood watch on the front porch, while the back entrance was left unprotected. Frank and Gino suspected the back was heavily fortified, making a guard unnecessary. To gain easy entry, they would need to disable the lookout at the front. Once inside, they planned to split up: Frank would head upstairs, and Gino would cover the first floor. Their immediate objective was to neutralize anyone inside while capturing enough people to question about Carlo's killing.

At 2 a.m., Sal, Frank, and Gino met at the garage. They loaded weapons and a backpack filled with incendiary devices into a customer's car left there for an oil change and tire rotation. As Sal drove to the Greenmount Avenue address, Frank and Gino put on rubber gloves and skull caps to cover their faces.

Sal said, "The house is on the right, about two blocks away."

Frank replied, "Drop us off a block away. Next, continue down the street, park a few houses past the target, and wait. When you see us coming, pop the trunk and be ready to leave as soon as we're inside the car. Keep your handgun ready in case we're followed."

"Okay, I understand. You guys, be careful. I'll be here when you need me," Sal reassured them.

Gino put on the backpack, and as soon as Sal came to a full stop, they exited the vehicle and started walking toward the house. Frank led the way, with Gino following about twenty feet behind. Frank planned to take out the lookout before they stormed in through the front door.

The lookout on the porch paid little attention to Frank as he walked down the sidewalk, his gun at his side, facing away from the lookout. As soon as Frank was directly in front of the porch, he quickly raised the silenced .22 and fired three shots into the lookout's chest. The only sound was the brass hitting the sidewalk. The lookout immediately collapsed, and Frank and Gino raced up the three steps to the porch. They paused at the door, listening for any movement inside. Hearing none, Gino slowly opened the front door, and both men entered.

Frank quietly ascended the stairs to the second floor, while Gino remained on the first floor. Gino spotted two men sound asleep on a couch in front of a still-powered TV. Seeing no one else, he positioned himself in front of the two men and kicked at their feet to wake them.

"What the...?" The first man mumbled, groggily looking at the gun pointed at him. His partner, also awakening, stared down the barrel and demanded, "Who the hell are you?"

Gino said, "Calm down, boys. You won't get hurt if you sit quietly and don't make a sound."

Meanwhile, Frank reached the top of the stairs and saw a large table in the middle of the room, covered in cash, drugs, scales, and money-counting machines. He noticed two doors down the hall, which were likely bedrooms. Frank approached the first door and peered in, spotting a man and a woman sleeping in bed. He then checked the second room across the hall, where another man slept. Frank shot the man as he slept, then turned his attention to the man and woman in the other bedroom. He yelled at them to get up.

Startled by the loud voice, both quickly opened their eyes. The man reached for a handgun on the nightstand, but Frank shot the lamp and said, "No, no. I want you both to get up and go into the room with the big table."

Frank herded the man and woman to a couch and called down to Gino, "I have two up here. Do you have any down there?"

Gino responded, "I have two down here. I'll bring them up."

Gino ordered the two men at gunpoint to go upstairs. When they reached the second floor, Frank said, "Sit next to them and don't talk."

Gino glanced at the table filled with paraphernalia and said, "Looks like we found the right place, buddy."

The man from the bedroom demanded, "Who the hell are you, and what do you want?"

Frank replied, "Keep your mouth shut. You'll find out soon enough."

Gino moved a chair from the table over to where their four captives sat. He said, "We're here for information. We don't want to hurt any of you. What we need to know is who was responsible for the hit on a bakery in Little Italy that killed our friend Carlo."

The man from the bedroom sneered, "We ain't saying shit. You have no idea who you're dealing with."

Gino calmly replied, "Well, I guess you're not going to tell us what we need to know, so you're of no use to us." He shot the man twice in the forehead.

Frank turned to the remaining three. "Let me ask you all the same question. Who was responsible for the Little Italy bakery hit?"

One of the men Gino had brought up stammered, "Hey, man, we had nothing to do with that."

Gino said, "We know that. However, we believe you can tell us who was responsible. Once we have that information, we'll leave, and you'll still be alive."

The woman, now trembling, said, "I have nothing to do with the business these fools are into. I was just his girlfriend. Now he's dead, and all I want is to get out of here."

Gino said, "If you help us out, we'll make sure you get out of here in one piece. But you have to help us, or you'll die."

The woman, shaking and crying, pleaded, "I don't know anything. How can I help you?"

Frank turned to the second man, who had been silent. "You don't have much to say. How about you tell us what we need to know?"

"I can tell you it wasn't us that hit that bakery. We're not in the protection business. Sure, we deal drugs, but that's it. You guys have the wrong place."

Frank said, "Maybe. But gangs always know what's going on in their territory. Now, are you going to tell us who was responsible?"

"I don't know, man. Even if I did, I wouldn't tell you."

Frank said, "Then you're of no use to us." He shot the man twice in the forehead. The woman, now in a full panic, had to be calmed down.

Gino turned to the last man and asked, "Tell us what we need to know about the bakery hit."

The man staring at the bodies beside him hesitated. "If I tell you, you promise you won't say I gave you the information? They'll kill us all for sure."

"We're not here to hurt you or your friends," Gino said. "They simply wouldn't cooperate, so now they're dead. If you help us out, you and this girl will be set free."

The man looked at Gino and said, "You need to look at the Mexican Sinaloa cartel. They're the ones taking over the area. We're also targets and will soon be pushed out of business. They're ruthless and have a large number of soldiers. They bring in 60-70 kilograms of cocaine monthly. They then transport the money back to California, from where they eventually send it to Mexico. If you plan on taking them on, you'll need a lot more help."

Frank said, "Well, we got what we came for. That means you're no longer any use to us." He shot the man dead.

The woman, now frantic, begged for her life. Gino said, "Now it's your turn to help us. Where do these guys keep the money?"

The woman, desperate, said, "What's not on the table is stashed in the compartment below the stove. The drugs are usually kept in the refrigerator freezer, wrapped in butcher paper."

Gino said, "Frank, go check it out. I'll keep her company. If she's lying, I'll kill her."

Frank went to the kitchen and opened the bottom compartment of the stove. He found bundles of cash, all counted and wrapped in bank wrappers. Each stack appeared to contain $10,000. He then checked the refrigerator freezer, finding several brown paper packages. When he opened one, it contained a kilo of white powder. Frank called out, "She was telling the truth."

Gino removed the six bottles of makeshift napalm from his backpack. He handed the empty backpack to the woman, instructing her to give it to Frank so that he could load the money and drugs.

There was so much cash that the backpack was full, leaving no room for the drugs. Frank asked the woman if there were any gym bags or backpacks in the house.

"Yes, in the bedroom, there's a gym bag. I can get it for you," she offered. Not trusting her, Frank said, "Show me."

The two walked to the bedroom, and the woman pointed to the gym bag in the corner. Frank emptied it and escorted the woman back to the kitchen. He instructed her to put all the brown-wrapped packages from the freezer in the gym bag.

Gino scoured the first and second floors, collecting several handguns. He carried them to the second floor and added them to the gym bag.

Gino asked the woman, "Are there any more guns in the house?"

She admitted that there were some in the second bedroom's closet. Gino checked and found two SG 550 assault rifles. He had to carry them, as they were too large to fit in the gym bag.

Once all the drugs, guns, and money were loaded into the bags, Frank shot the woman behind the ear, killing her instantly.

Gino put on the backpack and grabbed three bottles of makeshift napalm. He instructed Frank to take the gym bag and three remaining bottles downstairs and wait by the front door. "I'll set off these three, grab the assault weapons, and meet you at the front door. Then we'll light the remaining bottles and head to the car," he said.

Frank nodded and made his way downstairs, standing by as Gino torched the second floor. Gino then quickly descended the stairs, and together they ignited the remaining three bottles, tossing them in different directions within the open space of the first floor.

The two men grabbed the gym bag and rifles, lowered their face masks, and walked toward the car where Sal was waiting. As Sal saw two figures approaching in the rearview mirror, he popped open the trunk. Frank and Gino dumped all their gear into the trunk, closed the lid, and climbed into the car. Sal drove away at a normal speed to avoid drawing any attention. Frank looked back toward the house they had just left, now fully engulfed in flames, lighting up most of the surrounding area.

Back at the garage, the boys unloaded the trunk and proceeded to Frank's house, which was the closest. They stored everything in the small basement, and Gino headed home. Sal was already on his way home, and Frank began walking to the bakery to start his shift. The plan had been executed flawlessly. Frank checked his watch; it was 4:55 a.m.

Frank entered the bakery and saw Diego hard at work.

"Good morning, Diego. How are things going this morning?"

Diego turned to face Frank and said, "Things are going well." He paused, then added, "Gee, Frank, you look terrible. Did you not sleep well last night?"

"No. I had a rough night and barely slept an hour. I'll be okay."

Diego returned to preparing the last batch of bread dough, and Frank began his bread baking routine.

As Frank was finishing his final batch, the morning news broke about a house fire on Greenmount Avenue. The media reported that it was a potential arson linked to organized crime. Frank realized they needed to be more careful as the police and FBI began investigating the blaze, suspecting it was connected to the escalating gang violence.

On his way to the garage, Gino stopped by the bakery and pulled Frank aside. "Did you see the news coverage of the house fire on Greenmount Avenue?"

"Yes, I saw it. We need to make sure we cover all our bases. The FBI getting involved will definitely put this event under close scrutiny."

"I agree. We should also stop by and inform Father Alonzo. This Mexican cartel is going to be too big for us to handle alone. I think we should ask Carlo's brother for some help. It wouldn't hurt if they could at least put some pressure on the drug trafficking. After all, the drug money feeds the cartel, and if we can slow the flow of money, we might be able to slow down their power and spread into our area."

Frank said, "Okay, I see where you're coming from. Let's talk to Father Alonzo tonight. However, I don't want us to lose focus on finding out who killed Carlo."

"I'm with you. My main goal will always be to find and eliminate those directly responsible for Carlo's death. But I won't shy away from anyone or any group that gets in the way."

After work and a quick stop at DeLuca's bar, Frank and Gino headed over to the rectory to see Father Alonzo.

"Come in, boys, and have a seat. I'm always glad to see you two."

Gino said, "Father, did you see the news today about the fire on Greenmount Avenue?"

"Yes, I did. This drug trade is terrible business. The news said they found five bodies in the ashes, and they suspect it was gang-related." Father Alonzo paused, looking at the boys in front of him. "That was you, wasn't it?"

Gino said, "It couldn't be helped, Father. We found out who was responsible for killing Carlo. It was definitely gang-related, specifically the Mexican Sinaloa cartel."

Father Alonzo leaned back in his chair, studying the boys. "I've heard of this cartel before. You're not planning to take on such a large, well-organized operation, are you? That would be suicide."

Frank said, "Father, we know it would be impossible to take on the entire cartel. We're only interested in taking care of those directly responsible for Carlo's death."

"That may be, Frank. But my understanding is that if you cut off one arm of the octopus, the other arms will still grab you."

Gino said, "We're here to ask if you could reach out to Carlo's brother Aldo for some help. He has connections that might help us divert some of the cartel's actions away from our mission."

"I see. I think I understand now. Let me speak to him. I'm sure he'll be more than happy to help, but I'm not sure exactly how. Well, that's not for me to ponder any further. I'll ask him for a contact in New York—someone you two can meet with and discuss business. That way, I'm out of the loop and don't need to know the details. How does that sound?"

Frank and Gino both nodded in agreement. Gino said, "You get us a name and possibly a phone number to contact, and we'll take care of the rest. Thank you for your help and understanding."

Father Alonzo stood to show the boys out. As they walked to the front door, he said, "You two be careful. I'll let you know what I find out from Aldo. In the meantime, stay out of trouble."

Father Alonzo called his good friend Aldo to discuss the urgent need for help in their small community in Little Italy.

"Good morning, Aldo. This is Francesco."

"Hello, my good friend. How are you, and to what do I owe the pleasure of this call from the United States?"

"Aldo, I have some news about your brother Carlo's case."

Aldo had been anxiously awaiting such a call and was growing increasingly impatient to avenge his brother's murder.

"I'm all ears, my friend. What do you have for me?"

Father Alonzo said, "We have some people here who managed to take out a small drug operation. During their mission, they discovered that the Mexican cartel known as the Sinaloa Cartel was responsible for Carlo's death."

"Yes, I'm aware of who they are. My associates in the States have had concerns about their rapid spread."

"Well, my friends here are specifically going after those who committed the crime against Carlo. However, they've requested that I contact you to see if you might be able to assist in their pursuit of justice."

"Of course. I'll do anything I can to help them with their mission. What kind of help are they looking for?"

Father Alonzo gave Aldo a summary of the situation. They ultimately needed his help in slowing the drug and money transport within the States, aiming to disrupt the flow of drugs coming in and the flow of money going from California to Mexico.

Aldo said, "I understand. That's not a bad plan. If the cartel is worried about their supply line being cut off, they'll likely focus on fixing that problem rather than worrying about smaller attacks on their people."

Father Alonzo cautioned, "You understand that this could also backfire. The cartel might respond by sending more people to the States to combat the supply line disruption."

"Yes, I understand that. But money fuels the cartel, and without a resupply from the States, they won't be able to pay their bills in Mexico. That could, and should, cause significant problems for them at home as well."

Father Alonzo said, "I need to put my two friends in touch with someone local whom you trust and who would be willing to help."

"That's not a problem. I know what you need and will text you back later today once I have confirmation. The man I'm thinking of is in New York. He's an outstanding member of our family, and I know he'll welcome such a challenge. After all, our members across the United States will appreciate the opportunity to earn more money. The man I'm speaking of is also an excellent coordinator. He'll be able to arrange for families from other states to get involved. You understand this is a huge undertaking and will take time to set up properly."

Father Alonzo said, "Aldo, I don't need any details. Just let me know who the contact in New York is, and I'll pass that information on to my people. The less I know, the better."

"Listen, my friend, I understand. Give me a few hours to make arrangements, and I'll send you a text with the name, code word, and phone number of my New York associate. Until then, Francesco, stay well and safe."

"The same to you and your family, my friend."

Later that day, Father Alonzo received a text message from Aldo. It simply read: Fabrizio Romano, followed by a phone number. The text also included a code word. When Gino and Frank called Fabrizio, they would need to provide the code word so he would know it was safe to talk to them. Once communication was established, they could set up a meeting to discuss details. The meeting would have to take place in New York, but that wasn't a problem since Baltimore was only a four-hour drive away.

Father Alonzo forwarded the text message to Gino and Frank. When they saw they were clear to set up a meeting with Fabrizio, they were relieved. With the help of a large organization, they could concentrate on their mission of finding those responsible for Carlo's murder.

Chapter 5

Diego, his wife Maria, and Sal were doing their best to keep up with all the orders from local restaurants. However, the demand for pastries and cakes soon became overwhelming. Diego decided to talk to Frank about the situation first thing in the morning.

"Good morning, Diego. How are you today?" Frank asked.

"Very busy, Frank. I think we need to have a talk," Diego replied.

"Sure, what's on your mind?"

"We're being inundated with orders from the local restaurants. They keep increasing their pastry and cake orders. The bread and roll orders seem to have stabilized, but we're now spending almost twice the amount on supplies just to keep up."

Frank nodded, "I know Sal only works part-time because he has to make all the deliveries. Your wife, Maria, has been putting in extra hours helping you and keeping the storefront running smoothly. And you're working sixty hours a week. I'm feeling the pressure too. I think what you're getting at is that we need more help."

"That's right, Frank. I think it's time to expand a little and bring on someone who can take over the dough-making, so I can focus more on the pastries and cakes."

"Diego, I agree. But I don't know anyone who can handle the dough-making process as well as you. Do you have any suggestions?"

"There's a new family that moved into the neighborhood up the street. The mother and father have a son who's about twenty. I spoke to him a few days ago, and he's desperately looking for work but has no papers. I think he can be trained to handle the dough-making process. We could try him out for a week or so and then decide whether to keep him on. What do you think?"

"Diego, you know I trust you and Maria with everything around here. Why don't you have a talk with this young man and see if he's interested? We'll pay him in cash for the hours worked. Just make sure he understands this is a trial period. If he doesn't work out, we'll have to let him go."

"Frank, I'll speak to the family this afternoon. If the young man is willing to come in at midnight tonight, I'll start his training. We should know in a couple of days if he's suitable and dependable."

"Okay, Diego. Let's do this. By the way, what's the kid's name?"

"His name is Miguel Ramírez, but he goes by Mikey."

After Diego finished his shift at the bakery, he stopped by the Ramírez apartment to talk to Miguel. Diego explained the situation and how the boss would give him a trial work week. If he proved he could do the job and was dependable, they'd agree to keep him on full-time. Diego also mentioned that he'd be paid in cash, so he didn't have to worry about his legal status.

Miguel's parents were in the room when Diego made the offer. Miguel was very interested and told Diego that, while he had no experience working in a bakery, he was a quick learner. Mrs. Ramírez was thrilled with the offer and said, "Mr. Diego, don't you worry. I'll make sure Miguel shows up for work every night at midnight." Mr. Ramírez added, "Yes, thank you for helping my family. I'm indebted to you, and I'll also make sure my son doesn't let you down. He's a good boy and will work hard."

Diego said, "Okay, we have a deal. Miguel will show up tonight at midnight, and we'll start his training." He extended his hand to shake Mikey's hand. As the Ramírez family walked Diego to the door, Mr. Ramírez said, "If you hear of any work for me or my wife, please let me know. We're not familiar with the bakery business, but I'm a pretty good mechanic and have worked on all types of cars and trucks."

Diego replied, "I'll keep my eyes and ears open for possible employment, but I can't promise you anything at this time."

"Understood. Thank you again for looking after my son."

Gino was hard at work at the garage when he took a break to call the train station. He wanted to know if it was possible for him and Frank to take the train to New York and back on the same day. The train ride would only take about three hours, and neither Frank nor Gino could have their cars out of storage and ready for a four-hour drive.

By taking the train, they could then take a cab to their meeting with the New York contact. After the meeting, they'd reverse their travel. Once Gino had the train schedule, he called Frank and said he was ready to make the call to Fabrizio and set up the meeting. Frank, busy with the bakery, said, "Okay. But we have to make this happen all in one day. I can't be away any longer than that."

After work, Gino and Frank stopped by DeLuca's for a beer. They then went to the back and sat at a table. Gino dialed the number he had been texted by Father Alonzo.

"Hello. Who is this?" the voice at the other end of the call asked.

"My name is Gino, and I have a word for you. The word is *'segreto'* (secret)."

"Yes, I was expecting your call. My boss said you and your friend need to have a conversation with me, correct?"

"Yes, sir, that's correct. We're in Baltimore and will take the train to New York. Once we're in the city, we'll take a cab to wherever you want to meet. After the meeting, we'll simply go back to the train station and return to Baltimore. Is that acceptable to you?"

"Sure, not a problem. When do you want to meet?"

"As soon as possible. Our needs are urgent and of a very personal nature."

"I understand, Gino. My boss gave me the rundown on the issue at hand. He too has a very immediate need to see his brother's death avenged."

Gino asked, "Would tomorrow afternoon be too soon for you, Mr. Fabrizio?"

"Tomorrow would be fine. And please don't call me Mr. My friends simply call me Fabio for short."

"Okay, Fabio. I have the train schedule in front of me. We can arrive at the New York train station at noon, 2 p.m., or 4 p.m. Which do you prefer?"

"I'll tell you what, Gino. You and your friend arrive at the New York station at noon. Take a cab or walk to Carmine's Times Square Italian Restaurant. The address is 200 West 44th Street. I'll meet you there, and we can have lunch, discuss business, and have you on your way in a few hours. Is that acceptable?"

"Absolutely. No problem. We'll see you tomorrow at Carmine's, probably close to 1 p.m., as I'm not sure how far that is from the train station."

"That's fine, Gino. The cab ride from Grand Central Station to Carmine's is about five minutes, depending on traffic. You can walk it in 10 to 15 minutes. I'll see you tomorrow."

Miguel (Mikey) was waiting at the door when Diego arrived to open the bakery. "Good morning, Mikey. Are you ready to make some dough?" Diego asked.

"Yes, sir. I'm ready. Show me what to do, and I'll do my best to keep up with your demands," Mikey replied.

"Okay, kid. Call me Diego, and we'll get along just fine. First, we check the list of orders Sal has prepared. This list shows how much bread and rolls each restaurant wants for the day. The numbers basically stay the same each weekday, but on weekends or during special events, they can change dramatically. Once we know how much to produce, we bring out all the ingredients from the back room and put them by the mixer. Then it's a matter of preparing the number of batches of dough we'll need. I do the math in my head, but you can use a calculator if you like. The last thing we do is pour the ingredients into the mixer using precise measurements. The machine will do the rest. It's not that hard, and you'll get the hang of it the more you do it."

"I understand what you're saying. Walk me through the first few batches, and I'm sure I can duplicate it."

Diego added, "At about 3 a.m., we'll get deliveries from our suppliers. We help them unload the truck and put everything in the back room. We pay them in cash, which we keep in a safe. Frank takes care of the ordering, and we're responsible for making sure we receive all the supplies before paying the driver. Once all the dough is made and has risen, we start forming the loaves of bread and stack the trays so Frank can start baking when he arrives at 5 a.m."

"Wow. You guys have this down to an exact science."

"There's no science involved. It's simply chemistry and hard work."

Mikey laughed and said, "It's a lot to absorb on my first day, but I can do it."

Diego said, laughing, "When Frank tastes the first batch of bread you've made, we'll know if you can do it!"

Frank and Gino were on the train headed to New York. As they traveled, Gino looked out the window while Frank was fast asleep. Gino knew Frank hadn't had much sleep since they raided the Greenmount Avenue house.

Frank woke up and said, "Wow, I must have been tired. That nap did me good. Let's just walk over to the restaurant for our meeting. The weather is nice, and I'd like to stretch my legs."

The streets of Baltimore were busy, but New York was a whole different beast. Cars, cabs, buses, and trucks were bumper-to-bumper in every direction. The air was thick with the smell of diesel, and the sounds of blasting horns filled it. The sidewalks were packed with people moving in every direction, like a beehive of activity. Everyone seemed to be in a hurry, weaving through the mass of humanity.

"There's Carmine's on the right," Gino said as they navigated the throngs of people to cross the street. Once they reached the front door, Frank said, "Now all we need to do is find Fabio."

Inside the front door of Carmine's, they looked around as if they were lost. A man in his fifties, about 5'10", wearing a dark suit, approached them and said, "Are you two tourists from Baltimore lost?"

Gino said, "Mr. Fabrizio, I take it?"

"Yes, but it's Fabio. Please follow me; I have a table in the back." The three men exchanged pleasantries and ordered lunch. Fabio then said, "Okay, let's discuss the issue at hand. I'll tell you what I know so far so you don't have to go over all the details."

Fabio told Frank and Gino that he had extensive conversations with Aldo. "His objective is the same as yours—he wants the people responsible for killing his brother, Carlo, punished." He then told them that he had people working to gather information about the Mexican Sinaloa cartel.

"We have our people in Florida checking on the trucking company the cartel uses to transport drugs and money. We also have our friends in California tracking how the money ultimately moves into Mexico. Once we've nailed down their supply chain, we plan to hijack the trucks, force the drivers to reveal where the drugs and money are hidden, and then destroy the trucks and the drivers. Our plan is to make it extremely difficult for the cartel to continue business as usual, while inflicting heavy property and cargo damage on those working with the cartel."

Frank and Gino were impressed with Fabio's grasp of the situation. Frank said, "You're very well-informed and have an excellent plan to deal a financial blow to the cartel. Aren't you concerned they'll retaliate against you and your people?"

Fabio looked at Frank and said, "Of course, we're concerned. In fact, we expect it. But if they retaliate, we'll respond by inflicting even more damage. We have a Plan B that targets them in Florida, where the drugs enter the country. We'll destroy their distribution centers there and in Mexico. This is a war. We have operations all over the country and have been successful for many years. The cartels are new players; they think they can just come in and take over what belongs to us. That, my friend, cannot happen. We must take the fight to the enemy and hit them where it hurts the most—in their wallet. It's all about the money."

Gino said, "We agree with your plan of action. While the cartel is busy fighting on one front, we plan to hit them on a second. We want to flush out the cartel's Baltimore operations one by one until we get to the individuals who killed Carlo. We'll inflict pain and suffering by using Sapper-style operations on their safe houses and warehouses. We won't make a big splash all at once; we'll strategically hit them one by one until they're all gone. Since we're a small operation, we can move quickly and quietly, adapting as we go."

Fabio was impressed with Gino and Frank. He said, "If you can do everything you say and keep it going by hitting small operations, you won't attract too much attention from the cartel's big players."

Frank said, "It sounds like we both have a plan to put into action. Our operations will begin as soon as we get back to Baltimore. We have a man gathering information on the next safe house location. Once we have that, we'll go in, extract information from those present, and leave no witnesses."

Fabio said, "I like it. Everything sounds good to me. Now, you guys are a small operation. Is there anything you need that I might be able to provide?"

Gino said, "Without being too pushy, we could use some explosives—preferably C-4 and blasting caps, or Semtex."

Fabio laughed and said, "Oh, I see you two are veterans. That's good. Now I understand why you want to use stealth tactics and are familiar with explosives."

Frank said, "Yes, we're well-acquainted with hit-and-run night maneuvers, and we're very familiar with C-4 and Semtex. If you can't help us with those items, we certainly understand."

Fabio laughed again. "Oh no, I didn't say I wouldn't help. I just wanted to make sure I wasn't dealing with amateurs asking for high explosives. You're certainly not amateurs. I can have these items delivered to you tomorrow if you'd like. I keep them in a warehouse in New Jersey. I'll have them delivered by truck. Just text me an address, tell me how much you need, and let me know if you have access to a forklift."

Gino said, "Yes, I have one at the garage where I work."

"Good. I'll send you a pallet with everything you need, including timers, fragmentation grenades, phosphorus grenades, and so on. You'll be well-equipped. If you need anything else, just text me a supply list, and I'll make it happen."

Gino said, "Thank you so much, Fabio. This generous offer will make our job much easier. I'll text you the details as soon as we're on the train back to Baltimore. Also, would it be okay if we stay in touch to keep each other informed about the progress, or lack thereof?"

"By all means, let's stay in touch. I must keep Aldo informed about the progress you're making with the primary mission. As you probably know, he has a very vested interest in your success. He assured me that he would provide you with all the assistance you need to complete the mission. If you need extra personnel for your raids, let me know a day in advance. I can send you two, three, or even five men at a time if you need them. You might want to consider that as a backup plan."

Gino said, "That's something we might take you up on, Fabio. If we want to hit two places simultaneously, Frank can take one of your men to hit one, and I can take another to hit the second. That would definitely drive the Baltimore police crazy!"

Fabio said, "I like the way you think, Gino. If the situation arises where you want to hit two places at once, let me know. I'd love to be part of that operation's planning."

After the men finished their meal and business discussion, Fabio said, "I'm glad we had this meeting. I wish you both much success and good luck in the days ahead."

Frank and Gino stood and shook Fabio's hand, saying, "We wish you and yours good luck and success. Together, we'll make Aldo proud and ensure the safety of our community."

On the walk back to Grand Central, Frank said, "That was a very productive meeting. I'm glad you took the lead on this, Gino."

"I agree. I was very impressed with Fabio. He seems like a man of action and is laser-focused on the problem."

The ride back to Baltimore was smooth, and both men were quiet. Gino broke the silence by saying, "I hope Sal has some good information for us when we get back."

Frank said, "I know what you mean. We need to have a target lined up for our next operation. I want to hit these bastards hard and fast."

Frank immediately went to the bakery, where Diego and Mikey were working double shifts while he was in New York. Sal and Maria were in the store, taking care of the line of customers.

Frank walked into the store and asked how things were going. Both Sal and Maria said things were busy as usual, with almost everything sold out.

"That's good to hear. I want you two to know that I think you're doing a great job. The customers seem to like you, and that keeps them coming back. In fact, things are going so well for the bakery, I'm increasing everyone's hourly wage by two dollars effective immediately."

Sal and Maria were stunned and surprised by Frank's announcement. The expression on their faces said it all.

Frank went back to the kitchen and saw Diego and Mikey cleaning up. Frank said, "Diego, I apologize for being so late coming back from my trip. It couldn't be helped. But I just told Sal and Maria that I'm increasing everyone's hourly wage by two dollars, effective immediately. That includes you, my friend. I appreciate how hard you work, and these raises wouldn't be possible without the extra products you've introduced to the menu."

Diego had a surprised look on his face as he said, "Thank you very much, Frank. We all appreciate your generosity and look forward to more success in the future."

"You're welcome, my friend. Now, how's the kid working out?"

Diego said, "To be honest, Frank, he's doing surprisingly well. The last loaves of bread are on the table. Check them out."

Frank looked at Mikey as he cut into a loaf of bread and tasted it. "This is good. Very good. But your bread is always good, Diego."

"I didn't make that bread. Mikey made it from scratch. He prepared the dough, formed the loaf, and baked it."

Frank looked at Mikey, who was anxiously waiting for his reaction. Frank took another bite of the bread and said, "Kid, you did good. This is excellent. Then again, you had a great teacher. If you can keep this quality up for the rest of the week, you've got yourself a job."

Relieved by Frank's response, Mikey said, "Yes, sir, Mr. Frank. Diego is an excellent teacher. I'm not as fast as he is, but I'll get faster as I get into the swing of things."

Frank said, "Call me Frank. And you're right—the speed will come with time, but the quality of the product must always come first."

Frank looked around and asked, "Did we get all our deliveries this morning, Diego?"

"Yes, everything was delivered. I had Mikey pay the driver in cash. We loaded all the supplies in the back, and Sal deposited all the cash in the safe."

Frank was impressed that the operation was running like a fine-tuned machine. He then said, "Okay, you two get out of here. I'll clean up the place and put in the supply order for tomorrow. You guys did a great job today and went above and beyond what was necessary. Go home and rest because we get to do it all over again tomorrow."

Chapter 6

Sal came into the bakery early because he wanted to speak to Frank in private. "Good morning, Sal. Is there something wrong with your watch? You're early for making deliveries." "No, I needed to talk to you about some information I discovered last night." "Okay, let's go into the back, and we can talk."

Sal said, "I heard something that may interest you and Gino. I was at a party last night, and two guys were talking about how they found a new distributor for cocaine. Apparently, these two guys were in the business of buying and selling on the street. One of them said he would take the other to meet with the seller after the party."

Frank asked, "Does it sound like this may be one of the distribution centers of the cartel?"

"That's what I was thinking. So, I left the party a little early and waited in my van. When I saw the two guys from the party get into a car, I followed them. They ended up going to a house in Baltimore County. It was a big house on a large, secluded lot. There were other houses in the area, but there was a good distance between them. I waited and watched for about fifteen minutes when another car pulled up, and two more men went into the house. Shortly after the second car arrived, the first two men I was following left the house, got into their car, and drove away. I was about to leave the area myself when another car came, and the same thing happened: two men entered the house as two men were leaving. All this went down between 1:30 a.m. and 2:30 a.m. After that, I left the area and went home."

Frank listened to Sal's report and said, "Give me the address of the house, and I will check it out in the early hours of the morning to see if this is a pattern. From what you described, it sure sounds suspicious, but we need more information before we go in there guns blazing."

Sal suggested, "Frank, I have a better idea. Why don't you and I go out to the house at 2 a.m. and pull into the driveway using a car that Gino supplies from the garage? We'll take a stack of cash we got from the Greenmount Avenue raid and try to make a buy. They probably won't care who we are as long as they see the cash."

Frank thought about it for a few seconds and said, "It's a risky plan going into an unknown situation like that, but it just might work. Let me talk to Gino and see if he can get us a car for tonight."

Sal went about his business of loading the delivery van and dropping off his orders at the local restaurants. Diego was busy in the kitchen working on cake decorating, and Mikey was occupied making dough and forming loaves. Maria was in the storefront working the counter, and as soon as Diego would bring out a tray of pastries, they seemed to disappear into the customers' hands. Business was very good, especially during the morning hours. Everyone wanted the fresh goodies while they were still warm.

After work, Frank and Gino met at DeLuca's bar for a beer. Frank informed Gino of what Sal had discovered and explained the plan they had devised to further investigate and confirm their suspicions. Gino listened but was not on board with the plan.

"Frank, you two will be going into that blind. That seems like a foolish way to gather detailed information."

"Okay, hotshot. What is your plan?"

"Simple. You and Sal go to the house with cash and try to make a buy. I will be close by with heavy armor in case you are walking into a trap. I'll get you and Sal a customer's car, and I will follow you to the location in a separate customer's car. At least in my plan, you and Sal will have backup."

Frank considered it for a second and said, "Okay, you're right. I like your plan better. I'll call Sal, and we'll meet you at the garage around 11:30 p.m. to take a ride out to this house. Once we're inside, we'll case the joint as best we can. If it is in fact a distribution center, we'll make a buy and get out as quickly as possible. If it belongs to the cartel, we will come up with a plan to take them out."

"Sounds good to me," Gino replied.

Frank then asked, "Did our New York friend make a delivery today?"

"Oh yes. I knew there was something else I wanted to tell you. Around 10 a.m., a panel truck pulled up to the garage, and the driver said he had a delivery for Gino. The boss called me and said there was a delivery for me, and it looked rather large. I went out to meet the driver, and he said, 'Do you have a word for me?' I said, 'segreto,' and he said, 'I have something for you from Fabio. You will need a forklift as it is rather heavy.'

"I unloaded the wooden crate, which was on a pallet, and put it in the back of the garage. Pasquale looked at the big wooden crate and asked, 'What is that, an engine?'"

Frank asked, "Oh boy. What did you tell him?"

"I was in a bind and decided to level with Pasquale. He has been good to me over the years, and if he had said to get that crate out of his shop, I would have done it in a heartbeat."

"Well, what did he say?"

"Frank, when I told him the crate contained things we need to pursue our quest for justice regarding Carlo, he didn't bat an eye. He said he didn't need to know any details and told me to throw a tarp over it and make sure no one gets near the box except you and me."

"Holy smoke, Gino. This is indeed great news. When we go in now, we will be well prepared to take out the bad guys."

Gino left DeLuca's and went home to get some sleep before meeting up with Sal and Frank later that evening. Frank also went home to rest but couldn't settle down enough to doze off. He called Sal and gave him the details of the new plan he and Gino had come up with. Sal was excited and said he would meet them at the garage at 11:30 p.m. He also reminded Frank to bring a bundle of cash so they could work their way into the house and make the purchase.

Frank said, "We need to look the part of big-time buyers, so wear a suit and tie."

After his shift ended, Diego went to Rossi's garage to talk to Pasquale. He wanted to let Pasquale know there was a man up the street who was a mechanic and looking for work. Diego told Pasquale the man did not have papers and that his son was now working at the bakery with him.

Pasquale said, "I have been thinking about bringing on some additional help, but they need to be proficient in transmission rebuilds and rear-end repair. If this man, Ramírez, is experienced in those areas, have him come see me tomorrow. What is his full name?"

"Antonio. Antonio Ramírez," Diego replied.

Diego then went to the Ramírez apartment and was greeted by Mrs. Ramírez.

"Hello, Mr. Diego. Miguel is asleep, but I can wake him if you need him."

"No, I am not here to see Miguel. I am here to see your husband. Is he in?"

"Yes, of course. Come in and have a seat. Can I get you something to drink while I fetch Antonio?"

"Some cold water would be nice. Thank you, and I won't be long."

Mrs. Ramírez returned with a glass of ice water, and Antonio followed closely behind.

Antonio asked, "Is something wrong, Mr. Diego? Did Miguel mess up?"

"No, not at all. Miguel is doing great and is a hard worker. Frank will be making him permanent at the end of the week. The boy learns fast. I'm here to talk to you, Antonio. You mentioned you were a mechanic. Do you have experience with rebuilding transmissions and rear-ends?"

Antonio looked puzzled but replied, "Why, of course. I have done that kind of work most of my life, along with engine rebuilds. Why do you ask?"

Diego said, "Do you know Rossi's Garage down the street?"

"Yes, I have seen it. It's a small garage, but they always seem to have cars and trucks on the lot."

"The owner, Pasquale, is looking for experienced help with transmissions and rear-end rebuilds. I told him you were a mechanic looking for work. He's in the process of expanding and needs additional help. He would like to talk to you tomorrow if you're available."

"Oh yes, I am certainly available. I can be there when he opens the garage. Does he know that I don't have any papers?"

"Don't worry about that. Pasquale is aware of your situation, and it doesn't concern him. He will pay you in cash if you're a good fit for the job."

Mrs. Ramírez said, "Don't you worry, Mr. Diego. I will make sure Antonio is there first thing in the morning."

Antonio added, "Thank you once again for looking out for our family, Mr. Diego. We are certainly in your debt."

"No need to thank me. You don't have the job yet. Meet with Pasquale and impress him. You can then work out the details of your job. I might suggest you tell Pasquale that you'll work the first week for half the salary to prove you can do the job. After that, it will be hard for him to turn you down. Besides, what do you have to lose?"

"That's a great suggestion. I will do exactly as you say. Given the chance to prove myself, I know he won't be disappointed."

Diego finished his water, said his goodbyes, and left the Ramírez apartment feeling satisfied that he had helped another family take a step toward stability.

Sal, Gino, and Frank met at the Rossi garage precisely at 11:30 p.m. Gino glanced at the two men and said, "You two look like you're heading to a formal event dressed like that."

Frank laughed. "We want to make it appear like we're big-time buyers. This is the best I could come up with."

Sal chimed in, "Gino, do you have some firepower in case we run into trouble?"

"Don't worry, my friend. If there's trouble, I'm well prepared. What I want you to do, Sal, is call me on your cell phone and leave it in your pocket on speaker. That way, I can hear what's going on inside the house. At the first sign of trouble, say the word 'Safehouse,' and I'll come in blasting."

Frank added, "We can't be carrying because they'll likely frisk us when we get inside, so you're our only way out, Gino."

"Don't worry, I've got your backs. I still think this is a risky plan, but it is what it is. Take these two pistols and leave them in the car before you go inside. Better safe than sorry. Let's go."

The two cars left the garage and headed toward the house in Baltimore County. As they approached, Sal pointed and said, "That's the house on the right."

Frank pulled into the driveway, and Gino parked about fifty yards behind them, near an adjacent home. Sal called Gino's cell phone, put it on speaker, and slipped the phone into his suit pocket. Frank looked at Sal and asked, "You ready, partner?"

"Yep. Let's get this done."

Frank and Sal exited the car and walked up to the front door. Before they could knock, the door opened, and a rough-looking man motioned for them to come inside. He then signaled for them to raise their hands to be patted down. While being frisked, Frank noticed two armed men on the side, watching them carefully.

When the pat-down was complete, one of the armed men asked, "What can we do for you?"

Frank said, "We're here to make a purchase." He slowly reached into his suit jacket and pulled out a stack of $100 bills, rubber-banded together.

"Come with me."

Frank and Sal followed the man down a hallway to a large room where a well-dressed man sat behind a desk. Two more armed men were in the room, sitting on a couch off to the side. The man behind the desk pointed to two chairs in front of him and said, "Have a seat."

Frank and Sal sat down, and the man said, "I haven't seen you two before. What's the nature of your visit?"

Frank replied, "We're here to make a purchase." As he spoke, he placed the stack of money on the desk.

The man eyed the money and said, "That looks like a large sum. What were you expecting to receive for that cash?"

Frank said, "We need two keys, uncut, and we'll be on our way."

The man glanced at his partners on the couch and smiled. He then turned back to Frank. "That's doable, but it'll cost more than what you have here."

Frank countered, "Here's the deal. We recently lost a supplier on Greenmount Avenue. The place was burned to the ground. We need a replacement, and I heard you were the man to talk to. If you're not interested in selling to us, we'll take our money elsewhere."

"Hold on there, Mr. . . . What's your name?"

Frank said, "I'm Mr. Smith, and this is Mr. Jones."

The man smiled. "Okay, Mr. Smith. Now, I didn't say we couldn't do business. I just need to be sure I'm dealing with the right people. Two keys are a lot of product for a one-time purchase."

Frank replied, "If you become our new supplier, we'll be purchasing two keys per week. With that kind of arrangement, our boss expects to receive discounted rates."

"Oh, I see. You want to arrange regular purchases on a weekly basis. You didn't mention that at first. Repeat buyers are always a good cash flow for us."

Sal added, "Our boss sent us to arrange regular deliveries. He's very cost-conscious and expects us to make a fair deal with assurances of delivery."

"I see. And who is this boss you're speaking of?"

Frank said, "Our boss wishes to remain anonymous. Do you tell your clients who you work for?"

"Of course not. However, my boss is as particular and cautious as yours appears to be. We can start this relationship with a first-time purchase agreement, with a guarantee of future weekly purchases. Is that acceptable?"

Frank nodded. "The terms are acceptable. My partner and I will visit each week on Friday to exchange cash for two keys of your product. As our distribution efforts increase, we may need to up our supply. Can you handle that?"

"Of course, Mr. Smith. We can supply all the product you need. However, if demand spikes dramatically, we may need a few extra days to fulfill the order."

"Understood. Those terms are acceptable. Well, that concludes our business tonight. If you could retrieve our product, we'll be on our way."

The man behind the desk signaled one of the men on the couch, who left the room and quickly returned with two small packages of drugs, placing them on the desk in front of Sal.

The man behind the desk asked, "Aren't you going to test the product?"

Frank said, "That won't be necessary. If the product is bad or has been stepped on, you'll only be hearing from our boss. You won't like how he responds. Are we clear?"

"Okay, big shot. I hear you. Sounds like your boss is meaner than mine."

Frank stood, signaling the meeting was over. Sal took the two packages of drugs, and they were escorted to the front door. As they walked down the hall, Frank and Sal took in as much of the layout as possible.

Once outside, Gino could see them, and everything looked fine. Frank and Sal got into their car. Sal took out his cell phone and said, "Gino, did you hear all that?"

Gino replied, "Yeah. That was quite a performance. Now, get the hell out of there."

As Frank and Sal pulled away from the house, Gino noticed another car coming from the side, following them. Gino called Sal and said, "We've got trouble. You're being followed by a gray SUV. I'm tailing the SUV at a safe distance."

Sal cursed. "Damn it. Things were going well, and now we've got a tail."

Frank said, "They might be coming to take the drugs we just bought. We could have been set up from the start."

Gino, still on speaker, said, "They could be following you to see where you're going. Or, like you said, they might be planning to rob you."

Frank said, "Gino, I'm heading toward the Beltway and taking I-83 North toward Sparks. If they keep following us, I'll exit at I-83 and take them to Prettyboy Reservoir, where we'll be away from any people or houses. I'll park by the dam, and when they approach, you'll need to be ready to take them out."

"Got it. Let's hope they break off before you get to I-83."

Frank looked over at Sal. "Reach into the backseat and grab the pistols. We might need them."

When Frank turned onto I-83, the gray SUV followed. "Gino, they're still on us."

"I'm still with you. I'm going to pass you and get to the dam parking area before you arrive. That'll give me time to set up before our company gets there. We don't know how many men are in the SUV, so this could get dicey."

"Good idea, Gino. I'm going to slow down a bit so you can pass. If you get a chance to look inside the SUV, try to get a headcount."

"Will do. Passing them now. . . No good, Frank. They've got black-tinted windows. I'm going to punch it and get to the dam parking area to set up in the woods."

Gino was well-prepared. He had a semi-automatic AR-15 with two extra clips of ammo. He raced up I-83, exited at Mount Carmel Road, and it was only a four-mile trek to Prettyboy Reservoir. The country roads were empty, so he made excellent time. When he reached the parking area near the dam, he pulled his car into the woods to partially conceal it. Then he took up a high ground position in the woods, overlooking the parking lot. He had a perfect view of the entire area, which wasn't very large. There were no lights, so it was pitch black, with only a sliver of moonlight.

Frank pulled into the parking area two minutes later and stopped the car. Within seconds, the gray SUV pulled in and stopped with its headlights pointing at Frank's car.

The driver and passenger opened their doors and stood outside the SUV, both armed. The driver shouted, "Get out of the car and get on the ground!"

Frank and Sal opened their doors but didn't exit. Frank yelled back, "What do you want?"

"Get out of the car and get on the ground!"

Sal shouted back, "Drop dead, asshole."

The passenger of the SUV fired at Sal's open door. Gino took aim and fired three times, hitting him twice. Shocked and confused about the source of the shots, the driver turned around and Gino immediately shot him.

Frank and Sal exited the car and walked toward the SUV, where the two men lay. Gino emerged from the woods and joined them.

Frank said, "Nice shooting, Gino. Let's grab their wallets, cell phones, and get the hell out of here."

Gino nodded. "Roger that. See you back at the garage."

Chapter 7

Antonio was waiting by the front door of Rossi's Garage when Pasquale arrived to open up for the day. He stood with his hands in his pockets, shifting his weight nervously from one foot to the other. As Pasquale approached, he gave the man a once-over, then offered a friendly smile. "You must be Antonio," Pasquale said, unlocking the door. "Yes, sir, Mr. Pasquale. I'm here about a job." "First off, just call me Pasquale, and come on into the shop. I understand you have experience working on rebuilds." "Yes. I've done engine, transmission, and rear-end rebuilds for many years. I'm very experienced with both automatic and standard shift transmissions."

Pasquale looked Antonio over and said, "I'm well aware of your circumstances, and I don't care as long as you do excellent work. I want to try you out for a week, and if you pass my evaluation, I'll bring you on full-time. I pay in cash, and I pay by the hour. The more hours you work, the more money you make. I don't skimp on parts; I only use quality parts because I guarantee all the work my shop performs. In other words, we do it right the first time. Are we clear?"

"Understood, Pasquale. I'm ready to start immediately."

Pasquale said, "There's a 2019 blue Chevy on the lot. Take the keys and drive her around the block. When you come back, we'll talk about your impression of what the problem might be. The owner says it doesn't shift out of second gear."

Antonio went to the lot and drove the Chevy around the block three times. When he returned to the shop, he handed the keys to Pasquale. Pasquale asked, "Well, what do you think? Was the owner correct?"

Antonio said, "No, not at all. That automatic transmission is three quarts low on fluid. I recommend that we top it off and take it for a test drive. I suspect the transmission is fine, except it has a terrible leak from the drain pan."

Pasquale was impressed. "Okay, Antonio. The supplies are located in the corner. To validate your suspicion, top off the fluid and give it a spin. If it shifts okay, I'll notify the customer. If he wants us to fix it, I'll order the gasket and filter kit to replace the ones in the car. However, I think you'd better put it on the lift to make sure we're not dealing with a cracked housing."

Antonio did as instructed and reported that there were no cracks. Pasquale called the customer, received approval to proceed, and ordered the parts, which were delivered shortly thereafter. Antonio did the work and test drove the car again. Everything was fine. Both the customer and Pasquale were happy.

Pasquale then gave Antonio two more cars to work on. Unfortunately, both vehicles needed the automatic transmission rebuilt.

Over the next few days, Antonio tore down and rebuilt two automatic transmissions. Pasquale went on the test drives with Antonio, and they were perfect. At the end of his fourth day on the job, Pasquale asked Antonio to come into the office.

"Antonio, you're a very good mechanic. I'd like to have you work full-time with us in the garage. As I first told you, I'll pay you by the hour in cash. Here's your first payment. Do we have a deal?"

Antonio was nearly in tears as he replied, "Oh yes, Pasquale, we have a deal. You've made me a fair offer, and I accept. You won't be disappointed."

"Great, Antonio. We have more work coming in this afternoon, so you're going to be very busy. You keep track of your hours, and we'll settle up each Friday."

Diego was busy in the bakery preparing pastries for the display cases. Miguel was now working unsupervised, making bread dough. He had proven to be a quick learner and a very hard worker. Frank was pleased with how well the bakery was doing. The local restaurants were asking for more pastries and cakes. Diego's wife, Maria, was now working extra hours doing cake decorations. Sal was constantly busy with deliveries and working at the storefront. With the Italian Festival only a few weeks away, orders were coming in faster than Frank could count. The business was good and improving.

The Baltimore County house where Frank and Sal made the drug purchase was concerned about their two men who followed the duo after they left the house. They were never heard from again, and now the police are at the door, asking questions about the two unidentified men found in a parking lot. The only identifier they had was that the gray SUV was registered to Miguel Sanchez at the Baltimore County residence.

Detective Matthew inquired about Miguel's SUV and took him to the morgue to see if he could identify the bodies. Miguel admitted the SUV was his but claimed he lent it to two cousins visiting from Mexico. He said they were going on a trip to Atlantic City, so he wasn't concerned when he hadn't heard from them. Detective Matthew wasn't buying what Miguel was selling. He said, "You need to make arrangements to have the two bodies shipped back to Mexico. The SUV is at the impound lot and will be held for forensics and kept as evidence pending further investigation."

Miguel was not happy about losing two of his good men. Since he was the one who met with Mr. Smith and Mr. Jones a few nights ago, he was very interested in finding out who they really were and for whom they worked. The timing of the meeting and the deaths of his two men were too much of a coincidence. Furthermore, he was concerned that the cops might be watching the Baltimore County house more closely. That would be bad for business, but they couldn't shut the operation down.

Frank, Sal, and Gino met at DeLuca's bar after work to discuss the events surrounding the Baltimore County home visit. Gino went through the wallets of the two men and discovered their names but no driver's licenses. Frank suspected they were illegal immigrants working as musclemen and hitmen for the man behind the desk. Sal went through their cell phones and managed to pick up frequently called numbers, as well as, more importantly, text messages.

Sal reported that based on his reading of the text messages, they were in constant contact with someone named Miguel. It was when he read the last few messages on one of the cell phones that a light went off.

"The cell phone texts show Miguel telling the owner that the marks are leaving the house. The time on the text corresponds exactly to when Frank and I left the Baltimore County house."

Gino said, "Then the man you met with in the house must be this Miguel character."

Sal commented, "That's how I see it too. But there's more."

Sal delved deeper into the text messages on both phones and managed to piece together a summary of events that immediately followed the drug buy.

"From what I can determine, this Miguel guy tried to contact the cell phone owners several times. These were all times after they had been silenced, of course. He then sent text messages to someone named Hector, copying the two cell phone owners. Apparently, Miguel was telling Hector they might have a problem with a buyer. The buyer was flashing a lot of cash and requesting future orders. Hector responded to take it slow and not involve the home office."

Frank said, "Okay. What do we know? We know the guy we met behind the desk is named Miguel. We are certain that Miguel is not the headman, as Hector appears to be giving him instructions. We also know the Baltimore County house is a distribution point but not the main headquarters. How does that sound?"

Gino said, "I think that sums it up pretty well. Now, what's our next move?"

Sal said, "I think we go back to the Baltimore County house, take out several of the inhabitants, and leave a few for questioning. We need to get someone to tell us where we can find Hector."

Frank thought for a few seconds and said, "I think Sal is right. We need to get in there, neutralize the majority, and question the survivors. Then we remove all the cash and drugs and torch the place."

Gino said, "Wait a minute. I agree with what Sal is suggesting, but if we can use Miguel's cell phone, we might be able to figure out who Hector is. I'll bet you a dozen of Diego's best pastries Miguel has messages to his boss on his phone."

"Excellent point, Gino," said Sal. "We take all the drugs and money from the house, but the real prize will be Miguel's cell phone."

Frank agreed with Gino and Sal. "Okay. How do you want to take down this Baltimore County house?"

Gino said, "We know they have traffic at all hours of the early morning. They have to have some downtime. Maybe we do this at daybreak rather than in the early morning hours when there's a chance of surprise buyers disrupting our assault."

Frank said, "That may not be a bad plan. Let's say we hit them just before sunrise tomorrow morning. We'll meet at the garage, take a truck or van, and show up at the house at 6 a.m. Gino, you bring a one-pound brick of C-4, a blasting cap, and a timer. When we're done gathering what we need, we set the timer for five minutes and leave the area."

Gino said, "I'll take care of the blast, but we need to get in the house and take out most of the competition, except for Miguel and maybe one or two others so we can interrogate them properly."

Sal nodded in agreement. Then said, "If we three hit the front door and scatter throughout the house using only silenced .22s, we should be able to blitz the house before they have a chance to react."

Frank added, "The only issue is if they have an alarm on the front door. That could make things a bit more difficult."

Sal said, "Not really. We have the element of surprise and if we move fast as lightning the alarm will be of little consequence."

Frank said, "We know the house has two stories, but we only saw the first floor. The bedrooms are probably upstairs. The room where they kept the drugs seemed to be on the first floor, across from the room with the desk and couch where Sal and I were. Here's what we do: we quietly make our entrance through the front door. Sal, you concentrate on clearing the first floor. Gino and I will go upstairs and go through every room, eliminating anyone we come in contact with—except for Miguel. We need him alive."

Sal said, "But they probably kept the drugs on the first floor. There's likely some type of guard there, don't you think?"

Gino said, "Sal has a good point. However, if we do this quietly and move quickly, they won't hear us coming. That means we have the element of surprise. If there's anyone guarding the drugs on the first floor, they'll be caught off guard when Sal makes his entrance."

Frank said, "Okay, change of plans. Sal, you and I will go upstairs and take out everyone but Miguel and one or two of his companions. We can wound them, but we cannot kill them. Gino, you hit the first floor and take out everyone you come in contact with. They're simply collateral damage. How does that sound?"

Gino nodded in agreement. Sal said, "I like it. We go in fast and hard, question a few folks, gather the drugs and money, and blow the place up. Sounds good to me."

Frank said, "This will work fine if we're quick and accurate."

They all agreed on the plan, shook hands, and headed home to prepare for the assault at daybreak.

Frank called Diego at home and told him he wouldn't be coming in at 5 a.m. because he had some business to attend to. However, he planned to be in around 9 a.m. Diego said it was not a problem, and he and Mikey could take care of the baking until Frank returned.

Gino called Pasquale and told him he needed a couple of hours off in the morning to go to a doctor's appointment. Pasquale had no problem with Gino's request.

Sal would have to use the delivery van for the trip to the Baltimore County house. There was no way to use a car or truck from the garage and have it back in time before Pasquale opened the shop. However, he would change the plates on the van so that it was somewhat untraceable.

Sal, Gino, and Frank met at 5 a.m. for their trip to Baltimore County. Gino had the explosives and silenced .22s in a large cardboard box. They loaded the van and drove through the downtown streets, where there was little to no traffic at that hour of the morning.

As they approached the target house, Gino put the explosive device into a backpack and strapped it on. The three then quietly exited the van, each armed with a silenced .22 plus extra magazines of freshly wiped-down ammo. As they walked toward the house, they put on rubber gloves and facecovering masks. They knew the house had to have security cameras throughout, which would be destroyed when the final blast and fire consumed it.

The three men reached the front door, and Gino used a small wrecking bar to pry it open. To their surprise, there was no alarm sound.

Gino immediately went left, looking for any signs of life. Finding none, he went down the hallway to the room with the desk. The door was closed, so he slowly turned the knob and opened it. Again, there was no one inside. He saw the door off to the right, where the drugs had been retrieved during Frank's and Sal's visit. He turned the knob slowly and opened the door. There were stacks of drugs and money on several tables, but once again, not a soul in sight.

Frank and Sal were on the second floor. Frank opened the first door on the left and saw two twin beds, each with a man sleeping in it. He shot them both dead.

Sal opened the first door on the right side of the hall and saw one man in a double bed. He shot him twice.

Both Frank and Sal worked their way down the hall, and each opened the second set of doors. Frank's room was empty, while Sal's room had two double beds, each with a man sleeping in it. Sal fired five shots, killing them both.

The pair continued down the hall to what would be the last set of doors. Frank opened the door on his side, and Sal opened the door on his side simultaneously. Frank had Miguel in his sights, while Sal had another man in a double bed. Frank yelled, "Get out of bed and on the floor now!"

Sal didn't need to say a word; the man he was targeting abruptly awoke and reached for a weapon on the nightstand. Sal shot him in the shoulder and said, "Get on the floor now!"

Frank and Sal scanned the hall they had just come down, looking for any surprise visitors. There were none.

Frank directed Miguel and the wounded man downstairs, where they met up with Gino.

Frank asked, "Anything down here?"

Gino replied, "Not a soul. I've been in every room on this floor. I even checked the closets to make sure. But I did find a huge stash of drugs and money in the room off to the right of the big desk."

Miguel sneered, "Do you have any idea to whom that money belongs? You people will be dead in 24 hours."

Frank said, "That's okay, asshole. You'll be dead in one."

Frank led Miguel to the room with the big desk, and Sal and Gino followed along with the wounded man. Frank made Miguel and the wounded man sit on the couch, then peeked inside the room on the right and said, "Good thing we brought a van to haul all this away."

Gino said, "Sal, go back upstairs and retrieve the cell phones and wallets of these two morons. You might as well bring down all of the weapons you find. It may be a good idea to check the closets of all the rooms while you're at it."

"Sure thing, Gino."

Frank and Gino now turned their attention to the wounded man. Frank asked, "Are you expecting any company anytime this morning?"

The wounded man simply nodded and said, "No. No one except us is supposed to be here. The others will arrive around noon."

"Good. That's very good to hear," said Frank.

Gino looked at Miguel and asked, "Who is Hector, and where do we find him?"

Miguel smugly said, "You'll find out who Hector is soon enough. He'll eat your liver for lunch."

Frank laughed and said, "That's too bad. You see, we also plan to find and kill Hector. But right now, we need some information about a hit on a small bakery in Little Italy."

Miguel had a puzzled look on his face as he said, "Is that what all this is about? You raid this residence after the murder of a baker? You've got to be kidding me."

Gino said, "We're not kidding one bit, and we never said a baker was killed. How do you know about a baker being killed?"

Miguel knew he had screwed up and tried to recover by saying, "I heard it on the news or read it in the paper."

Frank said, "Nice try, asshole. We know it was you and your boys who killed that baker."

Gino looked at the wounded man and asked, "What do you know about the baker that was killed?"

The wounded man replied, "I wasn't involved in that. I can't tell you what I don't know."

Frank looked into Miguel's eyes and said, "I'll ask you one more time: What do you know about the killing of a baker in Little Italy?"

Just then, Sal came into the room with several cell phones, handguns, and wallets in a pillowcase. He said, "I have another pillowcase full of handguns by the front door. This place is an armory."

Frank said, "Let Miguel pick out his cell phone so he can make a call."

Sal held open the pillowcase with the wallets, cell phones, and some handguns, and asked, "Which one of these cell phones is yours?"

Miguel looked into the bag and said, "The black one with a red cover. Who am I supposed to be calling?"

Gino said, "No one. We just needed to know which phone was yours so we can read your text messages."

Miguel was angry as hell and started to get up off the couch when Frank shot him in the upper leg. Miguel, now wounded, sat back down on the couch, applying direct pressure to his leg.

Gino looked at the wounded man Sal had shot in the shoulder and said, "If you can't tell us who killed our friend the baker, you're of no use to us."

The wounded man replied, "I don't know who did that."

Gino shot him twice in the head.

Frank said, "Sal, get the van and bring it up the driveway. We have a lot to load up. Our time here is getting us nowhere fast."

Sal headed out the front door to retrieve the van. He pulled it up the driveway and opened the two back panel doors before going back into the house.

Frank said, "Gino, set up the blast in the center of the first floor. If Miguel doesn't come up with the right answer to my question, I'll kill him, and we can load up the van."

"I'll take care of it, Frank. Then we really need to get a move on."

Frank turned his attention to Miguel and said, "This is your last chance. Who killed the baker?"

Miguel was in pain but managed to say, "You fools have hit the wrong house. We had nothing to do with that job."

Frank shot him in the foot of his good leg and said, "What house is responsible for the baker's death?"

Miguel, fading fast and in great pain, whispered, "The house in Laurel."

Those were Miguel's last words before he passed.

Frank and Gino began carrying the loads of cash to the van. As they were running out of space, Gino said, "We'll never fit all those drugs into the van."

"I agree," Frank replied. "We take what we can and leave the rest to burn. Besides, it'll be a good story for the cops when they arrive."

With the van packed to the ceiling, Gino set the timer on one pound of C-4 for five minutes. The three men climbed into the van and drove about a mile down the road. Frank pulled the van over, and they waited for the explosion and smoke to rise. Then they headed back to Little Italy, where they had to unload the van at Frank's house so Sal could make his deliveries later. It was now 8:30 a.m.

While in Frank's basement, Gino asked if Frank had been able to get any useful information out of Miguel. Frank said, "Yes. He said the house responsible for the bakery disaster is in Laurel. I believe he was telling the truth."

Sal said, "I'll go through Miguel's cell phone, and we can meet up at DeLuca's place after work. Who knows what we may discover about this guy Hector and the new location in Laurel."

Everyone agreed, and they each went their separate ways to start the workday.

Chapter 8

Sal, Frank, and Gino met at DeLuca's bar after work to have a beer and discuss their next moves. After grabbing their beers, they headed to the back of the bar to sit at a table. Frank began, "Before we get into our next steps, I have a proposal." Gino, with a grin, replied, "Oh boy. Frank's been thinking again. This can't be good." Sal laughed and added, "Yep. Every time Frank has an idea, we know we're getting dragged into it."

"Okay, wise guys, listen up," Frank said. "I'm concerned about the huge amount of cash and drugs in my basement. I think we need to do something about it, so here's what I propose. First, with the Italian Festival coming up, I suggest we make a $10K donation to Father Alonzo. We'll slip the cash in the poor box and make it appear like an anonymous donor contributed to the church. Second, we each take $20K for personal use—just don't deposit it at the bank. Stuff it under your mattress, and we'll make it our rainy day fund. Third, I'd like to pay $1K bonuses to Diego, Mikey, and Maria. They've been working like crazy, and I want to give them something for their efforts. Lastly, I think we should contact Fabio in New York and ask if he wants the drugs we've accumulated. We've got close to sixty keys of white powder, and I really want it out of my house. What do you guys think?"

Gino listened carefully and responded, "I don't have a problem with anything you said—until we get to giving the drugs to Fabio. How do we do that? We can't just mail it in a box."

Sal chimed in, "I agree with Frank's plan. Moreover, after the cash is disbursed, there will still be over $200K left for operations. As for Fabio, why not ask him if he wants the drugs? If he does, have him send someone to pick it up. We're talking about a street value of a couple million dollars or more. I bet he'll jump on it with both feet."

Frank smiled. "Good points, guys. Gino, how about you give Fabio a call and let him know what we've been doing, give him an update on the raid we pulled in Baltimore County, and let him know we have some more leads to follow in Laurel—specifically a guy named Hector? Lastly, make the offer to give him the drugs if he can arrange for pickup."

Gino nodded, "I'll take care of that tonight. Besides, I'd like to hear what Fabio and his men are up to."

Frank said, "Alright, we're all in agreement about the cash and drugs. Sal, would you mind making the drop in the poor box at St. Leo's?"

"No problem. Glad to do it. I'd love to see the look on Father Alonzo's face when he checks the poor box."

Frank added, "When we leave here, come by the house to pick up your share of the cash. Now, Sal, did you find anything interesting on Miguel's cell phone?"

"Oh boy, where to begin," Sal said. "Miguel had a ton of text messages on his phone. I had to download and print them out because they were getting complicated. Anyway, he had hundreds of texts with Hector, and there was one phone number in the log with almost as many calls. The area code wasn't familiar, so I looked it up. Apparently, when calling Mexico from the U.S., you enter 52—the country code for Mexico—then dial the area code and finish with the 7-8-digit Mexico phone number. Miguel was calling a number in Monterrey, Mexico. I dialed the number using Miguel's cell phone, and the person who answered said, "Torres residence." Who may I say is calling?'"

"I said it's Miguel. Is Hector there?"

"One moment, please. Then I hung up."

Frank nodded approvingly. "Good thinking, Sal. We now have a name and location—Hector Torres in Monterrey, Mexico."

Gino added, "I'll pass this information to Fabio since his men are working the California-Mexico connection. This is good news for all of us."

Sal said, "There's more good news."

"Do tell," Gino encouraged.

Sal continued, "I also saw a lot of text messages to a local number. The area code is 257 in Laurel. I figured I'd try the number like I did for Miguel, but it was a no-go. When I dialed, the voice on the other side simply said,

'What's up, Miguel?' So I hung up. I don't have a name or address yet, but there are other numbers with the same area code. I'll try them all to see if I can get a name."

Frank could see Sal was disappointed. "Sal, you did good. Don't worry about it right now. We can all help with making the calls to the other numbers, and maybe we'll get lucky and catch a name. We have time on our side for now."

Gino added, "Yes, we have time, but not as much as you think. When the news gets out about a Baltimore County house blowing up, filled with bodies and drugs, these folks in Laurel will wise up and clam up."

Sal suddenly had an idea. "Hold on. When the news hits, I bet the person in Laurel will call Miguel's cell phone to see if he's okay or involved. The story should be on the local news at 6 p.m. How much do you want to bet Miguel's cell phone starts ringing?"

Frank glanced at the clock. "It's almost six now. I guess we'll see if Sal's hunch is right."

Gino suggested, "What we should do is answer the phone and act like we're Miguel. Maybe lead the caller into a conversation that will get us a name of someone in the Laurel operation."

Sal agreed, "It's worth a try. We'll see soon enough. Miguel's phone has been off for several hours, so they may have already tried to call or text him. I'll check it out—just give me a few minutes to boot up the phone."

Sal put the phone on the table and took a long drink of his beer. The phone went crazy with dings as text messages flooded in. "Holy cow," Sal said. "The noon news must've picked up the story about the Baltimore County house explosion. All these texts started coming in at 12:15."

Gino asked, "What are they saying, Sal?"

"'Call me right away. Marco.' The number has a Laurel area code."

"'Are you guys okay? Philipe.' The area code is 301."

"'Hector wants you to call him ASAP. Juan.' Another Laurel area code."

"On and on they go. There must be twenty texts between 12:15 and 1 p.m."

Frank suggested, "Sal, why not respond to the one from Marco? Say, 'I know several Marcos. Who is this?'"

Sal did as instructed, and the message came back: "It's Marco Rodríguez, you fool. Are you okay?"

Frank smiled. "Now we have a name for someone in Laurel."

Gino added, "Do the same for the guy named Juan."

Sal sent the same message to Juan, who immediately responded, "It's me, Juan Alvarez. Call me as soon as you can."

Frank said, "You're batting a thousand, Sal. Well done. We now have two names to run down in Laurel."

Gino said, "Laurel is only 21 miles from here. It's less than a thirty-minute drive on a good day. Why don't we take some of the drugs down to Laurel and use them to gather information? If we hit a club and let it be known that we have a couple of keys for sale, it might set off some alarms."

Sal was cautious. "That's a risky plan, Gino. If we happen to attract an undercover cop's attention, we'll be doing hard time for distribution."

Frank agreed. "Yeah, it's a bad plan. However, if we can find either Marco or Juan and approach them with a proposal to sell, we might find out where the distribution center in Laurel is located."

Sal said, "I like that idea better. Why don't I go down to Laurel, hit a few clubs, and let the bartenders know I have some product to sell? But I'll only talk to a man named Marco Rodríguez. Then I'll take a seat at the bar and have a few drinks to see if I'm contacted. If no one approaches me, I'll leave and hit another club. Bartenders are usually well-informed about who's who in the area, especially when you hand them a $100 bill."

Frank said, "I like it, Sal. But I'd like to be outside in the parking lot as your backup. You can leave your phone on speaker, and I'll monitor the conversation from my car. That way, if they want you to go for a ride, I can follow."

Gino agreed that Sal's plan was better, though it still put him at risk. However, they all knew that drug trafficking posed a risk.

Father Alonzo was hearing confessions on his regular evening schedule. "Before I begin, Father, I tried to put a dollar in the poor box, but it's jammed."

Father Alonzo replied, "Thank you for telling me. I'll check it out after confessions."

When he finished hearing confessions, he went to lock up the church and check the poor box. As he approached, he saw a piece of paper stuck in the slot. Father Alonzo removed the paper and reached into the box. His hand touched cash. He counted the money—$10,000—and there was a note with it that read, "For the Italian Festival. Please use it wisely. Sincerely, An Anonymous Donor."

Frank met Diego, Maria, and Miguel when he entered the bakery at 5 a.m. He called them together for a brief announcement. "You've all been working very hard, especially in my absence. I have a thousand-dollar bonus for each of you," Frank said, handing each person an envelope. To say they were stunned would be an understatement. Diego shook Frank's hand, saying, "Thank you for being so generous." Maria gave him a big hug, wiping tears from her eyes, while Miguel was simply speechless. Frank felt good about offering the bonuses to his crew. They were hardworking and well-deserving of such treatment. The bakery wouldn't be as successful as it was without the dedicated staff he had assembled.

Gino made the call to Fabio in New York. "Hello, Gino. How's the hunt for justice going down there in Baltimore?" Fabio asked.

Gino summarized the activities regarding the Baltimore County house and told Fabio about the information they discovered about a man named Hector Torres in Monterrey, Mexico, who they suspected was the head man. Gino went on to mention the lead they had in Carlo's murder and how it might be tied to a drug distribution center in Laurel, Maryland.

"Wow, slow down, Gino. I'm trying to write this down as you speak. That's a lot of good intel, my friend. Please go on."

Gino continued, "We've managed to confiscate over 60 keys of supposedly uncut cocaine. We're not interested in the drug trade, nor do we feel comfortable having so much product in our possession. We thought of offering it to you as compensation for all the hardware you sent us. Would you be inclined to take possession of these drugs?"

Fabio replied, "I understand your concerns about possessing so much product. I find your offer very respectful but totally unnecessary. However, if you insist, I'll take ownership of the product so you can keep your hands clean."

Gino said, "Thank you, Fabio. We've discussed how to get this large amount of product to you but have drawn a blank on how to do it safely."

"Gino, if you can box the product into a few plastic, non-see-through containers like the ones you get at Walmart, I'll have them picked up by a van. You text me when you're ready for the pickup and the location. I'll then text you the day and time to expect the driver. I'll also give you a code word for the driver so you know it's safe to make the transfer. The driver won't be alone—he'll have heavily armed men with him, so don't be alarmed. How does that sound?"

Gino replied, "That's a perfect solution, Fabio. I'll get right on it. The sooner we get rid of this stuff, the better I'll feel."

"I understand, my friend. If this is truly an uncut product, we're talking a street value in the millions of dollars. That even makes me nervous."

Gino was pleased with how the conversation was going with Fabio. The man was full of good ideas, and Gino now felt a sense of gratitude for the help Fabio had previously provided to Frank and him.

Fabio then said, "Are you finished, Gino? I have some information to share with you as well."

"Yes, please continue."

"Okay, my men in Florida have stopped three tractor-trailers on I-95. They managed to get the drugs and money from the vehicles, kill the drivers, and incinerate the trailers and their contents. We've infiltrated a Yellow Freight trucking company, and one of their employees supplies us with the schedule and truck numbers to look out for. So far, it's working well, but this won't last forever—the cartel will find another trucking company to replace them. Then we'll have to start all over again in Florida. For now, though, we're making an impact on distribution from Florida. Next, our California folks are working with a few border guards who supply us with intel on the trucks going into Mexico. This has been a difficult task so far, but with the information you provided about Hector Torres in Monterrey, we can zero in on that location. That will make our job more laser-focused. Thank you for supplying that bit of information. I'll let you know how it goes from here. My guess is we'll soon be able to get eyes on this Hector Torres. You'd be surprised how much people will talk when offered a few hundred American dollars."

Gino said, "Thanks for sharing the info, Fabio. I'll be texting you in a day or so regarding the product pickup location. Goodbye, my friend."

"Ciao, Gino."

Frank and Sal headed to Laurel to fish for information using a customer's car supplied by Gino from the garage. Their first stop was at Nuzback's Bar. Frank stayed in the car while Sal went inside and found an empty seat at the bar. It was 10 p.m., and the place was crowded, mostly with people in their 20s and 30s.

The bartenders were busy filling orders for the waitresses and tending to the bar's customers. The music was loud, and the dance floor was at capacity. The place was so noisy that Sal didn't think Frank would be able to hear anything from his cell phone speaker.

A bartender finally approached Sal and asked, "What can I get you?"

Sal replied, "A Miller Lite and some information," as he handed the bartender a folded hundred-dollar bill.

The bartender quickly returned with the beer and asked, "What kind of info are you looking for?"

Sal said, "I have some product to sell, and I can only speak to a man named Marco Rodríguez. Can you get word to him that I'll be here for the next hour? If he shows, I'll give you another bill. If he doesn't, I'm out of here."

The bartender looked directly at Sal and said, "Stand by."

Frank, outside the car, could hear the music from inside the bar. It was definitely loud. The noise from the club made it nearly impossible for him to hear the conversation Sal had with the bartender. His only hope was that things were going well and that they could both get out of there quickly.

Sal noticed the bartender he spoke to was on the phone. After about twenty minutes, the bartender said, "The man you're looking for is coming through the door now—the one in the green shirt."

Sal slipped the bartender another hundred-dollar bill. As the bartender caught the eye of the man in the green shirt, he pointed toward Sal.

As the man in the green shirt approached, he said, "You're looking for me, I hear."

Sal replied, "If you're Marco Rodríguez, then yes. Miguel told me you were the man to talk to about buying and selling product."

"So, you know Miguel?"

"Yes, and I'm really sorry to hear about the trouble they had today. I was shocked to hear the news. That's why I'm here—I need to find another distributor to replace Miguel."

"What kind of business are we talking about?"

Sal said, "I have a sample in my car. I've got two keys of uncut cocaine, and I can get much more if you're interested."

"Yes, I see. I'm sure we can do business, but I'd need to have your samples tested to ensure they're pure and uncut."

"Not a problem. Let's go to your tester and get this over with right now. My boss has authorized me to gift the two keys if, after testing, you agree to purchase two keys per week at the going rate."

"Who exactly is your boss, offering such a generous deal?"

"Now, you know better than to ask that. After all, I haven't asked you who your boss is, have I?"

"I see we're two men who think alike. Okay, get your samples, and I'll take you to our tester. It's only a short ten-minute ride from here. If the sample tests good, we can arrange future deliveries."

As Sal and Marco were walking toward the door, Sal said, "I have the samples in my trunk out back."

Frank could hear that part of the conversation and exited the car, walking a short distance to hide behind a dumpster. Sal and Marco soon approached the car, where Sal opened the trunk and retrieved a brown paper bag containing the drugs. As he closed the trunk, Sal said, "Let's take your car since I have no idea where we're going."

"Not a problem. My car's around front."

Frank could clearly hear the conversation now, and as Sal and Marco rounded the corner, he climbed back into the car and waited for them to leave so he could follow at a safe distance.

Marco was right when he said it was a short distance. It only took eight minutes for Marco to pull into a driveway leading to a huge house on two acres of well-manicured landscape. Frank stopped short of the massive house and listened to the conversation.

Marco led Sal to a large room on the left side of the front door. Inside, it looked like a laboratory. Several people were working at different lab stations. Marco directed Sal to the rightmost station, where an Asian woman was working on a project. Marco handed the bag to the woman and said, "Chen, test this for purity."

"Yes, sir, Mr. Marco. Right away."

Marco said, "This won't take long. Let's go to the other room and have a drink while we wait for the results."

Marco led Sal out of the lab area and into what appeared to be the living room. There was a fully stocked bar against the wall.

"What's your pleasure? Hey, I don't even know your name."

"I'll have a beer, and my name is Sal Delgado."

"One beer coming up. Have a seat."

As the two men were drinking, another man approached the bar and asked, "Who's this, Marco?"

"This is Sal. He brought us a sample of his uncut product, which is being tested in the other room. He's interested in supplying us with two keys a week of uncut product if everything tests okay."

The newcomer said, "My name is Juan. Glad to meet you, Sal. What's this sample going to cost me?"

Marco chimed in, "He's offering us this two-key sample as a gift for future business."

Juan was surprised at this interesting proposal.

Sal said, "My boss authorized me to make this offer in hopes that we can do a great deal of future business."

Juan said, "I'd very much like to meet this boss of yours and sit down to dinner."

Sal replied, "I'm sorry, Juan. My boss has always remained anonymous in these types of transactions. That's the way he wants it, and I do as he wishes."

"Very well, I understand, Sal. Please tell him I'm grateful for this opportunity to do business together."

Just then, Chen entered the room and said, "The test results are 99.8% pure. This is some of the best we've seen in a long time—much better than what we've been getting from China."

Juan said, "Well, Sal, I think that closes the deal. Let's do business. Marco, take care of our new friend and make all the necessary arrangements for weekly deliveries."

Juan extended his hand to shake Sal's and said, "Good evening, Sal. Marco will be your contact from this point forward."

Frank, listening to the conversation, was impressed with how Sal improvised on the fly. He then headed back to the club so he could park the car and wait for Sal to be dropped off.

Marco drove Sal back to the club and dropped him off at the front door. Sal told Marco he wanted to go back into the club for a while.

Marco said, "Sure thing. I can't join you, as I have other business to attend to."

The two men exchanged cell phone numbers and promised to keep in touch. Sal went into the club, and when he was sure Marco had left the area, he left and walked around the back to meet up with Frank.

Frank said, "Sal, you're a natural. That was beautiful the way you improvised on the fly."

Sal climbed into the car and said, "Frank, I was never so scared in all my life. But we pulled it off. Now let's get the hell out of here."

Chapter 9

Gino went to Walmart and purchased two large, solid blue plastic tubs. He and Frank packed sixty kilos of cocaine into the tubs and secured the lids with several plastic tie-wraps. If needed, they kept six kilograms aside as bargaining chips. Gino texted Fabio, informing him that they had two large containers ready for pickup and provided Frank's address. Fabio texted back, confirming that a gray panel van would arrive at precisely 8:30 a.m. on Friday to pick up the containers. The code word was "Cannoli."

After work, Sal, Gino, and Frank met at DeLuca's Bar for a beer and to update Gino on the fishing expedition in Laurel. Frank said, "Gino, you should have seen our boy Sal in action. He had those Laurel boys fooled from the get-go. He was really impressive."

"That's great to hear. But did we learn anything new?" Gino asked.

Sal replied, "We learned that the guy I met at the club wasn't the main man. Marco Rodríguez is just a pawn. The man I met inside the house seems to be in charge, and his name is Juan. I didn't get a last name, but I'd bet it's Juan Alvarez. The house is huge—more like a mansion. They took me to a testing lab on the right side of the house, and it's a top-notch setup. They had at least five stations working on various things. The lab appeared to be where they test, mix, and package the drugs. I'd estimate the lab takes up most of the right side of the house on the first floor. They even had a huge exhaust fan, so I suspect they're cooking meth in there too. I didn't see the second or what appeared to be a third floor of the house. I did get Marco's cell number so we can set up the weekly delivery of two kilos. I told them the cost would be the going rate, whatever that is."

"Thanks, Sal. You did a great job, as always," Gino said. "But how do we plan to take down such a sophisticated operation? This place will certainly have security cameras and alarms. We can't just walk in and take out folks like we did at the Baltimore County house. The place is too big."

"I agree, Gino," Frank said. "We need a new approach for this house."

Sal had been listening patiently to Gino and Frank go back and forth when he interrupted, "I have an idea. Why don't we reverse the operation we did on the Baltimore County house?"

Gino looked puzzled. "What are you talking about, Sal?"

Sal explained, "We hit the lab side of the house with one of those LAW rockets we got from Fabio. That will send the place into panic mode. People will flock to the lab area, suspecting an internal explosion of some sort. While they're rushing to the lab, we blitz the place and take out everyone in that area. That will probably be most of the residents. Then we can search the rest of the house for survivors or stragglers. Finding Juan will be a challenge, though. We need him for questioning."

Frank nodded. "I like the first part about making it seem like there was an explosion in the lab. Sal's right: those in the house will surely run to the lab to see what happened. The building will be on fire, and smoke will fill the lower floor. But I think we should hit the third floor with a second LAW rocket and simply wait outside the front and back of the house, taking out those fleeing the fire and smoke. From what I could see from a distance, there's a parking area at the rear of the house. My guess is that's where the survivors will go to escape the action."

Sal nodded and said, "Good points, Frank. I like your plan better. But with the place in flames, we won't be able to confiscate any guns, money, or drugs. We'll have to rely on the fire to take care of most of that."

Gino thought for a moment before saying, "How do we ensure we get this Juan character out of all the chaos?"

Frank responded, "First, we do this just before sunrise. That will help keep the number of inhabitants to a minimum. Second, we launch the two LAW rockets simultaneously to create more confusion inside. Gino hits the back, and I take the front. Sal, when the explosions occur, you drive up the driveway, get out, and help me take out anyone exiting through the front door. Meanwhile, Gino takes care of anyone trying to escape from the rear. We'll have to be careful not to kill Juan, but we do need to get him out of there for questioning; maybe even grab one or two others. Finally, we ensure the place burns to the ground by tossing in two Willie Pete grenades as we leave with our prisoners."

Gino nodded. "Sounds like a solid plan, except for one thing. There's no way to guarantee we'll get Juan out for questioning. After all, that's the main point of doing this. We need to find out if his operation was responsible for killing Carlo."

"Gino's right," Sal said. "We need a plan that ensures we get Juan in our hands."

Frank thought for a moment and then said, "Well, I have another idea, but it's much riskier. Especially for Sal."

"Let's hear it," Gino said.

"Okay, here's the plan: We do the operation at night, around 8 or 9 p.m. Gino, you make your way through the landscaping around the house so you're not detected, armed with two LAW rockets. Sal, you drive up to the house in a van and park outside the front door. I'll be hiding in the back of the van, armed to the teeth. You go inside with your two-kilo weekly delivery, keeping your cell phone on speaker so Gino and I can listen in. You head to the bar, hopefully with Marco, and ask for a drink. Then, you tell Marco that your boss has a personal message for Juan. Marco will get Juan, and now we should have you, Marco, and Juan at the bar. As soon as we hear Juan's voice, Gino hits the third floor with a LAW rocket. Panic will immediately set in, causing chaos in the house. You pull out a gun and escort Juan and Marco out the front door into the van. Once you're outside, Gino hits the lab area with the second LAW rocket.

I'll secure Juan and Marco in the van. Gino will rush to the van, toss two Willie Pete grenades through the front door, and then climb into the driver's seat. You and I will take out anyone leaving through the front door, and we'll get out of there before the grenades explode."

"Not bad, Frank," Gino said. "If for some reason Sal can't get Marco and Juan in the same location, we abort the plan. No harm, no foul."

"Good thinking, Frank," Sal added. "Like Gino said, if I can't get Marco and Juan together, I'll just make the delivery, get paid, and leave. We'll pick up Gino on the way out."

Frank said, "If everything goes according to plan, we only have one more thing to decide."

"What's that, Frank?" asked Gino.

"Where do we take our captives once we leave the area? We need a secure place where we can question and then eliminate them."

Sal thought for a few seconds and said, "Why not take them out to the Prettyboy Dam area? At that time of night, there will be no one around, and it's very quiet."

Gino said, "I'm okay with that. We'll question them, waste them, and leave them in the parking lot for the vultures."

"Sounds good to me," Frank replied.

Gino said, "Okay, we have a plan and a backup plan if Sal can't get the main targets in the same location at the same time."

Friday morning, Sal and Gino were waiting on the front steps of Frank's house. At exactly 8:30 a.m., a gray van pulled up, and the man in the passenger seat said, "Are you Gino?"

"Yes, I am. Do you have a word for me?"

"Cannoli."

Gino said, "Very good. Come with me into the house; we have two large plastic containers for you."

The man in the passenger seat exited the van. The sliding door opened, and another man also exited. That left the driver and one other man in the back of the van, who was heavily armed.

The four men went into Frank's house, where Sal and Gino lifted one container while the other two men from the van lifted the second container. All four men went outside and loaded the van.

Once the van was loaded, the two men from it climbed back inside, closed the sliding door, and left.

Sal said, "Not very talkative, were they?"

Gino laughed and said, "No, but at least we got that stuff out of Frank's house. I feel much better about it now."

Sal said, "Gino, are you going to have a van for us to use tonight?"

"Yes, we have the choice of two: one white and the other gray."

"Good," replied Sal. "I'll text Marco and tell him I'll drop off the two-kilo delivery at about 8:30 p.m. tonight. I sure hope Frank's plan works out. I have to tell you, I'm a bit nervous about it."

"I'm nervous too about you going into that house alone. But if by some chance everything goes according to plan, we'll be alright. If you're not able to get the two guys into the same location at the same time, we abort and come up with another plan. We'll get what we need sooner or later for sure."

Frank was at the bakery, doing his bread-baking duties. Diego and Maria were busy mixing pastry dough and decorating cakes. Mikey finished up his dough-making and then helped Diego mix the ingredients for the pastries. They all knew their parts and managed to stay out of each other's way.

Frank asked Diego if he thought they needed more space to expand the kitchen. Diego said, "It would be nice to have another oven and mixer, but we don't want it to be too far from the existing gear."

Frank said, "Suppose we expand out to the side and make that our storage area for supplies. Then we take out the wall that's currently dividing the kitchen from the supply room and install the mixer and oven in that space."

Diego said, "Oh yes, that's a great idea, Frank. That way, we can keep the baking and mixing operations together for better efficiency. Expanding and moving the supply area is also a great improvement. Do you think we can get the construction done without disrupting what we have going on now?"

Frank said, "Let me talk to Mr. Perez. He's a contractor who's done a lot of remodeling in Little Italy homes. If he says he can do the work without disrupting current operations, we'll move forward. I'll also have to see if I can order a mixer and oven that meet our needs. They might not be the same model, but they may actually be better than what we have now."

"Sounds good, Frank. Good luck with Mr. Perez."

Gino was hard at work at the garage. He was helping Antonio remove a large dump truck manual transmission that needed to be rebuilt. It was heavy work and sometimes required three men to maneuver the huge piece of equipment. Gino said, "Antonio, this is probably the biggest transmission I've ever seen."

Antonio replied, "I've worked on much bigger pieces of equipment over the years. And to tell you the truth, it doesn't get easier as you age."

Gino laughed at Antonio's comment as they continued to muscle the transmission out of the truck and onto a workbench. Once that was complete, Antonio went to work stripping it down and replacing the gears and other parts necessary for the rebuild.

At the end of the day, Antonio finished the rebuild and told Pasquale they'd be ready to reinstall the next day. He would need all the help he could get to muscle the equipment back into the truck.

Frank called Mr. Perez and asked him to come by the bakery to provide an estimate for an expansion. When Mr. Perez arrived, Frank greeted him at the door and quickly explained his vision for the project, emphasizing that it was crucial not to disrupt the bakery's existing operations.

Mr. Perez nodded thoughtfully, taking out his measuring tape and clipboard. He and his son, Julian, carefully took measurements, inspecting the structure from all angles while jotting down notes. After about an hour of assessing the site, they reconvened with Frank at the front of the shop.

"This is a big job," Mr. Perez began, "but we can certainly handle it for you." He then detailed their plan for the expansion, outlining how they would build a new section without interfering with the day-to-day activities of the bakery. He assured Frank that they would put up temporary walls to keep the dust and noise to a minimum and work in phases to avoid any downtime.

Frank listened attentively, impressed by Mr. Perez's thoroughness and attention to detail. "That sounds like exactly what I need," he said. "What's the price?"

Mr. Perez glanced at his notes. "For the new building, knocking down the existing wall, adding storage shelves, and installing sliding barn doors between the two structures, the total comes to $25,000."

Frank raised an eyebrow but nodded. "That seems reasonable, Mr. Perez. I'll pay you in cash—half upfront and the other half upon completion. Does that work for you?"

"That's fine with me," Mr. Perez replied. "When do you want us to start?"

"How soon can you fit me in?" Frank asked.

Mr. Perez smiled. "I can have a crew here to start the foundation work next week. Once that cures, we can immediately begin constructing the new section. The whole job should take about ten workdays, weather permitting."

Frank nodded, satisfied. "That sounds perfect. I'll have your cash deposit ready tomorrow morning."

With the agreement in place, Mr. Perez and Julian packed up their tools and left. Frank immediately went online to search for a supplier for the new oven and mixer he needed to equip the expanded bakery. To his surprise, the process was smoother than expected. He quickly found a reliable supplier, placed an order, and scheduled delivery for three weeks out—just in time for the completion of the construction.

The total cost for the new oven, mixer, and delivery came to another $8,000. Frank took a deep breath, mentally calculating the investment. It was a lot of money, but he was confident it would pay off in the long run. With the expansion underway, he could increase production and ensure that his bakery continued to serve the community, just as Carlo would have wanted.

Frank looked around the bakery, imagining the changes to come. It would be a lot of work, but it felt good to be taking action, to be doing something tangible to honor his friend's memory and keep the business alive.

Around 5 p.m., Gino received a call from Fabio.

"Hello, Fabio. What's up?"

"Hello, Gino. I have some information for you. But first, I must tell you that my men arrived back in New York around 1:30 p.m., and they said the pickup went smoothly. Again, I want to express my gratitude for your generous gift."

"You're welcome, Fabio. We're glad it all went smoothly."

"Okay, now for some news. The tip you gave us about Hector Torres in Monterrey, Mexico, worked out beautifully. Our friends at the border flagged each truck heading to Monterrey, and my men have intercepted five so far. They've confiscated over 80 kilos of cocaine and well over a million dollars in cash."

"Wow, that's a hell of a lot of loot. This Hector operation has to be huge. You can only imagine how much business he does in a year."

"Oh, I agree. It's a big operation, probably the biggest in the country right now. But there's more."

"Please, go on, Fabio."

"My men found Hector Torres's final location by accident. They were following one of the trucks into Monterrey and couldn't find a decent place to pull them over, so they kept following it. The truck led them to a compound on the outskirts of Monterrey. This is no small place—it's a fortress with two houses and warehouses inside the walls. It's heavily guarded, with what looks like a small army of personnel."

"Sounds like an impenetrable fortress."

"Maybe so, but we're working on a plan to either take them down or at least destroy much of what they have. This will take time, but we're on it. In the meantime, we think Hector will start having his trucks escorted by armed men to safeguard their cargo."

Gino replied, "I guess that'll put a stop to your men hijacking the shipments."

"Not entirely. They can only provide escorts on the Mexican side of the border. On the U.S. side, we still have control over what happens. We're working on a plan with our trucking insiders to get the schedule of trucks headed for Monterrey. Before they reach the border, we can intercept them anywhere in the United States. We've got many irons in the fire. At the very least, we'll put a dent in Hector's supply chain."

"Well, it sounds like you and your men have this supply line figured out. My friends are planning a hit on the Laurel distribution center later tonight if things go as planned."

Fabio said, "That's good to know. After all, we need to find out who was responsible for killing Carlo. That's our main goal."

"Understood, and I agree. We'll know more by tomorrow. By the way, do you have any plans to take out this Hector character?"

"Oh yes. We're setting up in a few houses around the compound. We need to gather more intel, figure out his movements, and determine the best time and location for the hit. We'll get him; it's just a matter of time."

Gino said, "Good to hear, Fabio. It sounds like you have everything under control. Thanks for the update, and good luck with the supply chain activities. Sounds profitable!"

"Take care, Gino. Yes, it's profitable, and our guys love taking these guys down. Ciao, Gino."

After work, Gino, Frank, and Sal met up at DeLuca's bar for a beer. They took their usual spot at a table in the back. Gino informed them of his conversation with Fabio earlier in the day.

"They're doing everything they can to disrupt Hector Torres's supply chain," Gino said.

"That's good news," Frank replied. "If they're concentrating on hijacked trucks, they're not looking at what we're doing in Maryland."

Sal chimed in, "You know, I've been wondering why we haven't heard of any repercussions for the two hits we've already pulled off. Don't you think that's a bit odd?"

"Maybe," Gino said. "But remember, the Greenmount job was a small, stand-alone operation. The Baltimore County job and the upcoming Laurel job, however, are big-time operations. One may not draw too much attention, but I bet we'll be under scrutiny after two major operations are taken down."

Frank nodded. "Gino's probably right, Sal. If we successfully take out two major distribution centers, someone's definitely going to start looking closer at what's going on."

Sal pondered for a moment, then said, "If things work out tonight and we get the information we need from Juan, is that the end of it for us? Once we take out the guys responsible for Carlo's murder, do we just stop and go back to normal?"

Gino replied, "You raise a good point, Sal. As I think about it now, I'd say yes. We're done when Carlo's murderer is silenced. What do you think, Frank?"

"I agree that we're done with our offensive moves. However, we still need to prepare for the next scum that tries to take over Little Italy. What I mean is we need to shore up our defenses and immediately take out anyone or any group threatening our community."

Sal said, "I see what you're saying, Frank. I agree with you. After Carlo's murderer is dealt with, we start shoring up our defenses for the next takeover attempt. There will surely be more down the road."

Gino said, "Okay, I agree with both of you. Right now, we have a few hours to rest up before we head to Laurel. Let's get some rest and meet at the garage at 7:30 p.m. We'll have time to load up the armor and go over the plan one more time before heading to the target house. It's been a long day for me at the shop, and I'm feeling pretty tired right now."

Sal laughed. "I hope you're not too tired to hump those LAWs into the bush and make solid hits!"

"Don't you worry about me, Sal. I've done this and more in the past with no sleep for days. I'll be there when you need me, smartass."

Frank smiled at the banter between Sal and Gino. "Stop it, you two. You're making me wonder what I've gotten myself into."

With that, the crew broke up and went their separate ways until the rendezvous time.

At 7:30 p.m., the three men met at the garage and loaded their gear. Once everything was secure, they headed to Laurel with Sal driving, Frank in the passenger seat, and Gino in the back by the sliding door.

The plan was for Sal to drive up the 150-yard driveway to the house. When he was about halfway up, Gino would jump out the side sliding door with two LAW rockets over his shoulders and two Willie Pete grenades tucked into his belt by the spoon handle. Gino would use the landscaping to make his way to the right side of the house, where the lab was situated, and wait.

When Gino was in position, he prepared the two LAW rockets for firing. He pulled the pin on the LAW, dropped the cover down, removed the sling, extended the tube, and moved the safety forward, ready to fire. He placed the first LAW beside him and prepared the second in the same manner.

Frank used Sal's phone to make a three-way call to his cell and Gino's cell phone. He then set Sal's phone on speaker and tucked it into Sal's top shirt pocket. Frank and Gino could now hear everything that was in close proximity to Sal's phone.

Sal pulled the van in front of the house, about twenty feet from the front door. He turned off the van but left the keys in the ignition. As he exited, he grabbed the paper bag containing the two keys of cocaine. Frank stayed in the back of the van, out of sight.

Sal entered the front door of the house and walked directly to the bar area, where he was immediately met by Marco. "I see you're right on time, Sal."

"Yes, Marco, I'm known for my promptness. Always on time, never late."

Marco laughed. "That's a good quality in our business."

Sal replied, "How about a drink before we discuss business?"

"Sure, let's head to the bar."

As the two men poured cold beer into their glasses, Sal said, "By the way, Marco, my boss asked me to deliver a personal message to Juan. Is he around?"

"Yes, of course." Marco picked up the phone at the end of the bar and dialed a few digits on an intercom. "Juan, Sal is here with a delivery and has a personal message from his boss. Can you come to the bar, please? Okay,

I'll let him know." Marco hung up the phone, saying, "He'll be here in a few minutes."

Sal said, "That's great. Here are the two keys, as promised." Sal handed the bag over to Marco. Marco signaled to another man in the large living room area to come over. When the man arrived, Marco handed him the bag and said, "Take this back to the lab and bring back the briefcase Joey has at his workstation."

The man took the bag and disappeared toward the lab for a few seconds before reappearing with a briefcase. He handed it to Marco, who opened it to reveal it was full of cash. "There you go, Sal. Transaction complete."

Sal closed the briefcase and placed it by his feet. Marco asked, "Aren't you going to count it?"

"No need to count money from a business partner. That's trust."

"Excellent," replied Marco.

Just then, Juan appeared and extended his hand to Sal. "Everything okay, partner?"

Sal replied, "Juan, things couldn't have gone any better."

That was all Gino needed to hear. He now knew Sal, Juan, and Marco were together at the bar. He raised the first LAW, aimed it at a set of French doors on the third floor, and fired.

The LAW rocket's sound was deafening, and the flash from the weapon's rear was blindingly bright. The projectile hit the glass French doors, entered the room, struck a wall, and exploded. The flash was intense, and the sound was deafening. Fire quickly engulfed the third floor, and the windows in the room where the projectile exploded shattered outward. Gino picked up the second LAW, ready to fire as soon as Sal and his two prisoners were in the van.

Inside the house, Marco yelled, "What the hell was that?" Juan said, "We've been infiltrated. Let's get out of here!"

Sal said, "Follow me. My van is right outside the front door." He grabbed the briefcase and started running toward the door, with Juan and Marco on his heels. As the three men exited the house, Frank told Gino to let the second LAW fly.

Gino aimed the LAW at the lab area and pulled the trigger. Another loud blast with a bright flash followed. The rocket pierced a double-paned window and exploded instantly, triggering several secondary explosions as the chemicals in the lab ignited. Fire consumed the entire lab area.

Frank now had Juan and Marco at gunpoint on the floor of the van. With plastic zip ties, Sal secured their feet and hands.

Gino grabbed the expended LAW tubes, covers, and shoulder straps, tossing them into the van as he passed by. He then pulled the pin on the two Willie Pete grenades and threw them deep into the house. He immediately turned and sprinted back to the van, climbed into the driver's seat, started the engine, and sped off as Frank slammed the sliding door shut. The van was about twenty yards away when the grenades exploded. Every window on the first floor shattered from the blast. The white phosphorus burned everything it touched. By the time the van reached the end of the driveway, the house was fully engulfed in flames and starting to collapse.

Gino headed north toward Prettyboy Dam, about an hour's drive away. In the meantime, Sal sat in the passenger seat while Frank guarded the captives.

Juan was the first to speak. "Who the hell are you, and what do you think you're doing?"

Frank said, "I'm Frank. The driver is named Gino, and of course, you know Sal. We're your worst nightmare. We just leveled your entire drug operation in less than six minutes. That's who we are."

Marco, looking dazed and puzzled, asked, "What do you want from us? We've just lost several friends, a ton of drugs, and cash. The people we answer to will come after you with everything they have."

Frank said, "Maybe. In fact, we're counting on it. But first, they have to figure out who we are. Right now, we're ghosts."

Juan said, "Okay, you destroyed the drugs, money, and our people. What do you want with us?"

Frank stared into Juan's eyes. "We want information."

"What kind of information?" Juan asked.

Gino said, "Hold off on the questioning, Frank. We're almost there."

Gino pulled the van into the parking lot at Prettyboy Dam. It was deserted, so he shut off the engine and looked over his shoulder at the captives.

Gino said, "We were sent to your location by some friends of yours. Apparently, you and your group are in the protection business. Not too long ago, your boys tried to muscle an old man in his bakery. Things got out of hand, and the baker was killed. Does any of this sound familiar?"

Marco glanced at Juan with fear in his eyes. "That was weeks ago, Juan!"

Juan snapped, "Shut up, Marco. They're fishing for information. Don't tell them anything."

When Juan finished, Frank shot him in the right foot. Marco recoiled, realizing they were in serious trouble. Gino said, "I'll ask again. Does any of this sound familiar?"

Marco quickly responded, "Yes. The baker refused to pay for protection."

Frank said, "Now we're getting somewhere." He turned to Juan. "All we want to know is who killed the baker in Little Italy. That's it."

Juan, now in pain, said, "Go to hell." Frank shot him in the left foot.

Sal said, "It doesn't look like Juan wants to cooperate. Just kill him."

Gino said, "Let him suffer for a while. We're not done with him yet." He looked directly at a very frightened Marco and asked, "How about you? Who killed the baker in Little Italy?"

Marco quickly replied, "It wasn't me. I had nothing to do with it. Another crew runs the protection business. We only deal in drugs and distribution."

Gino looked at Frank. "Another crew, huh? Now we have to start all over again."

Juan shouted, "Be quiet, Marco! Don't say another word." Frank shot Juan in the left arm.

Juan was suffering from intense pain. The more Frank tortured Juan, the more Marco talked.

Marco said, "You've got the wrong guys. You want Santiago, not us."

Frank asked, "Where do we find this Santiago?"

Again, Juan told Marco to shut up. Frank had enough, and he shot Juan in the right arm. Juan began bleeding out and grew weaker. Marco watched in fear as Juan passed out and died.

Marco said, "Santiago has a small farm in Westminster. I was only there once. Juan handled most of his business. Check his cell phone."

Diego pulled the cell phone from Juan's pocket and handed it to Sal. "See what you can find on this."

Sal scrolled through the contacts and text messages. "Here it is—Santiago Hernández."

Marco immediately said, "Yes, that's him—Hernández. That's the guy you want. He handles the protection side of the business."

Frank said, "Well, we have a name and a location. Do we need this guy anymore?"

Gino said, "No." Frank looked at Sal. Sal said, "No"

Frank shot Marco in the head, killing him instantly. The men dragged the two lifeless bodies out of the van and left them in the parking lot. Sal confiscated their cell phones and wallets while Gino closed up the van. Then, they headed back to the garage.

Chapter 10

With the cash, Sal put the cell phones and wallets he had confiscated from Juan and Marco into the briefcase. He and Gino began cleaning out the van to remove all traces of blood. Frank took the briefcase and went home to get a few hours of sleep before his shift started at the bakery. It was almost 1 a.m. when Sal and Gino finished cleaning up the van. Just as they were about to leave, they noticed flashing blue lights up the block. Sal said, "What is that all about?" Gino replied, "I have no idea, but it looks like they're at DeLuca's place." Within seconds, sirens blared, and more police cars pulled up to the scene. Several people who lived nearby were already coming out of their homes to see what was going on.

Sal said, "Let's go up there and see what's happening. It looks serious."

As they made their way up the block, they could see an ambulance in front of DeLuca's place. On both sides of the street, a crowd was forming by the bar. Sal asked one of the onlookers, "What's going on?"

"The DeLucas were hit. They're taking the old man out now on a stretcher. We don't know what happened to the old lady," the person replied.

Sal went over to Gino and relayed what he had heard. Gino said, "You don't suppose it's those Westminster boys again?"

Sal replied, "If it is, we have our work cut out for us. Those poor folks don't deserve to be treated like this."

"Let's not jump to any conclusions just yet," Gino cautioned. "I'll go across the street and nose around. You do the same on this side. We need to piece this together so we know the facts."

Sal noticed the glass in the front door of the bar was shattered—possibly broken by the police to gain entry. He also saw Mr. DeLuca being loaded into the ambulance, his face a bloody mess. There was no sign of his wife, but the forensics team was already entering the bar. Sal thought to himself, *This can't be good.*

Gino was hearing all kinds of speculation about what had happened at the bar, but he couldn't make sense of the rumors. He noticed a news truck parked halfway down the block. The reporter and camera operator were making their way closer to the action.

As Gino returned across the street, the police began pushing the crowd back and putting up yellow crime tape. Police cars were coming and going, and the news crew was kept away from the bar but was still broadcasting live, reporting the incident as breaking news. The streets of Little Italy were now full of curious residents trying to find out what was happening at DeLuca's.

Father Alonzo arrived on the scene and managed to get close enough to see Mr. DeLuca in the ambulance. He must have identified himself as the parish priest, as they allowed him to enter the ambulance to be with Mr. DeLuca.

Sal said, "It seems odd that the ambulance is still here. Why haven't they taken the old man to the hospital?"

Gino replied, "I hate to say it, but since they let Father Alonzo in there with him, he may be administering Last Rites."

Frank arrived on the scene and found Gino and Sal. "What the hell happened?" he asked.

"We don't know for sure. There are rumors flying all over the place," Sal replied.

Gino added, "Father Alonzo is in the ambulance with Mr. DeLuca, but we haven't seen his wife. The forensics staff are inside, not the EMTs. That can't be good."

Frank, surveying the scene, asked, "You don't think this was another hit, do you?"

"Sal and I were just talking about that when you showed up. I sure hope not. But if it is, that might support some of the things Marco was saying a few hours ago."

Detective Matthew approached the ambulance just as Father Alonzo was leaving the now-deceased Joey DeLuca. "Father, do you have a minute to talk?" he asked.

"Hello, Detective. Yes, of course," Father Alonzo replied.

"Father, we have two deceased here—the man in the ambulance and a woman inside the bar."

"This man's name is Joey DeLuca, and he and his wife Mary ran the place for many years. You say there's a deceased woman inside. I should go in and administer Last Rites."

"One second, Father. We need to notify the next of kin as soon as possible. Do you know who that might be?"

"The DeLuca's have a son. His name is also Joseph. They call him Joey Jr."

"Do you have any contact information for the son?"

"No, I'm sorry. Joey Jr. moved away several years ago. Somewhere close by—a place called Mount Airy; I think."

"Okay, Father, that helps. I'll have an officer take you inside as soon as the forensics team is finished."

Detective Matthew summoned a police officer. "The Father needs to administer Last Rites to the woman inside."

"Well, hello, Father Alonzo. It's Freddy Amato. Do you remember me?" said the officer.

"Freddy, of course. So you're a police officer now. Good for you," Father Alonzo replied.

Detective Matthew asked, "I take it you two know each other."

Freddy said, "Oh yes. I grew up around the corner from here. Everyone knows Father Alonzo. However, it's a very sad situation we have here, Father. The DeLucas were such nice people. I remember them well."

Detective Matthew added, "I need to notify the next of kin, and Father Alonzo said they have a son. Do you know where he lives?"

"Father Alonzo is right. They have a son named Joey Jr. Last I heard, he worked for Carroll County—in the Parks Department. No, wait, that's not right. He worked for the Carroll County Tax and Assessments Department. Unfortunately, they're closed on Saturday and Sunday, Detective."

"Thank you both. I'll make a few calls and wake some folks up to get the contact info for Joey Jr."

Father Alonzo said, "You want to ask for Joseph Alfonso DeLuca, Jr. That's his full name."

Two hours passed before Father Alonzo could administer Last Rites to Mary DeLuca. She had been beaten terribly, and Father Alonzo felt sick to his stomach. After finishing his duties, he rushed outside for fresh air.

Detective Matthew approached and asked if he was okay. "Yes, thank you. I will be fine. I just don't understand why the animals who did this were so brutal. That poor woman never hurt a soul in her life. I hope you find out who did this terrible deed, Detective. They deserve to be punished."

"I'll do my best, Father. Also, this appears to have some similarities to the Carlo case a few weeks ago. I'd like to renew my request for any information you may come across that could help bring these people to justice."

Father Alonzo nodded and walked back to the rectory, sad and angry about what he had witnessed.

Gino went to the garage to start work. He was tasked with helping Antonio lift a massive transmission into the underside of a dump truck. It required everyone in the shop to accomplish the task, as the regular car transmission jack wasn't powerful enough, and a suitable jack was too expensive.

Once the transmission was safely bolted into the chassis, Antonio finished the connections and filled the fluid levels. When he was done, he asked Pasquale if he wanted to go for a test drive. Pasquale said, "Sure. Let's see what she can do."

Antonio drove the dump truck out of the city and onto the freeway, shifting through all the gears and pushing 70 MPH on the open road. Pasquale said, "She sounds good, Antonio. Let's get her back to the shop before you get a ticket."

Frank met up with Mr. Perez to give him the down payment on the expansion project. Frank told Mr. Perez he had a new mixer and oven coming in three weeks, so he had better be ready. Mr. Perez replied, "Not a problem if it doesn't rain. Once we have it under the roof, it can rain all it wants, but the foundation and the roof are the two critical parts of the construction."

Frank said, "Understood. I'll ask Father Alonzo to pray for a dry spell."

Joey Jr. was at Della Noche Funeral Home, making arrangements for his parents' funeral, mass, and burial. As he was leaving, he ran into Sal.

"Hey, Joey, how are you doing? I am so sorry about your parents being taken out the way they were."

"Thanks, Sal. I just made the final arrangements, and Father Alonzo will perform the mass and gravesite services."

"That's good to know, Joey. Did your folks have a final resting place?"

"Oh yeah. They bought plots years ago at Holy Redeemer. Good thing they did, too. That place is almost full."

Sal said, "Joey, what I'm about to tell you stays between you and me."

"Sure, Sal. You know me. I've had your back since grade school."

"Well, Gino, Frank, and I are looking into what happened to your folks. We think it's tied to what happened to Carlo, the baker, a few weeks ago."

"No kidding. The cops never mentioned that when they talked to me."

"Cops? What are they going to do? They're overwhelmed and understaffed. Anyway, arc you still working for the County?"

"Yes. I work for Carroll County, why?"

"If I give you a man's name, can you look up any property records you have on file for him. We have a guy we want to question about the murders but don't have an address. He lives in Westminster someplace."

"Sal if it will help find the people that killed my parents, you bet I will help. Listen. Take my cell phone number and text me with the name. In a few days I will check the property tax records and let you know what I find."

"That's great Joey. I look forward to hearing from you and I will keep you informed of any developments."

"Okay Sal. Good seeing you again. By the way, if you need any help with this guy, let me know. I would love to get my hands around his neck if he is responsible for killing my parents."

As Sal was walking away, he turned and said, "By the way, Joey, if anyone comes around asking questions, let me know ASAP."

Joey nodded, and the two went their separate ways.

After work, Sal, Gino, and Frank met at Velleggia's Restaurant because it had a bar and lounge. They ordered a beer and sat at one of the tables in the rear. They then ordered dinner and talked about their next move. Sal filled them in on the conversation he had with Joey Jr. He told them he would send Joey Santiago Hernández's name so he could do a search of the tax and land records. "We should have an answer in a couple of days."

Gino said, "That's good news, Sal. I didn't know you knew Joey Jr."

"Oh, yes. We were in grade school together."

Frank said, "Well, let's hope he comes through with an address. Once we have that, we can do some reconnaissance and come up with a plan."

Gino said, "I can't wait for the opportunity to have a conversation with this Hernández character. By any chance, did Joey say what he was going to do with the bar?"

"No, we didn't get into that. He has enough to worry about right now. After all, what's the rush?"

Frank said, "Sal, I would like you to stop by later and pick up the cell phones we took from Juan and Marco. There may be information in their texts that ties in with this Hernández guy."

"Sure thing, Frank. I will do that tonight. Speaking of Juan and Marco, I have not seen anything on the news about it."

Frank and Gino agreed that they too hadn't heard about it or a house in Laurel blowing up. Sal said, "Maybe it's just covered locally, or it was a busy news day and never made the cut."

Frank said, "Guys, the briefcase Sal took from the Laurel house contained $75K. We each get $25K, and you can pick it up whenever you want. I'll be using mine to expand the bakery."

Gino said, "I didn't know you were actually going through with the expansion idea."

Sal said, "Oh, he is going through with it, alright. They will be breaking ground for the foundation next week, weather permitting."

Gino said, "That's great, Frank. The business is really taking off for you."

At Sunday mass, Father Alonzo spoke about the horrible deaths of the DeLucas. He also announced the plans for the viewing, the mass, and the burial. Everyone in the church knew the DeLucas well. Father Alonzo said, "After the cemetery service, everyone is welcome to come to St. Leo's Hall, where we will have food and drinks. The wake will be paid for by the local restaurants in Little Italy."

In Monterrey, Mexico, Hector Torres was having a meeting with his two top lieutenants. Hector was furious about the news that in the past month, fifteen trucks with drugs and cash had failed to make it to Monterrey. He said, "I want to know who is hijacking our merchandise. Do either of you know what's going on?"

Lieutenant Pablo said, "We know you are upset, boss, but we simply have not been able to nail down who is responsible. The trucks are sometimes hit while still in the United States, and others in Mexico. We do not suspect either government to be at fault. It is most certainly another cartel trying to take over territory."

Hector looked at Pablo and said, "Do we have any information to support your statement that it is another cartel trying to move in? Of course not. Otherwise, we would be at war."

Hector turned to the second lieutenant. "What do you have to say, Juan?"

"Boss, I think Pablo is mostly correct. Someone is trying to take over, or at least muscle into our territory. However, I think the most likely candidates are the Colombians."

Hector had an inquisitive look on his face as he said, "Interesting. The Colombians, you say. Now that makes some sense. They are always trying to expand into new markets, especially Clan del Golfo (The Gulf Clan or AGC). Yes, this makes more sense."

Pablo said, "Boss, we do not have anything solid on whether the Colombians are making a grab for territory. However, I agree it is more likely they are behind this than another Mexican cartel. We need to gather more information."

Hector said, "I agree. We need more information. Here is what I want you two to do. Get your best men on the street to find out where the Colombians are operating right now. Then I want them to grab as many of them as they can. The higher in the organization, the better. I want them brought to the compound and interrogated. We will get to the bottom of this."

Pablo and Juan nodded in agreement. Then Hector said, "There is one more thing we need to discuss. It has come to my attention that we've also lost two East Coast distribution centers in the past month. Pablo, this falls under your jurisdiction. What the hell is going on?"

Pablo had anticipated this question and was well prepared. He pointed to a screen and turned on a small projector in the middle of the table. "This is the news coverage of the Baltimore County and Laurel drug houses going up in smoke. These pictures show a distinct outward blast that could only be caused by explosives. In other words, these were not accidental lab miscues. These were military explosive-type operations. They were precise, quick, and resulted in total destruction."

As Pablo turned off the projector, Hector asked, "Are you saying the American military destroyed these houses?"

"No, not at all. I am saying all the information we have gathered from both sites tells us military explosives were used by a small group that can quickly get in and out undetected."

Juan added, "Pablo and I discussed this with the men we have in the area, and they agree it was more like a military strike force operation. We also think the Colombians may be behind this, along with the truck hijacking, to disrupt operations for our cartel."

Hector thought for a few seconds and said, "Okay. Again with the Colombians. We need more information. Do as I tell you. Grab some of these Colombians and bring them to the compound. This is going to start a war between us and the Colombians for sure. I hope your men are ready for what soon may be ahead."

After the meeting, Juan and Pablo came up with a plan to have two groups of men round up some Colombian drug traffickers. The crews wouldn't have to travel to Colombia since several small clusters were operating around Mexico City. These small groups were never a threat to the Mexican cartels in the past; they mostly consisted of offshoots of crews who wanted to leave Colombia and branch out on their own. However, maybe they recently decided to expand, but they certainly would not have the organization to take on truck hijacking and drug distribution centers. The key to the plan was to extract information from them and possibly get contacts of the men in the know in Colombia. Once Pablo and Juan had good intel on where some key members were located, they could send in their folks to have them extracted and brought back to Mexico by sea and ground. Juan was very interested in turning a few of these local Colombians into soldiers for the Mexican cartel. He believed that money speaks for itself and outweighs loyalty.

Gino received a call from Fabio. "Hello, Fabio. Are things going well in the trucking business?"

"Hello, Gino. Yes. We hit thirteen trucks from Florida to California and another two in Monterrey. We have also been gathering a ton of information on this Hector character. We now have a good idea of his schedule and the places he visits most often. It won't be long before we have a big enough picture to take him out.

"How about you? Did you get the Laurel folks taken care of?"

Gino replied, "Fabio, the Laurel hit went off like a well-oiled machine. However, we could not link them to the Carlo murder. We did manage to extract valuable information from two key players. We are pursuing that now. In the meantime, we had another tragedy."

Gino told Fabio about the attack on the DeLucas and how they were brutally murdered at their small bar in Little Italy.

Fabio said, "I am sorry to hear this horrible news. But the good thing is you basically confirmed it wasn't the Laurel folks since they were eliminated. Concentrate on your new lead and follow the clues. You and your crew will get to the right people as soon as possible. In the meantime, is there anything I can do for you? Do you need any supplies?"

Gino thought for a few seconds and said, "A few more LAWs would be helpful, and some type of timed incendiary would also come in handy. There's no rush on this, Fabio. We have much more work to do before we go after this new prospect."

"Okay, Gino. I'll see what we have at the warehouse and let you know when to expect delivery. We will deliver to the same garage, and I'll text you a code word well in advance."

"Sounds good, Fabio."

"Gino, what is the name of the new target you are after?"

"His name is Santiago Hernández."

Fabio repeated the name twice and said, "Although that is a common name, it does sound familiar. Let me do some checking here. If my memory is correct, he was one of the guys we ran out of New York a few years ago. He was in the protection business. I'll call you back in a day or so after I talk to some of my guys."

"Thanks, Fabio. Talk to you later."

The funeral mass and trip to Holy Redeemer were a huge success. The entire community of Little Italy attended the DeLucas service in force. Back at St. Leo's, the wake was packed with people celebrating the lives of the DeLucas. Sal went up to Joey Jr. and introduced Frank and Gino. Joey said he would be back to work the next day and would text Sal the information he found on Santiago Hernández's property. Frank assured Joey that if this Hernández guy was responsible for Carlo and his parents, they would make it right. Joey thanked the three men for taking such an interest in pursuing justice.

Chapter 11

Joey Jr. looked at the county records database when he returned to work. He found two properties listed under Santiago Hernández's name. Both were in Westminster, about a half-mile apart. The first was a 40-acre plot designated as agricultural, with two houses and a small barn. The second was a 6-acre plot, also designated as agricultural, but with no house—just a huge barn structure supposedly used to store farm equipment. When Joey did a Google Maps query, he got a bird's-eye view of the properties. He bundled all the information, including the Google links, into several text messages and sent them to Sal.

Mr. Perez was setting up the foundation framework. Concrete was scheduled to arrive late in the afternoon. Diego, his wife, and Sal were extremely busy in the storefront. Customers were lined up, and Sal was now making two deliveries a day to all the restaurants. The pastries and cakes were a huge hit, with no signs of slowing down. Frank was spending almost two thousand dollars each day on supplies. As soon as they were unloaded at the bakery, they were mixed, formed, baked, and sent out the front door. Gino, of course, was always busy at the garage. He had managed to secure a fleet of trucks from a construction company. Mr. Pasquale had no choice but to invest in a larger lift and truck transmission jack. Antonio was working six days a week and loving it.

The DeLuca bar and restaurant had remained closed since the attack. Joey's cousin was interested in taking over the operation, with his wife and daughter handling the kitchen duties. Before they took over, they wanted to do some renovations. Mr. Perez was selected to do the work, but they had to wait until he finished the bakery expansion. Everyone was glad to hear that the DeLuca's bar and grill would be reopening.

Gino received a call from Fabio with an update on the shipment of armaments. They would be delivered on Friday afternoon, and the code word was "Tiramisu." Gino thanked Fabio in advance for the order. Fabio continued, "Gino, I have more good news about our friend Hector Torres. We're in the process of sending in more men with heavy armor to take out the entire Torres compound. It's slow going because it's difficult to move so much equipment without being detected. My guess is we'll be in a position to wipe him out within thirty days."

Gino replied, "Oh, that's great news, Fabio. I wish your men good fortune and a safe assault on that devil."

"I have more news, Gino."

"Please continue, my friend."

"I was correct in my recollection of your target, Santiago Hernández. I checked with my guys, and we agreed that your Santiago is the same guy we booted out of New York a few years ago. This guy was brutal when it came to enforcing his protection racket. The merchants in the area were so scared of being killed that they ultimately agreed to his terms for payment. Those who didn't pay weren't just vandalized and robbed—they were killed outright. This is someone you need to be very careful about pursuing. I know you have good reason to go after him, and my boss told me if you fellows don't take care of it, he wants us to come down there and do the job."

Gino said, "Don't worry, Fabio. We will take care of this for sure. We believe he's not only responsible for Carlo's death but also for the DeLucas.'"

"Okay, Gino. Good luck and stay in touch."

"Will do. Ciao, Fabio."

After work, Sal met up with Gino and Frank at Velleggia's Restaurant. They ordered a beer and then a hearty dinner. Sal updated Frank and Gino on the information he received from Joey Jr. He then showed them the Google links that Joey had provided. As he showed them his phone, Frank said, "This is a great aerial view of both properties. We'll have to have a closer look, but that huge barn looks like it has fuel tanks right next to the building."

Gino said, "That makes sense since it's supposed to house farm equipment. Probably one tank for gasoline and the other for diesel."

Sal said, "Boy, is that a convenient spot to place a timed charge." Gino and Frank nodded in agreement.

Sal then pulled up the aerial view of the main plot. Two houses were clearly visible in the picture. On one side of the lot, there seemed to be woods, then an open pasture of sorts, and then the two houses, which were about 30 yards apart.

Frank said, "Those woods may be our best starting point. However, I don't like that open field between the tree line and the houses."

Gino chimed in with a possible solution. "Suppose we set some timed explosives at the big barn down the road. If we do it right, we'd light up the sky for miles. We set the timers for, say, 30 minutes. That gives us time to drive up the road and enter the woods. We wait for the explosion at the big barn and then make a dash from the woods toward the house. I bet as soon as the big barn goes up in flames, most of the people in the two houses will head toward the burning barn. It will be a diversion for us. We then blitz the big house, take positions inside, and wait for whoever returns. We'll have the element of surprise on our side and hopefully capture them for a nice chat. What do you think?"

Frank said, "I sure am glad you're not mad at me, Gino." Sal laughed, saying, "Yeah, me too. That's not such a bad plan."

Frank said, "Okay by me, except we have to assume the biggest house is where our target lives. I'm guessing the second house is for his crew. Why not set the timed charges on the big barn for an hour? We then somehow make a stealth visit to the smaller home and plant another charge for, say, ten minutes after the first one goes off. That way, we eliminate anyone still in the second house, and when the others return, they have to come to the big house where we're waiting."

Gino said, "I get what you're saying, but that means one of us has to get to the second house undetected, plant the timed device, and get to the big house and hide, waiting for the rest of us to take over the house."

Sal said, "Hold it. Try this on for size. We first set up timed explosives on the big barn as suggested earlier. We give them an hour. The three of us head up the road and go through the woods, while you two wait. I'll make my way to the second house, plant an explosive device, and hide somewhere close to the big house. When the big barn goes up in flames, the inhabitants of both houses will probably go see what's happening. If Gino can set the device I plant at the small house to be remotely detonated, timing is no longer an issue. When you two think most of the people have gone to the fire down the road, you detonate the explosives at the smaller house. Now we have maybe five minutes for you two to make the run toward the big house. I'll already be there and can ensure we have an entry point—front door, back door, or window, whatever works. The three of us take up positions in the big house, waiting for those returning from down the road. I suspect they'll ooh and ahh over the second house being totally destroyed before coming into the big house. We then take them at gunpoint and start the interrogations."

Gino said, "I like your plan, Sal. I most certainly can rig up a remote detonation device, but I'm not sure about the range. We can modify your plan a little by having me and Frank on the move as soon as the guys exit the houses and run toward the big barn."

Frank said, "We're forgetting one thing. When that big barn goes off, it will draw a lot of attention. Hell, the guys in the house could have called 911 on the way to the barn to see what happened. That means fire trucks and possibly cops will be en route sooner than we'd like. When they see the second house burning, they'll most likely turn their attention there as well, and now we're trapped."

Gino said, "You certainly raise a good point, Frank. We definitely need an exit plan. However, we're just tossing around ideas and haven't laid eyes on the place yet. Why don't we table this discussion and take a ride out there to check the place out before making any final decisions?"

Sal said, "Frank, Gino is always the one doing the thinking. I'm in. Let's go. From here, at this time of night, we could be there in forty-five minutes."

Juan and Pablo sent six men in three SUVs to Mexico City. Their mission was to split up and locate Colombians involved in the drug trade, then transport them back to Hector's compound. It didn't take long for the crews to discover a few clubs notorious for drug dealing. They would lure the unsuspecting Colombians out to their SUVs as if they were going to make a large sale. Once they are outside the club, they simply grab them at gunpoint, bind their hands with plastic zip ties, load them into the SUVs, and return to the compound. At the compound, the captives will be housed in a holding area usually reserved for torturing snitches.

The first two crews returned to the compound within 24 hours. The third crew arrived at noon the next day. In total, the three crews managed to abduct six Colombians.

Juan and Pablo entered the holding area late in the afternoon. All six men were bound to chairs around a large table, with four heavily armed guards watching over them.

Juan began the conversation once he and Pablo sat down across from the captives. "We have brought you here for a purpose. Our intent is not to harm you but to ask for information. When we're through, we will take you back to Mexico City."

Pablo instructed one of the guards to cut the zip ties from the captives' wrists so they could drink from several plastic water bottles placed in the center of the table. Their ankles were still bound.

After eagerly drinking the water, Pablo said, "Bring them more water. They seem to be very thirsty."

When additional bottles were placed on the table, each man took one and sipped as Juan began questioning. "We operate the Sinaloa cartel. Recently, several of our trucks have been hijacked. We need to know if you have any information that might help us find those responsible."

The six men appeared relieved yet confused. One of them said, "We're not involved in that kind of business. We buy and sell drugs, yes, but hijacking trucks is not something we do."

Another man added, "We are small operators who left Colombia for a better life. We certainly wouldn't steal from the Mexican Sinaloa cartel or any cartel. That would be suicide."

Pablo responded, "We understand your confusion. We suspect that Colombians are trying to muscle into our territory. We need to know who might be running these operations. Do any of you know who the main Colombian players are in the area?"

One of the captives replied, "We are not part of any Colombian cartel and have no contact with any of their operatives."

Pablo said, "Here's what we want you to do." He signaled a guard to bring over a box and place it on the table. "Inside this box are six burner cell phones. Each of you take one."

The captives complied.

"Turn over the phones; they are numbered 1 through 6. We're not interested in your names. When you check the contacts, you'll see two phone numbers—mine and my partner Juan's. Do you understand so far?"

The captives, still puzzled, nodded.

Juan continued, "We want you to go back to business as usual but keep your eyes and ears open for any information about Colombian cartels operating in the area. When you have the information, call one of those numbers and identify yourself by the number on your phone. Tell us what you've discovered, and we'll verify it. If your information is good, we'll call you on the burner phone and set up a drop at the same club you were taken from. You will be paid $20,000 for your information."

The six captives smiled, looking forward to working for the Mexican cartel.

Pablo glanced at one of the guards and said, "Cut them loose and load them into the SUVs. Drop them off where they were picked up."

As the six captives walked towards one of the SUVs, one of them turned to Juan and said, "This is dangerous work for us. But if you keep your end of the bargain, we'll be satisfied."

Sal, Frank, and Gino picked a customer's SUV from the garage lot and headed onto I-83, then I-695 E and I-795 N. As they approached the small town of Westminster, Gino punched the address on his phone for detailed directions to the Santiago Hernández properties Joey Jr. had sent to Sal. It was still daylight, but the sun was setting. As they got within a mile of their destination, Gino said, "This place is really out in the sticks."

Frank replied, "That could be good news for us."

Gino said, "The first address is coming up on the left now. Slow down, Sal."

As Sal slowed the SUV on the country road, he said, "There are the two houses. They're only about a hundred yards from this road."

"Keep going, Sal," Frank instructed.

Gino added, "There's the second property, and that barn is huge." As they passed the barn on the right, he continued, "I can see the two fuel tanks on the side of the barn, too."

Frank said, "Keep going straight, Sal. Let's see what's nearby these properties."

After driving another two miles, they came across a gas station with an attached convenience store. Frank said, "Pull in there, Sal, and park."

Sal did as suggested and asked, "Why are we stopping here?"

Frank replied, "I have an idea. Sal, you and I will go into the convenience store and buy some soft drinks. Gino, ask to use the bathroom, and while you're in there, see if there's a place to hide a timed explosive."

Gino agreed, though he added, "Okay, but I still don't see what you're driving at, Frank."

When the three men climbed back into the SUV, Frank said, "It's now too dark to see much of anything. Let's head back toward the properties. Sal, stop on the side of the road by the big barn."

"Okay, boss. Whatever you say."

Sal pulled the SUV to one side of the road and noticed a driveway leading right to the barn. "Do you want me to pull in there, Frank?"

"Sure, why not. Turn off the lights and let's see if anyone comes out to greet us."

The men waited patiently for five minutes. Then Frank said, "I don't see any security cameras, and the barn looks completely dark inside. Let's take a closer look and see if we can get a peek inside. There are windows all around the structure."

The three exited the SUV. Frank said, "I'll go left, Gino right, and Sal around the back. Take a quick look, and let's get out of here."

After their reconnaissance, the men returned to the SUV. Sal backed out of the driveway, turned on the lights, and headed back to Little Italy.

Sal said, "When I looked inside the back of the barn, I was surprised. They had some low-level lighting, maybe from battery chargers or safety lights; I'm not sure. However, there was enough light to see at least twenty classic or antique cars and trucks in the back. The barn seemed to be divided into two sections: one for the cars and another for farm equipment."

Gino added, "I also saw that it was divided. I could see all the big farm equipment in the front, but I couldn't get a good look at the back."

Frank said, "Alright, it's clear the barn is divided. That means we have to attack both areas simultaneously to be effective."

On the road, Gino asked, "So, what was that all about, Frank? Do you have a new plan?"

Frank replied, "Yes, I do. How does this sound? We go back to the gas station, and Gino plants a timed explosive device in the bathroom set to go off in two and a half hours. Then we return to the barn, plant timed explosives on the two fuel tanks, and break through a window to plant a couple more, set to go off in four and a half hours.

Next, we head up the road past the two houses and pull into the woods. Gino and I will wait while Sal plants a remote-detonated device on the smaller house and hides.

When the gas station blows, all the emergency services and probably some cops will rush to the scene two miles away. If that blast gets people curious enough, Gino and I will head to the big house and blitz the place. If not, the sound of the blast and sirens should at least make them gather outside to see what's happening.

We herd everyone into the big house and question them. We'll have about two hours before the big barn blows. Then, we take out everyone we've rounded up, head back to our vehicle, and leave."

Sal replied, "Well, it's a plan, but I think we need some modifications."

"Go ahead, spit it out, Sal," Gino said.

"Here's my idea. We do what Frank suggested until we reach the woods. Then, instead of waiting, all three of us head to the small house and quietly take out everyone there—around 2 a.m. when they're likely asleep. We use the silenced .22s. Once everyone's neutralized, we plant the remote device and move to the big house, where Santiago Hernández is probably sleeping.

We take positions outside the house, wait for the fireworks and sirens to stir the occupants, then round them up for questioning. This way, we don't have to worry about anyone coming out of the smaller house or whether the people in the big house will head to the gas station commotion."

Gino nodded, "See, Frank? Sal just simplified the plan, and I think it makes sense. We still have about two hours to gather information from the people in the big house. When we're done, we leave a timed device in the center of the house, set for thirty minutes. Then we return to our vehicle, blow the small house remotely, and leave. The big house will blow shortly afterward."

Frank thought it over and said, "I agree, Sal's plan is better. And I agree that we should do this in the early morning hours. The only unknown is whether Santiago Hernández is in the big house."

Gino replied, "True, but if he isn't, we'll get the others to tell us where he is."

Sal said, "I think we have a solid plan to either get Santiago or find out where he is. Aside from that, Santiago probably ordered the hits, but he never had a hand in carrying them out. I want to make sure we get the bastards who actually murdered Carlo and the DeLucas."

Gino replied, "That makes perfect sense to me as well. Taking out Santiago is a bonus. Our real targets are those who did the actual killings of Carlo and the DeLucas."

Frank added, "I agree. We need whoever is in that big house to confess the murders. I want them to suffer—a lot. As for Santiago, I just want him to get a dose of his own medicine. I want him to beg for his life. I want him to watch all his prized possessions in that big barn go up in flames."

Gino said, "One last thing, guys. When all the bad guys are dead, we might as well search the place for drugs and cash before we watch it blow up."

Sal and Frank nodded in agreement.

Chapter 12

Mr. Perez and his crew began framing the structure for the bakery's expansion. The noise was a real distraction to those inside, but everyone understood it was necessary. Frank went outside around 4 p.m. to check on the progress as the crew was packing up. They had framed and sheeted the four walls, and the roof rafters were in place. Frank was very satisfied with the progress so far. He said, "Mr. Perez, it looks good. You and your crew made quick work of the framing."

"Yes, this is not a big job, not like building an entire house, but we managed to move it along. Tomorrow, we will put on the sheathing, tarpaper, and shingles. For the most part, that will make us watertight. We can easily finish this job in the next five days. Right now, I'm worried I won't have the barn doors in time, but that won't hold us up. When they arrive, we can come back and install them. I'll be erecting a plastic temporary wall at the end of the week, so when we take out that existing wall, none of the dust gets into your workspace."

Frank replied, "Well, you seem to have it all under control. If you think there's anything we might be missing or some improvement we should make, let me know. We can then talk about it."

"Okay, Frank. There is one thing you might want to consider: a large exhaust fan for the kitchen side of the bakery. When that oven goes full blast, I bet it gets quite warm in there. When you add a second oven, it's really going to get hot in there."

Frank said, "That's exactly what I'm talking about. That's a great suggestion. You tell me the cost, and I'll give you the cash upfront for that addition. Besides, it sure will be better for us when there are two ovens going."

"Okay, Frank, I'll have my son check out what's available as far as industrial-sized fans and factor in the labor to install it and the electrician's costs to bring it up to code. I'll let you know in a day or two. There's no rush right now; we have plenty of other work to keep us busy."

Gino received a text from Fabio. He was sending a delivery of armor to the garage. A gray van would arrive at 2 p.m., and the code word was "Tiramisu." Fabio also mentioned that a forklift would not be needed; the shipment was in three easy-to-handle wooden crates.

When the shipment arrived, Gino placed the three wooden boxes in the back of the shop. Pasquale asked what had been delivered. Gino replied, "Nothing for the shop. I'll have these moved today." Pasquale simply nodded and said, "Good. I don't want to know what you're up to, Gino," then walked away.

After work, Sal and Frank came by the shop. The three men each took a crate and walked the short distance to Frank's house, where they put them in the basement. When Gino opened the crates, he exclaimed, "Holy smoke. We have everything we need to make some nifty bombs."

The crates contained three LAW rockets, three pounds of Semtex, detonators, timers, and a dozen thermite grenades.

Sal asked, "Do you guys know how to use that stuff safely?"

Gino said, "Watch this." He explained that the military uses thermite grenades to destroy vehicles and equipment, whose high heat renders them inoperable. Gino molded Semtex around a grenade, inserted a detonator into the soft Semtex, and wired the detonator to a timer, bundling everything together with tape—a small, powerful, portable explosive package. Frank jumped in, and between him and Sal, they made six explosive bundles in less than thirty minutes.

Sal said, "That was fast and easy. We can use them inside the big barn. That should take care of the car collection and the farm equipment."

Frank added, "It will not only take care of the cars and farm equipment; it will burn the place to the ground. Thermite is badass when it comes to melting equipment."

Juan received a call from burner phone number five. "Hello, number five. What do you have?"

The caller said, "I've been snooping around and discovered that there are two high-ranking Colombians who make monthly visits to Mexico City. They stay at The Ritz-Carlton and always have a Luxury Suite."

"That's terrific, number five. Do you know when they'll be there next?"

"My information is that it's always the last week of the month. They stay for only a few days, then fly back to Colombia. While they're at the Ritz, they have several visitors who come and go at all hours of the night. I have a friend who works in the Ritz's kitchen. He told me they order food and drinks at all hours."

"Okay, number five. This is great news. Here's what I want you to do: the next time the Colombians come to the Ritz, have your friend tell you the day they arrive and the suite number. You then call me with those two pieces of information. You do nothing else. I will take it from there, and if your information is correct, I will text your burner phone to set up a time and place for my men to pay you the reward. Do you understand everything I just said?"

"Oh yes. I'll do as you said. Goodbye."

Juan called Pablo and updated him on the conversation he had with burner phone number five. Pablo said, "That is great. We know they'll arrive in the last week of the month. That's only two days from now."

Juan replied, "That's plenty of time. Here's what we'll do: we'll send four of our best men to the Ritz and get a couple of rooms tomorrow. They'll reserve the rooms for a week. Now they'll be in position. When caller number five tells me the Colombians have arrived and the suite number, I'll call our men on the scene, and they can find out what they are doing there."

Pablo said, "Good plan, Juan. I think two men should reserve a room, and the other two should reserve a suite. That way, we can keep an eye on who comes and goes from the Colombians' suite."

"Excellent idea, Pablo."

Pablo then added, "However, I am very curious as to why they are there. Since they fly from Colombia and back, they are not bringing in drugs or taking back large amounts of cash. Very puzzling."

"I see what you mean, Pablo. Unless they have connections at the airport for their luggage to be handled in a special way, I too am baffled. I guess we'll soon find out."

Juan said, "I'll get the guys packed up and on their way to the Ritz. I'll also have a briefcase with $20K for them to hand over to number five if this turns out to be a legitimate claim."

"Sounds good to me, Juan. We'd better update Hector as well. He may have other ideas in mind."

When Juan and Pablo entered the meeting room with Hector, he was on the phone. He signaled for them to take a seat at the conference table. When he finished his call, he sat at the head of the table and said, "Well, more bad news. I was just informed that two more of our trucks did not show up as scheduled today. This is really starting to get on my nerves. What are you two here about?"

Juan updated Hector on what they had planned for the Ritz over the next few days. Pablo also explained how they planned to monitor the traffic coming and going from the suite. When they were finished, Hector said, "Very good. Maybe now we will find out if the Colombians are behind this hijacking mess. Do either of you have plans to bring these two Colombians back to the compound?"

Juan replied, "We don't know how this is all going to play out. If it is possible to safely bring them back to the compound, we will do so. However, I suspect we will be leaving a terrible mess in one very nice Executive Suite."

"Well, it is what it is. Do what you think is best. Just get some answers. We are losing a lot of cash and product with all these hijackings, not to mention the losses at the two distribution centers in Maryland."

Juan and Pablo left the meeting with high hopes of finding the answers Hector was seeking.

Over the next few days, Gino, Frank, and Sal prepared for the raid on Santiago's properties. They had reviewed the plan several times and believed they had everything covered.

They would use one of the customer's SUVs that had four-wheel drive because they would ultimately have to park in the woods. Frank was keeping a close watch on the weather. If rain was forecast, they would cancel the operation because they couldn't afford to get stuck in the woods when it was time to depart. As it stood, they planned to meet at the garage Sunday morning at 12:30 a.m. They would load up the SUV and be at the gas station/convenience store by 1:30 a.m. for Gino to set the two-hour timed explosive in the bathroom drop-down ceiling. They would then go to the big barn, gain entry through a glass window, and set the six thermite explosives with four-hour timers—three for the car collection and three for the farm equipment. They also had three C-4 explosives with four-hour timers for the two fuel tanks outside the barn and a large one for inside the center of the barn floor. The last two explosives were half a pound of C-4 each with 30-minute timed devices—one for each of the houses on the big property.

On Saturday after work, the guys met at Velleggia's Restaurant for a beer and a meal. Again, they went over the plan until Sal finally said, "I think we all know what to do on this thing. Can we stop talking about it while we eat?"

Frank said, "Sal, a plan is just that—a plan. We may have to improvise because plans seldom work out exactly as they are laid out."

Gino chimed in, saying, "I think the planning process is important, but on the job, it's everyone thinking on their feet in case something goes wrong."

Sal threw up his hands, saying, "Okay, I get it. Can we just eat? I want to get some rest before we meet at the garage in a few hours."

Juan received a phone call from one of his trusted men, who had been sent to the Ritz. His name was Tomás. "Hola, Tomás."

"Hola, Juan. We are checked in at the Ritz. This place is really very nice. The suite they gave us is at the end of the hall on the floor with the other suites, so we should have a good view of the folks coming and going. The place is so expensive I doubt many of the suites are occupied."

"That's good, Tomás. It's better for us if there aren't a lot of occupied suites. I want you to try and get a picture of the folks who come to visit the Colombians. Text the picture to one of our guys in the lobby. When our guy spots the man in the picture you sent, he is to follow him. I want to know where he goes after leaving the Ritz. I suspect he will go to his car, so we need to have one of our guys ready to pick you up outside the Ritz so you two can follow the target. We don't want to do anything with the visitor just yet—just find out where he goes. We can settle with him later. When our two guys return to the Ritz, we wait for another visitor and do the same thing. Our goal is not only to extract information from the Colombians in the suite but also to find out who and why they are meeting with. Do you understand?"

"I got it, Juan. Makes good sense to me."

"Also, Tomás, if possible, Hector would like to bring the two Colombians back to the compound. If it's not possible, you know what to do."

"I understand, Juan. I'll see how things go and let you know."

Frank, Sal, and Gino met at the garage, loaded all their ammunition into an SUV, and headed to the gas station/convenience store. Gino had also packed rubber gloves and three LED headlamps, charged and ready to go. They would need them inside the big barn, which was dimly lit.

At the gas station, Sal and Frank went inside to buy snacks while Gino went to the bathroom, where he set a timed explosive for two hours and placed it in the drop-down ceiling. It was light enough to not buckle the ceiling tile but powerful enough to blow the place apart.

The three met back at the SUV and drove two miles to the big barn. Sal turned off the lights and pulled into the driveway that led to the barn. The men exited the SUV, wearing their headlamps and carrying the explosives. They made their way to the side of the barn where the fuel tanks were located. Sal broke one of the lowest windows and climbed inside. He turned on his headlamp and made his way to a door that led outside, allowing Frank and Gino in.

Sal rushed to the back of the barn and placed his three thermite explosives on top of the vintage cars and antique vehicles, spacing them about twenty feet apart. Frank ran to the barn's front and placed his three thermite explosives on the large farm machinery. In the center of the barn, Gino placed his large charge on the floor. When everyone was in place, Gino yelled, "NOW!" The three men set their charges' timers to four hours.

Gino was the first to exit through the side door, where he placed an explosive on each of the fuel tanks and set the timers for four hours. Frank and Sal raced to the side door, met Gino, and the three jumped into the SUV. Sal backed out of the driveway onto the country road, turned on the lights, and drove past the two houses about a hundred yards away, pulling into the woods. He drove far enough in so that any passing vehicles would not spot them.

The three men exited the SUV. Gino was armed with two explosives for the two houses on the property, and all three had silenced .22s. They jogged toward the smaller house. Gino checked his watch; they had less than an hour before the gas station explosion.

The three men quietly approached the front door of the small house, making entry by breaking a small pane of glass and reaching in to unlock it. Inside, Sal and Frank rushed upstairs while Gino searched downstairs. Their goal was to take out everyone in the house. Sal and Frank opened bedroom doors and shot anyone they saw. Gino found no one downstairs, so he headed upstairs, meeting Sal and Frank as they came down.

Frank said, "There were only three men upstairs."

Gino replied, "No one downstairs."

Frank asked, "Gino, what's the time?" referring to the gas station explosive.

Gino checked his watch. "Nine or ten minutes. Let's get into position at the big house."

They rushed down the stairs and jogged to the big house, taking positions behind the shrubbery lining the porch. Gino checked his watch again, then looked at Frank and Sal, holding up one finger to indicate the gas station's detonation time.

About a minute and a half later, the gas station exploded. It was loud, and soon there were secondary explosions, likely from the gas pumps and propane bottles stored there. Within 30 seconds, lights came on in the big house, and 30 seconds later, five men appeared on the front porch.

Sal, Frank, and Gino popped up from their hiding places, aiming their guns at the men on the porch. Sirens could be heard in the distance, growing louder. Frank instructed the men to go inside the house. He directed them to the living room, making them sit on the couch and side chairs. Sal rushed upstairs to check for anyone else and returned, saying, "We're clear upstairs. This is it."

Frank asked, "Gino, how much time do we have?"

Gino checked his watch. "One hour, ten minutes."

One of the men on the couch asked, "Who the hell are you? Do you know who you're messing with?"

"Shut up," hollered Frank.

Gino said, "Who we are is not important. We're here for information. Tell us what we need to know, and you live."

The same man replied, "Information? You broke in here and pointed guns at us, and now you want information? We're not telling you squat!"

Frank said, "Since you have such a big mouth, I guess you're Santiago?"

The man who had been talking was flushed. He said smugly, "Yeah, that's right. I'm Santiago. Who the hell are you?"

Frank shot Santiago in the left foot. The other four men looked terrified. Santiago cursed at Frank, trying to stop the bleeding.

Gino said, "You see, my friend here has a very short fuse. So you'd better listen to what we ask and tell us what we need to know."

Frank looked at Sal. "Go upstairs and grab all the cell phones and guns you can find. Stuff them in a pillowcase and bring them back."

Sal hurried upstairs, searching the rooms. Frank turned his attention to the five men. "A few weeks ago, a baker in Little Italy was murdered. Shortly after, a couple running a bar in Little Italy were also murdered. We're here to find out who did it."

The five men looked worried. Santiago sneered, "Are you telling me you're here because a few old folks refused to pay for protection? Is that what this is about?"

Gino said, "We never said anything about paying for protection. But now we know we've got the right people."

Frank added, "Yep, big mouth just put his foot in it."

Santiago, still smug, said, "So what? Those folks wouldn't pay, so we sent a message to the rest of those wops in the area."

Gino's face turned red with anger. He looked Santiago in the eyes and said, "Those wops were our friends. Now we're going to give you a dose of your own medicine." Gino picked up a metal poker from the fireplace, walked over to Santiago, and struck his knees hard enough to crack bone. Santiago screamed in pain, and the other four men looked terrified.

Sal returned from upstairs with two pillowcases filled with cell phones and handguns, along with two Uzi machine pistols. Without looking at Gino, Frank asked, "How much time do we have?"

Gino checked his watch. "Thirty-five minutes."

Frank looked at the four scared men on the couch. "Which one of you was in on the Little Italy raid?" No one spoke, so Frank shot the first man in the left knee. "I'll ask again. Which of you were in on the Little Italy raid?"

The second man on the couch, his voice shaking, said, "It wasn't me, mister. I was here. Those two on the end were responsible for the Little Italy territory." The two men on the end started sweating profusely. One yelled, "Shut up, you idiot! Don't say another word!"

Frank shot the man who had spoken in the left knee. "So you like hurting and killing old people, huh?" He shot him in the right knee. "How do you like it now?" Gino approached the man with both knees bleeding and struck his shoulder with the iron poker, shattering his collarbone. Then he did the same to the other shoulder. Frank took out his cell phone and took pictures of the five men.

Sal asked the only unharmed man where the money was kept. Without hesitation, he pointed to a door across the living room and said, "In there." Sal opened the door and turned on the light. Gino and Frank heard him exclaim, "Mother of God, that's a lot of cash."

Frank yelled, "Bag it up, Sal."

Sal returned to the center of the room saying, "Frank, we're going to need more bags to carry all that cash. Go take a look."

Sal trained his pistol on the men, while Frank checked the money room. He came back, saying, "You're right, Sal. Check out that pickup truck outside and see if the keys are in it."

Sal went outside. There was no key in the ignition, but when he pulled down the sunvisor, a set of keys fell to the floor. He started the truck, left it running, and went back inside. "I got it running, Frank."

"Okay, Sal, grab some bed sheets from upstairs and start loading the cash. We'll drag them out to the pickup when we're done here."

Gino heard more sirens heading down the road toward the gas station. He looked at his watch. "Frank, fifteen minutes."

Frank turned to one of the men on the couch. "Did you have anything to do with the Little Italy hit?" The man shook his head vigorously.

Gino said, "He's lying, Frank." Gino struck the man's shin, breaking his leg.

Santiago, barely audible, said, "You'll pay for this."

Frank replied, "You don't get it, do you? Don't you know who sent us? It was your friend Hector Torres. That's right, Hector told us all about you boys."

All five men were shocked to hear that their boss had ordered the raid on their house. One said, "Why would Hector do that? We send him a great deal of money every month."

Frank looked at Gino and asked, "Time?" Gino checked his watch and replied, "Five minutes."

Sal was busy loading stacks of cash onto the bed sheets spread out on the floor. Gino tapped his watch and said, "Time to go, Frank." Gino and Frank shot four of the men dead, leaving Santiago the last survivor, badly battered. Frank said, "In a minute or two, you'll hear a huge explosion. That'll be your big barn going up in smoke, with all your prized cars, trucks, and farm equipment."

Santiago had a look of hate in his eyes and muttered, "Oh no. Not my cars. They are priceless." Frank smirked, "Well, not to us, asshole."

The sound of the big barn blowing up was so fierce, it shattered the windows in the house. Several explosions followed within a minute or two of the first. The sky lit up bright red, filled with fire and smoke. Without hesitation, Gino shot Santiago dead.

Gino turned to Frank. "You help Sal. I'm going over to the small house to set the explosives for thirty minutes. I'll come back and set the timer for this house too. Then we load up all the cash we can and put it in the pickup truck outside."

Gino took off running to the small house while Frank helped Sal load the cash into the pickup truck. Frank said, "Sal, you take this truck back to the garage. Gino and I will set the explosives here and head to the SUV. We'll only be two or three minutes behind you. Get going."

Sal jumped into the pickup just as Gino was returning from the small house. He took off down the country road, passing more emergency vehicles rushing toward the big barn.

Gino set the timer, and he and Frank grabbed the pillowcases full of cell phones and guns, then sprinted to the SUV hidden in the woods. They backed out onto the country road and sped toward the garage in Little Italy, passing more fire trucks heading to what had once been the big barn. A few minutes later, as they drove two miles down the road toward Westminster, they heard a couple of explosions close together. The two houses were now destroyed.

As Frank and Gino headed toward Baltimore, Frank said, "I think we did good, partner."

Gino nodded. "I'm satisfied we got the right people this time, Frank. I'm sure Fabio will be pleased. I'll text him now to let him know we avenged Carlo's death. His brother Aldo will finally have some peace."

Frank added, "Don't forget Joey Jr. I'm sure he'll be glad to know he helped us avenge his parents' deaths."

Gino replied, "But we still have unfinished business with Hector Torres. He's the one behind all of this."

Frank was silent for a few moments, then said, "You know what, Gino? You're right. This isn't over until Hector is dealt with."

Chapter 13

Juan received a call from cell phone number five. His informant told him the Colombians had checked in and were in Suite 1607. Juan immediately texted Tomás the information so he could start his surveillance. One of his men was stationed in the lobby, and another was near the hotel parking garage. Tomás would take the first watch while his partner slept in the other room.

Tomás replaced the peephole with a device known as a peephole cam. The device was wirelessly connected to his cell phone, allowing him to operate many functions. He could zoom, take snapshots, and record while watching the feed on his cell phone.

The two Colombians were actually in Suite 1613, just a few doors down the hall. Through his cell phone camera setup, Tomás could see the two men coming down the hall. He managed to capture several snapshots of them as they entered their suite. A porter was right behind them, wheeling a cart that appeared to have two suitcases on it. All three entered the suite, and a moment later, the porter exited and returned to the elevator at the center of the hall.

Now it was a waiting game. Tomás's partner, Alejandro, woke up from his nap and ordered room service for them both. It had been close to two hours since the Colombians went into the suite.

The food order was delivered, and Tomás and Alejandro ate while watching the cell phone camera, which was set up in the center of the table. As they were about to finish their meal, Alejandro said, "We have movement in the hall." Both men looked and saw a man carrying a briefcase stop at Suite 1613 and knock on the door. Tomás took several snapshots of the man, who appeared to be in his late 30s. He was dressed in a three-piece suit and didn't look like any drug dealer they were used to seeing. The door opened, and the man in the suit entered.

Tomás sent a text to his man in the lobby with the attached picture. The text simply said, "I will let you know when he is on his way."

About an hour later, a second man was spotted coming down the hall. He too was well-dressed, in a business suit and carrying a briefcase. Tomás captured a few snapshots of the man as he was let into the suite. Again, Tomás sent a text to the man in the lobby, with a picture of the second man attached.

Alejandro said, "This is going to get interesting if the two men leave the suite at the same time. Who do we follow?"

Tomás replied, "I think we go with Mr. Three-Piece Suit if that happens."

Another hour passed, and the door of the suite opened. The man in the business suit left the room and headed to the elevators. Tomás sent a text to his man in the lobby, Enrique, saying, "Man number two is on his way down."

Enrique, having the picture of the man on his phone, compared it to the people exiting the elevator. He quickly spotted his man and began following him. Keeping a safe distance, he called his partner in the parking garage to inform him they were on the move. However, the business-suited man did not go toward the parking garage. He kept walking down the street and, after traveling two blocks, entered a large bank on the corner. The building was Citibanamex (Citibanamex, part of Citigroup, and one of the oldest and largest banks in Mexico).

After waiting outside the bank for ten minutes, Enrique decided to go inside and look around. He went to one of the side tables and pretended to fill out a deposit slip while carefully surveying the area. He saw his target sitting at a desk in one of the side offices with glass walls. Enrique thought to himself, *This guy works here.* He left the bank and immediately called Tomás while heading back to the Ritz lobby.

"Yes, Enrique, where did he go?" Tomás asked.

"You are not going to believe this, but he did not go to the garage. I followed him down the street for a couple of blocks, and he went into a bank — the Citibanamex, to be exact. I waited a few minutes and then went in because he never came out. He works there. I saw him sitting behind a desk in an office."

Tomás, confused at the news Enrique just delivered, said, "Okay, Enrique. Go back to the lobby and wait for the three-piece suit guy to come down."

Alejandro took one look at Tomás and could see he was puzzled. "What's wrong, Tomás?"

Tomás told Alejandro what Enrique had just described on the phone. Alejandro, now also with a puzzled look on his face, said, "What the hell is going on here? A banker meeting with Colombian drug lords? This makes no sense."

About thirty minutes later, the three-piece suit man left the Colombian's suite and headed to the elevator. Tomás texted Enrique again.

Enrique recognized the target and followed him. He went in the opposite direction from the first man. Again, the man did not go to the garage. He walked a few blocks around two corners before entering a jewelry store. Enrique waited for about ten minutes, and the man never exited, so Enrique went into the store. A man behind the counter asked, "Can I help you?"

Enrique took off his watch and said, "Do you do watch repairs?"

"Why, of course. That is a fine timepiece you have."

Enrique said, "I managed to scratch the face. Can you replace it for me while I wait?"

"No problem, Sir. That will only take a few minutes. Wait here, and I will be right back."

The counterperson took the watch to the back. Enrique saw the three-piece suit man he had followed; he appeared to work there. He was doing something in the back of the store, but Enrique was sure he was either an employee or the owner.

A few minutes later, the counterperson returned, gave Enrique his watch, and told him the price for the new crystal replacement. Enrique paid and left the store. As he walked back to the Ritz, he called Tomás and gave him a report.

Tomás thanked Enrique and told him to return to the Ritz lobby. Again, Tomás was baffled by what had just occurred. He told Alejandro the story, and Alejandro was puzzled, too.

Shortly after, a porter was spotted rolling a food cart to the Colombian's suite. Apparently, they had ordered room service.

Tomás texted Enrique and told him and his partner to take a break and get something to eat. He also told them to go to their room and get some sleep. He would call if there was any more activity.

No other visitors came to the Colombian's suite until 11:30 p.m. Alejandro woke Tomás and said, "We have movement."

As the two men watched the cell phone footage, they saw two men, wearing suits and carrying briefcases, stop at Suite 1613. They entered just as Tomás managed to get a few still photos.

Tomás called Enrique and his partner and told them to get into position. He sent a photo of the two men via text.

The two men were only in the suite for about ten minutes. They left and headed for the elevator.

Enrique spotted them exiting the elevator and heading to the garage. Enrique called his partner and said, "Two men are on the way. I'm right behind them. Watch for the car they get into and pick me up at the garage entrance. We need to follow them."

With Enrique and his partner following the two men at a safe distance, he called Tomás to let him know they were following the car with the two men who had left the Colombian's suite. "Good work, Enrique. Remember, just follow them and see where they go. Don't do anything else."

After following the car for twenty minutes or so, it pulled into a gated compound. Enrique and his partner stopped about a half-block down the street. The place the car went into had high walls, and on top of a hill sat a huge house. They took some pictures and waited for another hour, but no one came or went from the compound, so they returned to the Ritz to get some sleep.

The next day, around noon, the entire process started again. The three-piece suit arrived, then the business suit arrived at the Colombian's suite. The three-piece left first and went to the bank. The business suit left and headed to the jewelry store. Later that evening, two men showed up, stayed for about ten minutes, left the suite, and drove to the compound with the huge house.

On the third day, Tomás was worried the Colombians would check out and fly back to Colombia. He called all his men together and said, "This whole thing doesn't make any sense. Those Colombians may check out today, so I think we go in and find out what the hell they are up to."

The three companions nodded in agreement.

The four men, armed with handguns, left Tomás's suite and went down the hall to the Colombian's suite. Tomás knocked on the door, and as it opened, the four men rushed in and made the two Colombians sit at a table in the dining area.

The two captives were terrified. One said, "Please don't hurt us. Take what you want."

Alejandro said, "Calm down and shut up. We are here for information. For whom do you work?"

"We work for Álvarez Téllez, of course. He is the head of the Clan del Golfo."

Tomás said, "So you admit you work for the Colombian cartel?"

"Yes, we do. Why do you sound so angry about who we work for?"

Alejandro said, "So we suspect you and the cartel are branching out into Mexico to buy and sell drugs. What we want to know is if your boss is also responsible for hijacking our trucks and destroying our distribution centers."

The two men from Colombia were baffled by the questioning. One said, "Drugs? We have no business dealing with drugs. We also have no idea what you are referring to when you speak about hijacking and distribution centers."

Tomás asked, "Then who are the men you are meeting with in this hotel every month? Do you expect us to believe there are no drugs involved?"

The two Colombians looked at each other, and one said, "You are very misinformed. I am a gemologist, a person who can evaluate and identify details in a gem that aren't visible to the human eye. My partner is a gem maker, a lapidarist, or a gem cutter. We are in the emerald industry. You observed men coming and going to deliver emeralds to us. We evaluate them, and then our banker pays for them. The emeralds are picked up and delivered to our boss, who gets them to Colombia. We are only the middlemen providing a service to Álvarez Téllez. There are no drugs involved. We strictly deal in emeralds and diamonds."

Tomás looked at his men and said, "Put the guns away, boys. I think we've been on a wild goose chase. There is nothing here to indicate these men are involved in the drug trade. I think the banker and the jewelry store visitor now make their explanation believable."

Tomás and his men left the Colombian's suite and checked out of the Ritz. On the drive back to the compound, Tomás called Juan and gave him a summary of the events with the Colombians. Juan listened to the report and said, "Well, the lead was good, but unfortunately, we were chasing the wrong rabbit. When you and your men get back to the compound, take a few days off. I am not looking forward to meeting with Pablo and Hector later today."

Tomás said, "Thanks, Juan. I will let the guys know. I also often heard about the illegal emerald trade, but I never knew how profitable it was until now. Perhaps you can suggest to Hector that this is something we should look into more. Anyway, I don't think we should pay cell phone number 5 for supplying us with this bogus lead. However, that is up to you and Pablo."

When Frank and Gino arrived at the garage, Sal was waiting for them. They unloaded the SUV and took the pillowcases filled with guns and cell phones, along with the bedsheets full of cash, to Frank's basement. When they finally counted the money, it totaled just over $1.5 million.

Gino said, "What are we going to do with all this money, Frank?"

"I have no idea. All I know is I'm very nervous about having this much cash just lying around. I think you and Sal should buy some boxes and take your cut. We can also make another deposit to the poor box at St. Leo's, if that's okay with you guys."

Sal said, "I'm okay with that, boss. If you want, I can take care of it when Father Alonzo conducts his evening confessions this week."

Gino nodded in agreement and said, "Another $10K would be nice."

Frank nodded in agreement, saying, "Okay Sal take care of it when you have some time."

Sal then continued, "We also have another problem. What do we do with the pickup truck I brought back from Westminster?"

Frank said, "Sal, why not take it over to the Inner Harbor and just park it in one of the metered spaces? As parking tickets accumulate, the cops will probably impound it in a few days. Just make sure you wipe it down so your prints aren't found."

"Okay. Good idea. I'll take care of it. It's a good night for a walk back from the Inner Harbor. By the way, I was listening to the radio while driving back from Westminster. The news came on, and they made it sound like this was going to be the biggest story in weeks. They had to call in fire departments from neighboring counties to help put out several blazes across a two-mile area."

Gino said, "Guys, we are also accumulating a bunch of guns. If this place gets raided, Frank will have a lot of explaining to do."

Frank replied, "I'm concerned about this armory we've built up too. However, we can't worry about that now. In the next few days, after things calm down, I'd like Sal to find Santiago's cell phone in the pillowcase to see if we can get any more information about this Hector Torres."

Sal said, "I'll take care of that after work in the next few days. It's a good idea, Frank. There must have been some type of communication between Santiago and Hector. Remember that one guy saying they sent a lot of money to Hector?"

Frank nodded. "That's right, Sal. Who knows? If we find anything important, it might help Fabio as well."

Gino chimed in, "We already know Hector Torres is behind all this trouble we've been having. Personally, I'd like to be there when he's taken down."

He continued, "Anyway, about the guns. Except for some of the sniper rifles and Uzis, we could probably have Fabio pick up the rest. I'm sure they could find some use for all these handguns."

Sal said, "That's a good idea, Gino. At least that gets them out of our hands and out of Frank's basement."

Frank said, "Gino, the next time you talk to Fabio, ask him if he wants them. It doesn't hurt to ask."

Gino said, "I'll pick up some of those big blue plastic containers from Walmart, like we used to package all the drugs. We can use three to divide the money and two or three to pack up all the handguns."

Frank and Sal nodded in agreement. Frank then said, "Okay, guys, let's meet at Velleggia's tonight and have a mini celebration."

Sal left Frank's house, took the pickup truck to the Inner Harbor, and then went home to bed. Gino also left, and he went home to get a few hours of sleep before going to work at the garage. Frank was exhausted and looked at the clock. It was 4:30 a.m., and he had a shift at the bakery starting in half an hour.

Meanwhile, in Colombia, Álvarez Téllez was hosting a birthday party for his wife at his estate. At the party, there was a band playing, lots of food, and over one hundred guests. As he was making the rounds with his wife to greet all the attendees, one of his lieutenants whispered in his ear that he needed to speak with him. Álvarez acknowledged the request and simply said, "In a few minutes, Nicolás."

After greeting several more guests, Álvarez excused himself and motioned for Nicolás to walk with him as he wanted to refresh his drink.

"What is it that is so important, Nicolás?"

"I received some disturbing news this morning from our folks handling the emerald trade."

"Disturbing? How so? Were they robbed or captured?"

"No, nothing like that. It appears four men from the Mexican Sinaloa cartel had our two men at the Ritz cornered and questioned them."

"Questioned them, you say? Questioned them about what?"

"It seems the Sinaloa cartel believes the Colombians are making a move on the Mexican drug trade. They specifically wanted to know who in the

Colombian cartel was hijacking their trucks and destroying drug distribution centers."

Álvarez had a puzzled look on his face, which then turned into a more worried expression. He said, "Why would they think anything of the sort? We have no interest in their drug business. Heck, we could probably buy and sell them ten times over. This makes absolutely no sense."

"I agree, Álvarez. I don't understand it either, but I thought I would bring it to your attention, just in case you want to heighten security on our operations."

"No. That is a good suggestion, but I think we need to have a meeting tomorrow to discuss this with the rest of the cartel. If the Mexicans suspect us of meddling in their business, there is surely going to be trouble. We must be prepared. But right now, we need to gather as much information as we can on this issue."

Álvarez went back to his wife's side, and they rejoined the festivities. However, he could not stop thinking about the issue Nicolás raised. The more he thought about it, the less it made sense to him. There must be more to the story. Much more.

Juan attended a meeting with Pablo and Hector to update them on the Colombian situation. Hector said, "Let's sit at the conference table, and Juan can tell us all about the mission to the Ritz."

Juan had a worried look on his face as he began the update. He said, "I am sorry to say we were not very successful in our mission. The men we sent did an outstanding job and were able to verify several things. First, and most important, the Colombians that meet every month at the Ritz in Mexico City have nothing to do with drugs or the drug trade. They are, in fact, emerald and diamond experts."

Hector was not happy with the initial comments. Juan continued, "Second, we still don't know who is responsible for the hijacking of trucks or the destruction of our drug distribution centers."

Hector's face grew red as his anger increased. Juan finished by saying, "Lastly, there is absolutely no evidence that indicates the Colombian cartel is trying to expand their territory into Mexico."

Hector slammed his fist on the table, saying, "This is terrible news, Juan. I admit when you and Pablo came to me and outlined your plan, it sounded good. However, we now know no more than we did before this exercise was put into action. In addition, it gets worse. Today, I was notified that our good friend Santiago and seven of his men were killed outside a small town called Westminster. Whoever was responsible not only killed all eight men but also destroyed all their property. There is more bad news. I heard from our Arizona supplier that two more tractor-trailers were hijacked and destroyed."

Pablo said, "Not to disagree with you, Hector, but we did learn several things."

"And what are these things you speak of Pablo?"

"We know the attacks on our trucks, distribution centers, and protection rackets are somehow related. We know for sure that the distribution centers and protection racket attacks are all in one small area in Maryland. The Baltimore, Laurel, and Westminster attacks are all within twenty-five miles or so of each other."

Juan chimed in, "Pablo may be on to something. If we exclude the hijackings for a second and concentrate on the three areas in Maryland, we may be able to conclude that those attacks were initiated and carried out by locals. There must be a thread that ties all three of those events together."

Hector thought for a few seconds, then said, "I see what you mean. A common thread must be there. We simply need to find out what ties those events together."

Juan added, "As for the hijacking of trucks, which does not seem to fit the MO of the other incidents. In other words, they may not be carried out by the same group. We may be dealing with two entirely different groups."

Hector said, "I see. That is entirely possible. Here is what I want you two to do: Juan, I want you to concentrate on the hijacking of trucks. Pablo, I want you to concentrate on what is going on in Maryland."

Juan said, "I think that is a good approach, Hector."

Hector continued, "Furthermore, Pablo, I want you to go to Maryland and personally look into this. Maryland is notorious for corrupt politicians and police. I bet you can flash some money around and find the connection we're looking for.

Juan, your task is more difficult due to the wide area of these hijackings. My guess is that they are not investigated beyond the state in which they occur. No one is looking at the big picture. I want you to focus on whoever is responsible for interstate crime. The FBI or the DEA would be my guess at this point. You need to find a way to feed them the information about the hijackings and get them to investigate how they are related. That will cost a great deal of money, but it will be worth it. Right now, we are losing a ton of cash and product. We cannot survive this way for long."

Juan said, "Maybe I simply call the DEA as an anonymous citizen and start feeding them bits of info. If I get the ear of the right agent, they will probably get a feather in their cap for bringing the issue to their attention."

"Excellent approach, Juan. I would go with the DEA because you can tell them that drug smuggling and large amounts of cash are involved. Like you said, if you get the ear of the right agent trying to make a name for themselves, you will have hit gold."

Hector felt much better about the situation now that they had a new plan. He finished by saying, "Juan, I want you to contact the number five caller. Pay him $2K as a small reward for his tip that did not pan out. I want to keep those eyes and ears on the Colombians, just in case they turn up something we can use. With that, go do what is necessary to put these issues to rest."

Chapter 14

A few days after the Westminster raid, Gino received a call from Fabio. "Ciao, Gino. I hope all is well with you and your friends." "Ciao, Fabio. Yes, we are doing well, thank you." "Gino, I am calling to tell you we are all set up to take out our nemesis, Hector Torres." "Oh, that is great news, Fabio. We were just talking about that the other day. We thought the last piece of the puzzle still unaccounted for was Torres."

Fabio said, "Gino, you are not going to believe what we plan to do. We have three locations around the Torres compound, each with two men. These men are well-trained in using drones—you know, the small ones people sometimes use for hobbies."

Gino asked, "Drones? For what purpose?"

"Gino, these men have been practicing for the past two weeks on a farm in upstate New York. They launch the drones and place them precisely where they want, using the video camera onboard. Each drone contains an explosive that detonates using the drone's batteries. It is absolutely ingenious."

"Please go on, Fabio. This is getting interesting."

"Each location has one drone equipped with thermite grenades, and another equipped with three pounds of C-4. Our plan is to launch six drones in the early morning hours when everyone is asleep. We will land two thermite drones on the roof of the big house and one on the roof of the smaller house. Then, we'll land one C-4-equipped drone at the front door of the big house and another at the front door of the smaller house. Everything is set up, and our men and equipment are already in place."

Gino said, "What an elaborate but effective plan, Fabio. However, don't you still have one drone unaccounted for?"

"Oh, yes. I forgot. The last drone, equipped with C-4, will land outside the largest outbuilding in the compound. You are very astute, my friend."

Gino pictured the air assault in his mind and said, "Fabio, if Hector is in one of those houses when you launch, he will be taken out for sure. What an ingenious plan! And your men won't be in harm's way. Absolutely brilliant."

"Thank you, Gino. Isn't this new technology great?"

Gino laughed, saying, "Yes, it is. But you still need qualified humans to make good use of it!"

Fabio said he had informed Aldo in Sicily about their success in Westminster. He was very pleased and asked him to convey his heartfelt appreciation for avenging Carlo's death. "The man is now at peace with the world."

Gino said, "That is good to hear. We didn't do it just for Aldo; we needed closure for our dear friend, too."

Fabio asked if Gino and his friends needed anything. Gino replied, "We have accumulated over fifty handguns from the raids we've carried out. We have no use for them and were wondering if you'd like them. They're packed in two blue plastic tubs."

Fabio said, "Sure. We can always use extra handguns, even if they are just throwaways. How about this? The next time I have a delivery near you, I will text you the pickup day, time, and code word. That way, I can kill two birds with one stone. In fact, in the next two weeks, we have a delivery in the Virginia area. Once I have the details worked out, they can pick up the containers on their way back to New York. I'll give you a few days' notice when everything comes together at my end. Thank you for thinking of us regarding the merchandise."

"Oh, that sounds great, Fabio, and you are welcome. Do you know when this air assault on Hector's compound will occur?"

"We're waiting for the first clear night with no rain, which should be in the next two or three days. One thing's for sure: the coroner in Mexico City is going to be very busy."

Gino laughed, saying, "Buona fortuna" (Good Luck), Fabio. "I'd love to be there to see that compound go up."

Fabio said, "Not to worry, my friend. We'll have aerial footage of the event to share. Ciao, Gino."

Pablo was in Baltimore, staying at a downtown hotel. He spent a couple of days observing the Inner Harbor area and the crime-ridden West Side of the city. He managed to find a couple of names from the Baltimore City Narcotics Division—men well-known to the West Side drug underworld. From his hotel, he used a burner phone to call the narcotics division and asked to speak to Sergeant Wilson. He identified himself as someone who had information about a large drug shipment heading to Baltimore. The sergeant was very interested and asked the caller to come into the station for further discussion. Pablo said he would only meet in person, but if the sergeant was interested, he should meet him at the Inner Harbor on the bench in front of the ice cream stand tonight at 10 p.m.

Sergeant Wilson asked, "How will I know who you are, and what should I call you?"

"My name is Mr. Smith. I'll be wearing a New York Yankees baseball cap."

The phone connection ended. Sergeant Wilson went to his partner, Sergeant Carl, and told him about the conversation. Carl said, "This sounds like a setup to me, Wilson."

"My thoughts exactly," responded Wilson.

"How do you want to play this?"

Wilson replied, "I think we should have several undercover guys in the area. The ice cream stand closes at 9, so we should be able to access that location. We'll need some guys at each end of the walkway leading to and from the meeting spot. That way, we'll have the entire area covered. I'll be wired, so you stay close by in the van, monitoring the conversation. I don't want to spook this guy. I want to hear what he has to say, and if it makes sense, we let him go but follow him."

Carl said, "Sounds good to me. However, if Mr. Smith does anything funny, we rush him and take him down. Agree?"

"Agree."

At 8 p.m., Sergeant Wilson and Carl assembled a team at police headquarters to go over the planned meeting at the Inner Harbor. Five officers would be involved. The police headquarters was only half a mile from the Inner Harbor, so they had plenty of time.

One of the officers in the group said, "This sounds like a setup from the get-go to me. Are you sure you want to go into this meeting alone?"

Sergeant Wilson said, "Yes, it does sound that way, but I think we have all the bases covered. Besides, I have you guys covering my ass."

Pablo went to a contact he'd met at Skullies, a West Baltimore bar. He managed to strike up a conversation and offered the man $2,000 on the spot if he could put him in contact with someone who had a motorboat. The person would be well-paid for just two hours of work. The contact told Pablo to stay put while he made a few calls.

After about twenty minutes, the contact returned and said, "The guy in the red shirt who just entered the bar can help you with this odd request." The contact left the table, and the man in the red shirt sat across from Pablo. "I understand you need a boat?"

Pablo said, "I need a boat with a motor and operator at the Inner Harbor by the ice cream stand. He should be in position by 9:30 p.m. tonight. At about 10:30 p.m., he will see me wearing a New York Yankees baseball cap and running toward his boat. He should have the engine started, and I will jump in. He will rush me to a location outside the harbor and drop me off. That's it."

The man in the red shirt said, "Odd request, but I can do this for you. The boat will be a small twelve-foot cabin cruiser. He will fly a bright red flag on top of the cabin. Are we clear so far?"

"Perfectly clear."

The red-shirted man continued, "Once you're on board, he will take you to a place about a twenty-minute boat ride away and drop you off at a dock. You'll see a black SUV with a driver there. He will pick you up and take you where you need to go."

Pablo said, "This is a good plan. I am prepared to pay you for your service, of course. How much is this going to cost me?"

The man in the red shirt said, "I will need $10,000 up front and another $10,000 upon delivery to your final destination."

Pablo thought the price was fair and said, "I need to go to my hotel and will return with the first payment within an hour. When the driver of the SUV takes me back to my hotel at the end of the trip, I will give him the final payment. How does that sound?"

"Okay by me. Do you have a car outside?"

"No. I took a cab from my hotel to this bar."

"If you like, I can have one of my men drive you to your hotel, pick up the cash, and save you a trip back here."

Pablo said, "Thanks, but no thanks. I have my own way of doing things. Wait here, and I will be back within an hour and a half with the down payment. In the meantime, you have some plans to put in place for this to work."

"Okay by me," said the red shirted man.

Pablo knew he had a man who could get things done. When he returned to the bar, he handed the man in the red shirt a paper bag containing $10,000. The man looked inside the bag and said, "Looks right to me." He then signaled another man over to the table and handed him the paper bag.

Pablo said, "Good, we are all set. Now, I have another opportunity for you if you're interested."

The man in the red shirt replied, "You can ask, and I can always turn you down."

Pablo explained that he was trying to find out who was responsible for the Baltimore County and Laurel drug distribution center killings. He was also interested in those responsible for the Westminster raid.

The man in the red shirt listened intently, now realizing he was dealing with someone with major drug-dealing connections. These three incidents were all gruesome and possibly had cartel ties. Now, the man in the red shirt was more cautious.

"I see. You're obviously a well-connected man. The incidents you asked about were indeed big news around here. However, as these things happen, they make the evening news and then disappear from the spotlight. The cops in this town are pretty useless when it comes to solving crimes. In fact, when drugs are involved, they just let the battling parties kill each other, so they don't need to get involved. In the end, what I'm telling you is that no one cares about those three incidents."

Pablo could see the man in the red shirt was a logical thinker. Pablo desperately needed the local knowledge he had. After a moment, he asked, "Are you able to help me find out how these three specific incidents are related?"

The man in the red shirt replied, "Why don't you take care of this boat and Inner Harbor thing first? When you're done with that business, come back to this bar and tell the bartender you're here to see Larry. He'll get word to me, and I'll meet you here to discuss this other task in more detail. In the meantime, I'll be checking on my own. Sound good?"

"Sounds good to me," Pablo said.

Juan was busy, too. He called the local DEA office in Orlando, Florida, and asked to speak to an agent who investigated intrastate drug trafficking operations. After several transfers, he was finally routed to Washington, D.C., to an agent named Miller.

"Agent Miller. To whom am I speaking?"

"Agent Miller, you're a very difficult man to contact."

"To whom am I speaking, and what is it you wish to discuss?"

"My name is not important. I have information that you might be interested in. It has to do with transporting large amounts of cash and drugs across several states and Mexico. Are you interested?"

Agent Miller caught the attention of another agent in the office and signaled him to pick up the phone and listen in.

"Why yes, I am interested in hearing what you have to say. Please continue."

Juan said, "Recently, there have been several—no, seventeen—hijacked tractor-trailers in the U.S. and four in Mexico. They are all related. All the shipments originate in Florida. Do you understand so far?"

"Yes. I am aware of some recent hijackings. However, they all occurred on the East Coast as far as I can tell."

"That's where you and your agency are missing the connection. The hijackings in Arizona, Virginia, New York, New Jersey, and Colorado are all related. There are probably several other states involved, too. No one is bringing all of the hijackings together. There are two major factors you need to investigate. First, all the hijacked tractor-trailers originate in Florida. That's where the drugs are brought into the country, and eventually, all the trucks are en route to California with a final destination in Mexico. Are you getting all this, Agent Miller?"

"Oh yes, I understand. However, what you are describing is a major drug operation across two countries and multiple states. That is a tremendous amount of territory to cover."

Juan said, "Exactly. That's why no one has taken the time or put in the effort to pull all the cases together."

"Okay, caller. I understand what you're suggesting. Now, why don't you tell me what it is that you want? Why such an interest in a huge drug operation?"

Juan thought his time was about up for the initial conversation. He said, "I will have more to talk about tomorrow. In the meantime, why don't you get to work on what I have already given you? Give me a number to call you directly."

Agent Miller gave his phone number to Juan. As he was about to ask more questions, the line went dead.

Agent Miller looked over at his companion and said, "Did you get all that?"

"Oh yes. If what he is saying is true, we have some serious breakdowns in our reporting of drug trafficking. We better let the boss know what just happened."

Agents Miller and Santoni requested a meeting with the director. The director, who had been in meetings all morning, granted them a sit-down at 4 p.m. At the meeting, Agents Miller and Santoni gave the director a summary of the conversation with the anonymous caller. The Director listened closely and then said, "Well, if these cases are in fact related, we have a serious problem. We are supposed to receive reports in this office regarding drug transportation across state lines. Those reports are supposed to be analyzed for patterns."

Agents Miller and Santoni nodded in agreement. The director picked up his phone and told his secretary to get the head of the analysis section to his office as soon as possible.

Within a few minutes, a female agent knocked on the Director's office door, saying, "You wanted to see me, sir?"

"Yes, come in, shut the door, and have a seat. Agent Sally Ming; these are Agents Miller and Santoni. They're going to tell you about a conversation they had today with an anonymous caller. I want you to listen. When they're done, we have some questions for you."

"Yes, sir," Sally replied and took a seat.

After Miller and Santoni finished updating Sally, the Director said, "Now, I need your staff to pull the reports of any and all tractor-trailer hijackings for the past six months. Then, analyze these reports, make follow-up calls to the local areas, and gather as much information as you can. When you are ready to discuss your findings, we need to have a sit-down to discuss the results."

"I understand, Director. When do you need this?"

"Since the anonymous caller will be contacting Miller tomorrow, we need the information right away. It looks like your folks are pulling an all-nighter. Oh, by the way, Agent Ming, be prepared to explain how we missed the possible connection to all these hijackings if the information we now have turns out to be true."

Sally Ming left the office and got her team working on the new assignment. The Director said, "You fellows go back to work. Make some calls to the local DEA offices in these cities and let them know what we're doing. Ask for their assistance in identifying a possible connection. Good job, boys. Now, get to work. Oh, by the way, Miller, make sure you're available for the caller when he makes contact. See if you can find out his motive for offering up this information. I smell a rat in the ranks of a cartel."

Frank was busy at the bakery when Mr. Perez came in to see him. "What's up, Mr. Perez?"

"Some bad news, I'm afraid."

"Okay, let's have it."

Mr. Perez said, "We erected the plastic wall as I told you we would. However, when we pulled out the ceiling portion, we found that the wall separating the spaces was loadbearing. This was an unexpected find. We need to install a large support beam before we can take down that wall."

"Okay. These things happen during construction. I understand. Is this something you can handle?"

"Oh yes, Frank. However, the cost to purchase the beam, support the roof temporarily, and install the new beam comes with added costs."

"How much more are we talking about?"

Mr. Perez bowed his head and said, "$7,000. That would cover the entire cost."

Frank could see Mr. Perez did not like delivering bad news to clients. He said, "Okay, Mr. Perez, I will have your money this afternoon. It is not a problem. My only concern is whether this will slow down the project. Remember, I have an oven and mixer coming in a couple of weeks."

Mr. Perez was relieved with Frank's handling of the problem. He said, "No, Frank, we will work nights to get the job done. It may not be acceptable to your neighbors, but we will stay on schedule. No problem."

Frank laughed and said, "Don't worry about the neighbors. I'll send them some baked goods to smooth out any disturbance of the peace."

Frank, Sal, and Gino met at Velleggia's Restaurant for a late dinner. Gino gave a summary of the conversation he had with Fabio. He said, "In the next day or two, Hector Torres will be dealt with, and that should close the book on the case. We will then have succeeded in avenging Carlo and the DeLucas' deaths. Fabio said Carlo's brother, Aldo, wanted us to know how much he appreciated our avenging his brother's death."

Frank said, "That is great news, Gino. The drone attack is a pure stroke of genius. If they pull this off, they deserve a medal." Sal chimed in, "I must admit, I would have never thought of that. I would have probably gone in with a small army and blasted the place. However, this solution is, in fact, brilliant, and not one of the good guys is put in danger. I am also glad to hear that Aldo is pleased. The man deserves to have some closure."

Gino said, "There's more. Fabio said he would text me in two weeks to pick up the handguns we stored in the basement. He plans to bundle it with some deliveries he has in Virginia. When that job is done, they will stop by and pick up the two plastic containers loaded with the handguns."

Sal said, "That works out perfectly. Now Frank can sleep better at night."

Frank asked, "Sal, how did you make out with that pickup truck from Westminster?"

"Funny you should bring that up. I went past there yesterday, and the truck is gone. I guess the cops had it towed like you said, Frank. It is out of our hands, so who cares what they do with it? It will probably show up in a police auction down the road. I also managed to drop $10,000 into the St. Leo's poor box last night. When Father Alonzo opens the box, I'd love to be a fly on the wall. I put a note in the box saying, 'To cover the expenses for services rendered for Carlo and the DeLucas.'"

Gino said, "Nice touch, Sal. I know Father Alonzo will make good use of the money." He continued, "I also contacted Joey Jr. and told him the people responsible for his parents' deaths are no more. I thanked him for the information he provided and told him we couldn't have done it without his help. He seemed very relieved and was happy to be involved." Frank and Sal nodded in agreement.

As the three men ate their dinner, Frank broke the silence by saying, "We have done what we set out to do. I am very content with our accomplishments." Sal and Gino agreed. Sal said, "What do we do now for excitement?"

Gino replied, "Well, I guess we could start a war with the Colombians?"

Both Sal and Frank laughed. Frank said, "I'd just as soon stick to baking bread."

Gino asked how the expansion was going. Frank said, "We had a minor setback with a load-bearing wall, but Mr. Perez is taking care of it. So far, we are still on schedule."

Sal said, "I was thinking, Frank."

Frank stopped him by saying, "Oh no. This can't be good. Every time Sal thinks, it costs me money."

Sal laughed and said, "No, seriously, I was thinking that when the expansion is finished, we are going to need more help. Running two mixers and two ovens at the same time is too much for you and Diego to handle."

Frank said, "I hear you, Sal, and I was thinking the same thing a few days ago. Unfortunately, I think we've tapped into all the available help in the neighborhood. We certainly can train someone to run the mixer, but I have no candidates for the job. Miguel is doing such a great job; I would love to have him train the new person."

Gino said, "You know what, Frank? I'll bet if there is anyone who knows who might be willing to help as a trainee, it would be Father Alonzo. He knows everyone in the parish and everyone's business. Why not ask him for a lead?"

Frank thought about it for a few seconds and replied, "Good idea, Gino. I'll speak to him tonight. That is a great suggestion."

Sal said, "Oh, by the way, I checked out the cell phones from the Westminster raid. I figured out which one belonged to Santiago. I went through all the text messages and emails and was able to confirm that there were many conversations between Santiago and Hector. What seemed odd was that Santiago kept asking to expand into other areas, but Hector denied his request every time. My gut tells me Hector wasn't that interested in the protection business. In fact, at one point, he outright told Santiago not to expand because it wasn't profitable for the cartel's primary business."

Frank listened to Sal, then said, "Maybe Santiago was going about this protection business behind Hector's back. Maybe that's why there was so much cash at that house. In other words, he was holding back funds from the cartel and keeping them for himself."

Gino thought for a few seconds and replied, "Maybe so. One thing's for sure—Santiago is out of business for good."

Chapter 15

Álvarez Téllez called a meeting of all his lieutenants at the main house. When everyone was assembled, he asked Nicolás to provide an update on what he had recently discovered regarding the Mexican Sinaloa cartel's interest in their precious stone business. When Nicolás finished, a puzzled look crossed the faces of all the lieutenants.

Álvarez said, "I can see that you are all puzzled by this information."

One lieutenant spoke up, "What makes the Sinaloa cartel think we are trying to expand into their territory? As far as I know, this is not part of our plans, nor has it ever been. Am I correct, Álvarez?"

"You are absolutely correct. That's why this is so puzzling. How could they have gotten such an idea to begin with? This is what I want to know: have any of you expressed to anyone the possibility of our cartel expanding into Mexico?"

The lieutenants still looked confused, and, one by one, they confirmed that they had neither heard nor said anything of the sort. This was news to all of them.

Álvarez continued, "This is my concern. If the Sinaloa cartel thinks we are trying to muscle in on their territory, they will resist and retaliate, just as we would if we suspected they were encroaching on ours. I want everyone to be extra cautious. If you suspect any Mexican interference in your area of operations, call me immediately. If you hear rumors of the Mexican cartel in any of our operations, call me immediately. We need to be vigilant until we know more about what they are up to. To be honest, I am still baffled as to how or why this entire matter surfaced. It concerns me, and I want to ensure that we have the facts before a war starts between us. Wars are costly and never end well for either party. Are we all clear on what we've discussed today?"

There was mutual agreement among all the attendees. As they departed, it was clear to Álvarez that none of his trusted lieutenants knew anything about expanding operations into Mexico.

Pablo checked his watch and decided it was time to walk from his hotel to the Inner Harbor. It would only take ten minutes, and he would still arrive a minute or two early. He took a seat on a bench near the ice cream booth, wearing his New York Yankees baseball cap. He checked his watch again—it was 9:59 p.m. Looking across the walkway to the docks, he spotted a cabin cruiser with a red flag waving in the wind. As he turned his attention away from the boats in the marina, a man sat down next to him.

"I take it you are the police."

"I am Sergeant Wilson, the man you contacted earlier. You called this meeting, so what's on your mind, Mr. Smith?"

Pablo said, "I suspect you are wired, and there are people listening to our conversation. I also suspect you're not alone, and we're being watched. Lastly, I suspect you plan to follow me when this meeting is over. How am I doing so far, Sergeant?"

"You are well informed, Mr. Smith. Now, why don't you tell me what you are here for tonight?"

Pablo laughed. "I am going to reach into my pocket and pull out a plastic bag containing a burner phone. There are no prints on the phone, and only one number appears in the contacts list. I will give you the phone, and you will call me using this phone tomorrow so we can exchange information."

Pablo retrieved the phone from his pocket and handed it to Sergeant Wilson.

He continued, "Now, I have very specific information about a large container ship that will dock at the Baltimore port. This ship has thousands of containers, and one of them holds a ton of cocaine. It would take an army to search all of the containers on the ships that dock there. I propose to give you the name of the ship and the number of the container with the drugs. Now, do I have your attention, Sergeant Wilson?"

"And what do I owe you for such valuable information, Mr. Smith?"

"I want information from you—specific information that will make my boss happy."

Sergeant Wilson was now curious about what information was being requested. "We may indeed be able to help each other. Please, tell me what specifically will make your boss happy?"

"My boss has recently lost many good men in your area—specifically in Baltimore County, Laurel, and Westminster. All these men operated a business and tragically lost their lives in a series of raids by a group other than law enforcement. We will trade the shipment data for information about who was responsible for these events. Do you understand what I am asking for now?"

Sergeant Wilson thought for a few seconds and said, "Okay. Now I get it. You are a stooge for the Mexican drug cartel. I don't care which one—they are all the same to me. You want me to tell you who or what group is taking out your drug centers in Maryland. How am I doing so far, Mr. Smith?"

"There is no need to be so insulting, Sergeant. I am offering you a good deal. Call me tomorrow with the information I need, and I will give you the ship's name and container number. Is that too hard for you to understand?"

Sergeant Wilson said, "First off, I am aware of the three incidents you asked about. We investigated and determined that those cases were closed. You see, Mr. Smith, when drug dealers kill other drug dealers, we have no incentive to bring them to justice. They are, in fact, doing society a favor. If those actions injure our citizens, then we take action. We do not waste our time or resources digging into drug dealer disputes. Quite the contrary—we are content to sit back and watch you kill each other. Is that too hard for you to understand, Mr. Smith?"

Pablo realized he would not get the information he needed from Sergeant Wilson. He checked his watch and saw it was 10:25 p.m. He stood up, saying, "I hope to hear from you tomorrow, Sergeant. If not, your streets will soon be covered in cocaine. I must leave you now."

Pablo took off running toward the dock and jumped onto the cabin cruiser. The boat's pilot took off immediately. Sergeant Wilson spoke into his microphone, "Damn. I didn't see that coming. He's long gone, fellas. Let's pack it up and head back to headquarters."

As the five-man team reassembled at police headquarters, Sergeants Wilson and Carl held a debriefing session. Carl said, "Well, I thought things were going well until Wilson here called out this Mr. Smith."

Wilson replied, "Hey, this guy was playing us. If I call him with the information he needs, he'll just hang up without giving us anything. Besides, his whole approach made it sound like he was bluffing about the shipment."

One of the other officers said, "I think Wilson is right. There may or may not be any drugs coming into the port. However, by the comments I heard, it sounds like somebody in Mexico is pissed off about losing drug distribution centers."

Another officer added, "Maybe. However, that only accounts for the Baltimore County and Laurel explosions. As far as I know, the Westminster raid had nothing to do with drugs."

Wilson said, "I think that is correct. We have nothing that ties all three of these crimes together, unless we missed something."

Carl suggested, "Maybe we should go over the Westminster explosion again, just in case there is something connecting the three cases."

Wilson agreed, "Okay, but let's not waste too much time on it. We have better things to do. As for this Mr. Smith guy, I'm chalking it up to a pissed-off Mexican on a fishing expedition."

Pablo made it to the dock, as promised by the man in the red shirt. The SUV was there to pick him up and take him to his hotel. When they arrived, Pablo left the SUV and returned a short time later to hand the driver a paper bag with the second and final payment for the job.

The next evening, Pablo visited a bar and told the bartender he was there to see Larry. He sat at a table nursing a couple of beers. The man in the red shirt, Larry, entered the bar and sat across from Pablo. "I take it all went well last night?"

"Oh, yes. Thanks for pulling it all together on such short notice. The plan worked perfectly."

Larry said, "You asked about some additional work regarding three specific incidents. Are you still in the market?"

Pablo replied, "Yes, indeed. To be clear, I don't have work for you; I need information from you. Do you understand?"

"Oh, yeah, I get it. You want to know who was behind the three raids in Maryland."

"That's correct. My boss wants to know who was responsible so we can take the appropriate action to ensure no more raids occur."

"I see," said Larry. "Why don't you tell me what you know about the three incidents and who you suspect is behind them? I will then be in a better position to help you."

"Fair enough." Pablo gave Larry a summary of what they suspected about the three explosive raids on their operations, often referring to the Mexican cartel suspecting the Colombians as the most likely culprits. When he finished, he asked, "Well, do you think you can help us figure out who was behind the three events?"

Larry had listened carefully. He then looked straight into Pablo's eyes and said, "I did a bit of checking last night and early this morning, just in case you decided to want such information. I had plans to make you pay handsomely for the information."

"And now you've changed your mind?"

"Let me give you some free advice. You're barking up the wrong tree. The word on the street is that the Colombians had nothing to do with your specific events. Nothing. Are we clear?"

Pablo was irritated but wanted to know more. "Go on. It wasn't the Colombians?"

"That's right. I don't know where you got the idea to suspect the Colombians, but it was totally false intelligence. Maybe someone wanted to misdirect your efforts, and from where I sit, that's exactly what they've done."

"Okay, let's cut to the chase. If it's not the Colombians, then who?"

"The Italians."

Pablo was shocked. "The Italians? What the hell do they have to do with this?"

"Look, man. You asked; I did some digging, and it all comes back to the Italians. Why? I don't know, and I don't want to know. The last thing I need is for those Italians to take a look at my operations. Listen, take your butt back to your boss, and tell him he was wrong. It wasn't the Colombians; it was the Italians. And I suggest you do it fast because the word on the street is they're not finished. I don't know what you all did to piss off the Italians, but you've got their undivided attention, and I don't need to be involved."

Larry stood up and left the bar. Pablo was left to ponder the revelation, unable to understand why the Italians were targeting the Mexican cartel.

Fabio's men were in position, and the weather was perfect for flying. The three two-man drone teams were armed and ready. They wore headsets to communicate with each other, allowing them to coordinate and detonate as precisely as possible.

At exactly 3 a.m., the teams launched their drones. The first team landed their two thermite drones on the roof of the big house. "Team One, in position," they reported. Team Two landed their thermite drone on the roof of the smaller house and confirmed their position as well. Team One and Team Three positioned their C-4 drones in front of the doors of the two houses, while Team Three also positioned another C-4 drone in front of a set of garage doors at the warehouse.

At exactly 3:04 a.m., the command was given: "Thermite, go!" As the bright white light of the thermite ignited on the roofs of the two houses, the second command came: "C-4, go!"

The explosions were loud, bright, and quite a sight for all three teams. The entire compound was lit up, and they could see the small house collapse into itself, engulfed in flames. Shortly after, the larger house began to fall, almost in slow motion. It must have been well-built, but soon it, too, was just a grounded fireball.

The warehouse, likely filled with chemicals or vehicles, suffered several secondary explosions. These continued for a few minutes as the rest of the structure slowly caught fire.

The three teams watched for several minutes, then decided to pack up their gear and rest before returning to New York the next day.

Fabio received a text message reading, "Mission accomplished. Video to follow."

At breakfast, Fabio was reading his messages and emails when he saw the update from Mexico. He immediately turned on the TV to check the international news. Sure enough, they were talking about the raid on the compound. At the scene, there was aerial footage of emergency equipment fighting several fires. There were more flashing lights than at a carnival. The reporter on the scene mentioned numerous casualties, with the count rising as firefighters sifted through the remains of what were once standing structures. The actual headcount would take days because of the vast area to cover.

Fabio checked his email and found a video attachment. It was a short, three-minute clip of the initial blast at the compound. He smiled and forwarded the text and video to Gino with a simple note: "Case closed."

Juan was the first to hear about the compound's destruction. He immediately sent a text to Pablo telling him to call. While they were talking, Pablo turned on the TV and searched for news reports about the compound. When he found one, he watched in horror. "Juan, I'm watching the news on TV. I see the compound burning."

Juan replied, "It gets worse. Hector and his entire family were asleep at home when the explosions occurred. Pablo, forget what you are doing and return home. We have serious business to discuss."

Pablo agreed to return immediately but first wanted to tell Juan about his conversations with a guy named Larry. When Juan heard what Pablo had to say, he was speechless for a few seconds, then replied, "The Italians? Pablo, are you certain that you have this information correct? What are the Italians doing when they are destroying our drug distribution centers? Oh no. Wait. Do you think they are involved with the compound explosion?"

Pablo was silent for a moment, then said, "I have no idea, Juan. None of this makes sense to me. I'm still not certain the information I was given is correct. Furthermore, I don't know who I can trust anymore. The entire situation is making me crazy. I'll be home very soon, and we can decide what to do next."

Álvarez was awakened by his housekeeper. She said, "Sorry to bother you, Mr. Álvarez, but there are men here to see you, and they said to wake you immediately." Álvarez put on a robe and went downstairs, where he saw two of his trusted lieutenants standing in the foyer. "What is so important that you had my sleep disturbed?"

"We have bad news and thought you would want to hear it right away."

"What is this bad news you speak of?"

"The main compound of the Mexican Sinaloa cartel was hit this morning. Everything and everyone inside were destroyed. In light of the meeting we just had with you, we thought this news could be bad for us."

Surprised at the news, he said, "Yes, you did well to come to me. Let's go to the other room and turn on the TV. There is probably coverage of this disaster."

The three men went to the living room. Álvarez directed one of the men to search the channels for news, then told his housekeeper to bring coffee and refreshments. As soon as they found a channel with international news, footage of the compound burning appeared. It was aerial footage from a news helicopter, and the reporter described the extensive destruction of not only the compound but also some surrounding homes.

One of the lieutenants said, "That looks more like a targeted bomb went off, like the kind the U.S. used in the Middle East. I think they are called cruise missiles." The other lieutenant asked, "Gee, do you think the U.S. is responsible for this?"

Álvarez replied, "Let's not get too carried away just yet. We don't know what we don't know. We need to take a deep breath and see what the news stations in Mexico report over the next few days. My big concern now is that those remaining in the Mexican cartel will think we were responsible. That brings up another question: Who will take over the Mexican Sinaloa cartel? Will they pursue us as their enemy, or will they be looking elsewhere?"

Gino texted Frank and Sal with news of the Mexican cartel compound's destruction. When Frank read the message, he simply smiled and went back to work, baking bread.

Mr. Perez had installed the new support beam and removed the existing wall, opening up the kitchen area. To keep the construction dust out of the bakery, they left the plastic wall up. Frank called Mr. Perez over to tell him how great the place would look with all the extra space. Mr. Perez replied, "We are doing some finishing work inside the new space, adding shelves and installing the garage and sliding barn doors. Once those three things are out of the way, we will tear down the plastic barrier and clean up the work area. You should be able to move in your new mixer and oven anytime now. As you can see, we have also finished installing the big exhaust fan. We still need the electrician to make the connections. I thought it best to have him handle the exhaust fan and the mixer motor at the same time. Later, a gas man will come in to run the extra line needed for the oven. Both the electrician and gas man will do their work at night since they have day jobs."

Frank was very pleased with the report. He told Mr. Perez that since he and his crew had remained on schedule and done such a good job, they would be rewarded with a $3,000 bonus once all the work and cleanup were complete.

Mr. Perez was surprised and very pleased. "Thank you so much, Frank. This is the first time in all my years in construction anyone has offered me a bonus. If you ever need more work done, please call me."

Frank met with Father Alonzo at the rectory after he had completed his confession duties at the church. "Frank, good to see you. Come in. What brings you to the rectory so late?"

"Thanks, Father. I have a request you may be able to help me with."

Frank explained that he wanted to hire someone to work in the bakery after the expansion was complete. "I was wondering if you knew anyone in the community who would be willing to be an apprentice of sorts. We would teach them; as a result, experience is not required. However, dependability, hard work, and a willingness to learn are critical."

Father Alonzo thought for a few seconds and then said, "I understand, Frank. You are good to come to me with such a request. Let me check with a few people, and I will let you know if I find a suitable candidate."

The next day, Frank was baking bread while Miguel was running the mixer for a new batch of dough when Father Alonzo came into the kitchen with a young girl, maybe sixteen or seventeen years old, following close behind. Father Alonzo said, "Frank, I want you to meet Gina. She lives around the corner with her mother and grandmother. Gina is not doing well in school, according to the nuns, and we all agreed she would be better off learning a trade and making money to support her family. I told her about your gracious offer to train someone in the bakery business, and she is very interested."

Frank and Miguel exchanged looks, and then Miguel said to Gina, "Not long ago, I too had no experience as a baker until Frank gave me a chance. Now I work six days a week and have also learned about pastry and cake making with Diego's help. If you work hard and learn what we have to offer, you can be very successful here."

Frank added, "Gina, I am willing to take a chance on you if you tell me you are up to listening and learning what we have to teach. You can begin tonight by showing up at the bakery at midnight. That's when the dough is made, and Miguel will be your primary instructor. Do you understand?"

Gina, a bit shy, managed to say, "Thank you for this opportunity. I understand and will do my best."

Frank said, "Thank you for bringing this young lady to see us, Father. I think this will work out fine if Gina puts in an honest effort. If she decides this is not the future she wants, there will be no hard feelings."

Father Alonzo looked at Gina and said, "This is a chance for you to learn a trade. Do your best, and good things will be in your future."

Gina replied, "Thank you all for this opportunity."

As Frank walked Father Alonzo out, he said, "She seems like a troubled teen. But I suppose we were all troubled teens at some point."

Father Alonzo laughed and said, "Frank, I see troubled youth all the time. However, if given the right tutoring and someone who cares, they can accomplish many things. Just look at yourself in the mirror, my son!"

Chapter 16

At 4 p.m., the Director of the DEA in Washington summoned Agents Miller, Santoni, and Ming to his office. The room was austere, with a large, dark wood conference table dominating the center. The walls were adorned with maps, charts, and a few framed commendations, but the tension in the air was palpable. The agents sat down, their faces a mix of anticipation and fatigue. The director, a seasoned veteran with gray hair and sharp eyes, wasted no time.

"What do you have for us, Agent Ming?" He asked, his voice steady but urgent. Agent Ming, a meticulous investigator known for her sharp analytical skills, cleared her throat and began. "My team worked through the night, sir. We reviewed all the tractor-trailer hijackings from all fifty states, contacted the local offices where these incidents occurred, and searched for patterns or links that might connect the cases. Initially, there was nothing concrete that proved a connection. But when we dug deeper into the police reports and ran several pattern recognition scenarios, we identified one compelling possibility."

The director leaned forward; his expression intense. "And what was that?"

Ming continued, her voice confident. "Each of the hijackings had an identical modus operandi. The trucks were stopped in remote areas, the drivers either complicit or coerced, and in every instance, the drivers were killed. The hijackers would then torch the tractor-trailers with their cargo. We found that in every case, the fires were set using the same accelerant, and all the burnt remains contained traces of a unique chemical compound. This compound matches the residue found in drug stashes seized from previous busts. The drugs in question, in all these incidents, originate from the same source in Mexico."

The Director's brow furrowed. "And you're certain all of these cases are connected by this chemical fingerprint?"

Ming nodded. "Yes, sir. The chemical signature is unmistakable. It all points back to a single source. What's more, that source is linked to a region in Mexico we've been monitoring for some time – a region associated with a series of recent drug busts that weren't directly tied to these hijackings until now."

Agent Miller, leaning back in his chair, interjected, "So you're saying you can link the hijackings together because the chemical analysis of the drugs is identical in every case?"

"Precisely," Ming confirmed. "All the drugs share the same chemical profile, which is too specific to be coincidental. These hijackings are part of a larger operation."

The Director's eyes narrowed. "Have you had any further contact from the anonymous caller?"

Agent Santoni shook his head. "No, sir. Not a word. He promised to call today with more information, but we've heard nothing so far."

The director sighed; his frustration barely concealed. "And what about the explosion in Mexico? The compound that blew up—do you think it's related somehow?"

Santoni nodded thoughtfully. "We heard about the explosion. With the new evidence from Ming, it seems more than likely there's a connection. The drugs flow from Mexico to Florida; money is laundered in California and sent back to Mexico. It's a complicated web, but there's a pattern emerging."

The director leaned back in his chair, raising an eyebrow. "That's a big leap, Santoni. Connecting these dots without more concrete evidence might be risky."

Agent Ming chimed in, "Not necessarily, sir. If you trace the flow of money and drugs, it all fits. The real question is: who is orchestrating this? Is it another cartel, perhaps from Mexico or Colombia? Or is it some other organized crime group taking advantage of the chaos to make a profit? We're still missing the key piece – the 'who' behind these operations."

The director drummed his fingers on the table, his mind racing. "Alright. Here's what we're going to do. Issue a bulletin to all agency satellites – we need immediate access to any information on recent tractor-trailer hijackings. Also, coordinate with local police departments. Let them know we're looking for any leads, and we're prepared to offer deals or reduced sentences for credible information pointing us in the right direction."

Agent Miller nodded. "That might be our best chance of finding out who's pulling the strings. Someone knows something, and they'll talk if the deal is sweet enough."

As the agents got up to leave, the director remained seated, staring at the stack of files in front of him. His shoulders slumped slightly, indicating the weight of the situation. If word got out that the DEA had missed the obvious connections between these cases, there would be hell to pay. The agency's reputation, his reputation, hung in the balance.

As the door closed behind the agents, he muttered to himself, "We'd better solve this damn puzzle before it blows up in all our faces..."

The bakery expansion was finally complete. The smell of fresh paint mingled with the comforting scent of warm bread and pastries. The new mixer, a state-of-the-art computerized marvel, sat gleaming in the corner, with more dials, knobs, and buttons than a fighter plane cockpit. Mr. Perez had received his bonus, and Gina was finishing her first week at the bakery. Everything seemed to be going smoothly—except for one small issue: the new mixer was more sophisticated than anything they'd ever used.

Miguel arrived for his midnight shift and noticed Gina already seated at a table, a determined expression on her face. She was surrounded by two thick manuals, her fingers tracing over the lines of text.

"Good morning, Gina. What are you doing in so early?" Miguel asked, wiping his hands on his apron.

Gina looked up, excitement sparking in her eyes. "Miguel, I've been studying these manuals, and it turns out this mixer is practically a genius. You can input a recipe, and it calculates the exact amounts and even the order in which they should be added. It'll sound an alarm when it's time to add each ingredient. It even knows how long to mix the dough for the perfect consistency."

Miguel whistled. "You understand all that computer stuff, Gina?"

Gina grinned. "Oh yes. I love this stuff. I wish they'd teach more computer science in school. This is the future."

Miguel chuckled. "Okay, kid. I'll get started on the dough for today's bread in the old mixer. You keep working on the new one. When you're ready to give it a go, let me know."

By the time Frank arrived at 5 a.m., the kitchen was alive with the scent of flour and yeast. Miguel and Gina stood side by side, looking at two large piles of dough.

Frank raised an eyebrow and approached them with a smile. "What are you two looking at? Haven't you seen bread dough before?"

Miguel laughed. "Gina figured out how to work that new mixer. She entered all the ingredients, and it told her the order to add them, the exact amounts, and how long to mix. When the dough was done, it even rang a bell. To compare, we just poured out one batch from the old mixer and another from the new one. So far, they look identical."

Frank leaned in, pushing his fists into both batches of dough, feeling the texture. "You figured this stuff out by yourself, Gina?"

Gina nodded, her face glowing with pride. "Yes, the manuals are very well written. The instructions are clear and concise."

Frank scratched his head. "Alright, then. The proof is in the bread. I'm going to shape loaves from each batch and bake them. Then we'll have a taste test. If they're the same, you've just earned yourself a raise, kid."

Gina's face lit up with excitement. "Oh boy! I love this kind of challenge."

Soon, the loaves were cooling on the table. They looked identical, with the same golden crust and soft, fluffy insides. Frank, Miguel, and Gina each took a slice from both batches. The taste and texture were indistinguishable. Frank grinned. "Alright, we need an outsider's opinion."

He called Diego into the kitchen. With a mischievous smile, he blindfolded him and handed him samples from both batches. "Diego, which one is from the old mixer and which is from the new?"

Diego chewed thoughtfully, then shrugged. "I have no idea. They taste the same to me."

Frank laughed. "Gina, you have a raise starting Monday."

Gina squealed with delight, doing a little dance around the table. Diego grinned and asked, "Gina, does that fancy mixer also work for pastry dough if you put in the recipe?"

Gina nodded eagerly. "There's no reason it wouldn't! If you give me the recipe and the order of ingredients, I'll see what it can do. And if I get stuck, the manufacturer offers technical support."

Frank clapped his hands together. "Go for it, guys. If this makes us more efficient and creates identical batches every time, then our quality control just went through the roof. Nice job, Gina."

Gina beamed, ready to tackle the next challenge. The bakery felt different, more alive, and there was a buzz in the air—a feeling that something new was brewing, something that might just take them to the next level.

Gino received a text from Fabio, the message short and direct: "Gray van at Frank's address to pick up handguns Friday at 1 p.m. Code word: 'rigatoni.'" Gino glanced at his watch; Friday was tomorrow. He had no time to lose. He was deep in the guts of an old Cadillac with a stubborn wiring problem, and the garage was swamped. No way he could be there for the drop. He decided to delegate. "Sal, I need you to handle something for me tomorrow at Frank's place."

"Sure thing, Gino. What's up?"

Gino explained the plan, his voice low but firm, giving Sal all the details. "Make sure they say 'rigatoni,' and keep your eyes sharp. I don't trust these guys, even with the code word."

Sal cracked a grin. "You got it, Gino. I'll be ready."

Friday came, and by 12:45 p.m., Sal was stationed on the front steps of Frank's rowhouse, leaning against the brick wall, eyes scanning the street. A light breeze stirred the stale summer air, carrying the scent of exhaust and hot asphalt. A few kids played hopscotch on the cracked sidewalk across the street, their laughter punctuating the steady hum of the city. Sal checked his watch, then shifted his gaze back to the street. Under his loose jacket, he felt the reassuring weight of the revolver tucked in his waistband. He didn't expect trouble, but in their line of work, you never really knew.

At exactly 1:00 p.m., a gray van appeared at the end of the block, rolling slowly down the street. Sal watched it approach, noting the make and model—nothing special, a generic panel van, perfect for blending in. The van stopped in front of the house, the engine idling. The passenger window rolled down, and a man in a baseball cap stuck his head out, his face obscured.

Sal pushed away from the wall, stepping closer. "What's your favorite pasta?" he asked casually, though his muscles were taut, ready.

The man in the passenger seat hesitated for a split second—a flicker of uncertainty in his eyes. Then he responded, "Rigatoni."

Sal gave a curt nod. "Good answer. Follow me. We've got two tubs downstairs, and they're heavy. Gonna take both of us to haul them up."

The passenger, a wiry guy with a thin mustache, climbed out of the van. His eyes darted around briefly before he followed Sal to the side door that led to the basement steps. Sal noticed the man's hand twitching slightly, the kind of nervousness he'd seen before in men who were new to the game. Sal kept his voice calm, his demeanor steady, as he led the man down the narrow, dimly lit stairs into the basement.

The basement smelled of mildew and dust, the dim light casting long shadows against the walls lined with shelves full of old tools, car parts, and boxes. Sal motioned to two large, blue plastic containers near the far wall. "Those are the ones," he said. "You take the front; I'll take the back."

The man nodded, but Sal caught the way his eyes lingered on the containers just a bit too long, as if calculating something. Together they lifted the first container, and Sal felt the weight of it—a solid, reassuring weight. "You good?" Sal asked.

"Yeah," the man grunted, his face tight with effort. They moved up the stairs slowly, and Sal kept his peripheral vision on the man's movements. One wrong move, one slip of the hand toward a concealed weapon, and Sal was ready to act. They reached the top of the stairs, and the man shifted to push open the door with his shoulder.

They carried the tub to the side of the van, and Sal took a moment to glance inside. Two more men were seated up front, eyes scanning the surroundings. No one spoke. The tension was thick. The first tub went in, and they headed back down for the second. Sal's mind raced, calculating, watching for any sign that something was off.

Back in the basement, Sal grabbed the second container, feeling the sweat on his palms, and they repeated the process. The man was still silent, his movements efficient but hurried. As they reached the top of the steps, Sal thought, *These guys are sure not much for conversation.*

The second tub slid into the van, and the passenger nodded to Sal. "That all?" he asked, a hint of impatience creeping into his voice.

"That's it," Sal replied. "Have a good one."

The van's door slammed shut, and it drove off without another word. Sal stood there, watching it disappear down the street. His mind was still alert. He waited a beat longer, then turned and headed back toward the house. Something about the whole exchange felt a little too clean, a little too quiet.

Meanwhile, back at the garage, Gino was elbow-deep in an engine, Antonio and Mark beside him, working on another car. "These electrical issues are getting more complicated each year," Gino muttered, frustration creeping into his voice as he struggled to find the source of a persistent short circuit.

Antonio nodded in agreement. "Maybe we should hire someone who knows how to diagnose these things with the newer, more sophisticated scan tools like the Autel MaxiCheck."

Gino wiped his forehead, grease streaking across his brow. "I know about these tools but knowing how to use them effectively—that's the hard part."

Antonio shrugged. "What you do is contact the local automotive trade school. They could send over some of their best students for a trial period. Those schools are always searching for shops to hire their graduates. Plus, they're trained on the best, up-to-date equipment."

Mark, Pasquale's son, chimed in, "I'll talk to my dad and see what he thinks. I'm sure I can persuade him to give these students a try. If we find one that's good, we hire him. We're spending way too much time chasing electrical issues. The right tool in the right hands will make us more efficient."

Gino nodded, but his mind was still half on the exchange with the van. "Yeah, that makes sense," he replied absently, but in his gut, he felt a nagging sense of unease. He needed to check in with Sal to make sure everything went smoothly. You never could be too careful in their line of work.

As the afternoon sun dipped lower, Sal finally called Gino. "It's done," he said simply. "But those guys, they were a bit too quiet. You know what I mean?"

Gino paused, tightening his grip on the wrench. "Yeah, I hear you. Keep an eye out, Sal. Something tells me we are being watched."

Luis Cabrera from Guadalajara was next in line to take over the Mexican Sinaloa cartel. Since the compound in Mexico City had been completely destroyed, Luis operated out of his home base. It was an elaborate setup—high walls, armed guards, surveillance equipment, and a labyrinthine structure to confuse intruders—but it was nowhere near the scale of the compound that once stood in Mexico City. Nonetheless, Luis was determined to reassert control, prove his leadership, and restore the cartel's dominance.

His first order of business was to call all the cartel lieutenants to a meeting. As the men filed into the dimly lit room, Luis sat at the head of a long wooden table. He was a soft-spoken man, calm and composed, but his reputation for ruthless efficiency was well known. When he spoke, it was in measured tones, his voice barely above a whisper, but every word commanded attention.

"At this first meeting, I need answers," he began, his eyes narrowing as he looked around the table. "Find out who was responsible for the destruction of our compound in Mexico City. I want names, locations, and alliances. Pablo and Juan, give us an update on your recent missions."

Pablo, a wiry man with sharp eyes, stood up. "We've been tracking chatter on the Colombians, but nothing definitive links them to the attack. No evidence has surfaced that suggests their involvement."

Luis nodded slowly; his expression unreadable. "Interesting. No evidence to confirm the Colombians...Yet we have new information pointing toward the Italians. Pablo, continue investigating this connection. See if it leads anywhere."

Juan, a heavier man with a thick beard, spoke next. "The hijacking issue seems to have resolved itself. All our shipments have arrived in Guadalajara without incident. If it starts up again, we'll act."

Luis leaned back in his chair, his fingers steepling. "Good. For now, focus all efforts on the Italians. We need to know who's moving against us."

The meeting ended, and the men dispersed. Luis watched them leave, pleased with the current direction but aware that time would tell if his leadership could steer the cartel back to its former strength. The losses in personnel, product, and cash over the past months had been staggering, but the Sinaloa cartel had weathered worse storms. They would survive this one too—if they could outmaneuver their enemies.

Meanwhile, Pablo was determined to get more information about the mysterious cases in Maryland. He knew there was a connection between the events in Baltimore and the chaos hitting the cartel. Flying back to Baltimore, he made his way to Skullies Bar on the West Side, a place where secrets stained the walls and hidden deals whispered from every corner.

Walking up to the bar, Pablo locked eyes with the bartender and asked to speak to Larry. He knew this was where he needed to start. After a tense thirty-minute wait, Larry entered, a wiry man with a face that had seen too many fights. He spotted Pablo immediately.

"What brings you back to our dark side of town, Mr. Smith?" Larry asked with a gruff but curious voice.

Pablo leaned in close, speaking just loud enough to be heard over the chatter around them. "I'm here on a fact-finding mission. No heroics, no bloodshed—just information. You point me in the right direction, and I'll make it worth your while. How does $100K sound?"

Larry's eyes widened slightly, but he kept his cool. "Alright, I understand the urgency. Tonight at 7 p.m., come back here. I'll introduce you to someone who can help—a crime reporter from the *Baltimore Star*."

Pablo frowned. "A reporter? How is a journalist going to help me?"

Larry smirked. "Just show up. Bring $10K in cash. You'll see soon enough. If you're satisfied with the information, there will be a second payment of $10K. And if it all checks out, I'll expect my $100K. We clear?"

"Crystal," Pablo replied, his mind already working through the angles.

At 7 p.m., Pablo returned to the bar. The dim lighting cast long shadows across the room, and the smell of cigarette smoke hung heavy in the air. He spotted Larry sitting at a table with a woman. She was in her late thirties, attractive, and carried herself with a confidence that suggested she had seen her fair share of the city's dark underbelly.

"Okay, I'm here," Pablo said, pulling up a chair. "How can you help me?"

The woman extended a hand. "I'm Marci, Mr. Smith. I write about crime for the *Baltimore Star*. Here's the deal: I'll approach the officers involved in the cases you're interested in. Tell them I'm working on a cover story about drug crime in the city. These cops love seeing their names in print—they'll spill details that never made it into the official reports."

Pablo arched an eyebrow. "And what makes you think they'll tell you what I need to know?"

Marci smiled. "I have access to certain files at the police department. I spend a lot of time there, and I can get into the system and pull confidential memos. It's risky, but I can do it. I'm betting I can find things the public hasn't seen—things that will help you put the pieces together."

Pablo leaned back, considering her offer. "How long will it take?"

"One or two weeks at most," Marci replied. "Maybe sooner if I get lucky. So, do we have a deal?"

Pablo thought for a moment, then handed her an envelope stuffed with cash. "There's my number. I'm heading back to Mexico tonight. Call when you have something. If your information is solid, you'll get your second payment. If it checks out, Larry gets his. We all good?"

Marci and Larry nodded. Pablo left the bar, feeling a flicker of hope. This was his best lead so far—a slim one, but better than nothing. As he stepped into the cool Baltimore night, he couldn't shake the feeling that he was walking along a razor's edge.

But that was how he liked it.

Chapter 17

Frank pulled Gina aside for a private conversation in the back office of his bustling bakery. The aroma of freshly baked bread wafted through the air as he spoke, his voice low but warm. "Gina, you've really been a diamond in the rough," Frank began, his eyes crinkling with pride. "You took on that new mixer contraption and made it sing. I also know you've trained Miguel to set up the recipes, and he's doing it on his own now."

Gina looked down at the flour-dusted floor, a bit embarrassed by the praise. After a moment, she looked up and met Frank's kind eyes. "I'm so thankful you took a chance on me, Frank. No one's ever given me the time of day, much less taken me under their wing and given me an opportunity to be successful." She wiped a tear from her eye, leaving a smudge of flour on her cheek. "If you'd let me, I think I could go a bit further. I've been taking some courses at the community college after work, and I'm sure I could automate our inventory and ordering process."

Frank smiled warmly, his weathered hands gripping her shoulder. "By all means, Gina. You have my permission to explore anything you think might help the business. I trust your judgment, and I trust you."

"Oh, Frank, it's so good to hear that coming from you. I won't let you down. I promise," Gina said, her voice thick with emotion.

Frank hesitated for a moment, his expression turning serious. "I heard from a little birdie that you had to cancel your cable at home because you were behind on payments. Is that true?"

Gina nodded, her shoulders slumping slightly. "Yeah. When my dad passed, my mom and grandma were left with very little income, and I didn't have a job. Money's been tight, so we cut off the cable service to save. Besides, my old computer died, so there was no way for me to keep up with the latest technology."

Frank reached into his pocket and pulled out an envelope, handing it to her. "What's this?" she asked, her brow furrowing in confusion.

"It's a bonus," he said, his eyes twinkling, "for all your hard work and for teaching Miguel. It should be enough to pay some bills and get your cable turned back on."

Gina peeked inside the envelope, her eyes widening in disbelief. "Oh my God, Frank, this is more money than I've ever seen at one time!"

Frank laughed, making a deep, hearty sound that filled the small office. "There's more." He reached down and handed her a box marked Dell Computer. "This is a company laptop for you to use to work on that inventory and ordering idea you mentioned."

Gina was speechless. She placed the box on the flour-covered counter and hugged Frank so tightly that he gasped for air. When their meeting ended, Frank said, "Okay, kid. Get out there and make us all proud."

As Gina left the office, her steps light with excitement, Frank's smile faded. He glanced at a hidden safe in the corner of the room, his thoughts shifting to the other side of his business—the side that allowed him to be so generous but also put them all at risk.

Later that day, across town at Pasquale's auto shop, the smell of motor oil and grease permeated the air. Mr. Pasquale, a stocky man with salt-and-pepper hair, gathered his men for a meeting in his cluttered office. The walls were adorned with vintage car posters and shelves filled with trophies from local racing events.

"We've had three students from the trade center come in and showcase their skills with various scanners," Pasquale began, leaning back in his creaky office chair. "What do you guys think? Are any of them fit to be hired after they graduate?"

Gino was the first to speak. "That's tough, Pasquale. They were all very good. In fact, I think all three were outstanding."

Antonio and Mark nodded in agreement. Antonio added, "Each of them had their own approach to the electrical problems we threw at them, but they all managed to solve them in the end."

Mark, Pasquale's son, chimed in, his young face eager to contribute. "Pop, I was impressed not only by their skills but also by how quickly they identified the problem areas and their understanding of wiring diagrams."

Pasquale nodded thoughtfully, his fingers drumming on the desk. "Well, we can't hire all of them. So, pick one. Also, make sure they're interested in doing more than just electrical work. We can't afford to have someone sitting around waiting for an electrical issue to come up."

Gino spoke up, his voice confident. "The kid named Tommy was very hands-on. He not only diagnosed the problem, but he also took the initiative to replace the part and test the results."

Antonio agreed, stroking his mustache. "Tommy seemed very eager to learn more, especially about rebuilding automatic transmissions. He wasn't afraid to get his hands dirty."

Mark nodded again, his enthusiasm evident. "Tommy is great, but he's got one thing: he's constantly asking questions. I swear he must have asked me fifty questions while I was working on the old Chrysler."

Pasquale smiled with a glint in his eyes. "An inquisitive kid is a good thing. I like the fact that he wants to learn more. Hell, he might be running this shop someday!" He paused for a moment before concluding, "Alright, I'll let the school know we'd like to hire Tommy after he graduates. In the meantime, he can work here part-time after school."

As the meeting dispersed, Pasquale caught Gino's eye and nodded subtly. They both knew that Tommy's eagerness to learn could be useful for more than just auto repair.

Pablo received a call from Marci, his voice low and cautious. "Only seven days?" Pablo commented, surprised by her efficiency. "That's much quicker than I expected. Would Monday at 7 p.m. at Skullies Bar work for you?"

"That's fine. See you then," Marci replied, her tone businesslike.

When Pablo entered the dimly lit bar, the smell of stale beer and cigarette smoke assaulting his senses, he spotted Marci and Larry seated at a corner table. He joined them, his movements fluid and controlled. "Did you find an answer to the puzzle?" he asked.

Marci handed him a thick manila envelope containing a report along with some crime scene photos. "You can look over these while I summarize what I found," she said, her voice low but clear. "First, the three incidents are definitely related. In fact, there was a fourth event that set this whole mess in motion—it happened on Greenmount Avenue."

She paused, making sure Pablo was following. "Before these four events, there were three murders in a small section of town called Little Italy: a baker and then a couple who owned a bar. These murders were listed in the police files as possible acts of protection rackets moving into the area. I followed that thread and interviewed nine police officers directly involved in each case."

Pablo nodded, his eyes scanning the documents as Marci continued. "My questioning led me to a few of the people the police had initially targeted as possible suspects. These suspects were eventually ruled out, but they suggested the police look into individuals from Westminster. Digging deeper, I discovered that Detective Matthew had been trying to get information from the local parish priest, Father Alonzo."

Marci leaned in closer, her voice dropping even lower. "I interviewed both men for my story on drug crime in the city. I'm 90 percent sure this priest knows more than he's letting on. In fact, Detective Matthew made several pleas to Father Alonzo to help him prevent a street war."

She took a deep breath before delivering her conclusion. "My conclusion is this: You need to get to Father Alonzo and make him tell you what he knows. That information will likely explain the brutal murders that happened just before all of your current troubles. My investigation also pointed to a Mexican crew in Westminster. You see, Mr. Smith, your people may have started this entire chain of events."

Pablo thumbed through the stack of papers and photos Marci had given him, his face impassive. Without a word, he reached into his pocket and handed her an envelope of cash. "You did well, Marci. Our business is complete. If you don't mind, I'd like some time alone with Larry."

"No problem." Marci left Skullies, the envelope tucked securely in her purse.

Pablo turned to Larry, his eyes hard. "I'm going to look into this priest, and if he can verify any of Marci's findings, I'll be back to pay you the agreed sum. Once you're paid, our business is finished. We won't be in contact again. Your name and this bar will never appear in what happens next. Are we clear? I was never here. Ever."

Larry nodded, a bead of sweat forming on his brow. "That's exactly how I want it. If Marci's right, you're in for one hell of a fight. You've already seen what these Italians are capable of, and trust me, it can get messy very fast."

Pablo returned to his hotel, the weight of Marci's report heavy in his mind. She didn't know that Hector had told Santiago several times to curtail his protection rackets. Now Pablo had to return to Mexico and relay this story to Luis Cabrera. However, before making his flight plans, he decided to visit Father Alonzo in Little Italy.

The sun was setting as Pablo approached the old brick church, casting long shadows across the quiet street. Father Alonzo was in the rectory doing paperwork when he heard a knock on the door. Looking through the glass pane, he did not recognize the man outside but opened the door and said, "Yes? May I help you?"

Pablo replied, his voice calm but authoritative, "Yes, Father, I need to speak to you about the recent deaths in your community, specifically at the bakery and the bar."

Father Alonzo hesitated for a moment before saying, "Please come in, and we can talk."

The two men sat in the rectory's sitting room, the air thick with tension. Pablo began, "I am from Mexico and work for a man who is inquiring about the three murders that occurred here. My boss is a very powerful man, the head of the Mexican Sinaloa cartel."

"I see," said Father Alonzo, his face a mask of calm. "And how may I help you?"

"We have lost many people and a lot of product since these unfortunate murders occurred. We would like to settle with those responsible for such acts of retaliation. Our information suggests that you know who they are."

Father Alonzo paused for a few seconds before responding, his voice steady. "You sound like a bitter man, Mr. Pablo. I know all about my parishioners' three murders. Of course, they were my friends. However, I cannot help with your request. I have no knowledge of those responsible, other than what I heard on the news."

Father Alonzo stood, signaling that he was done with the conversation. But Pablo had other ideas. He shouted at Father Alonzo to sit back down. When he did, Pablo said, his voice menacing, "Father, you are going to tell me what I need to know, or this is going to become very unpleasant."

What Pablo didn't know was that Father Alonzo was no altar boy his entire life. He had been brought up on the streets of Sicily and, as a young man, had been part of the mafia. He remained friends with Aldo, who still ran the organization.

Fearing for his life, Father Alonzo grabbed the six-inch crucifix hanging around his neck and lunged forward with surprising speed, jabbing it into Pablo's throat. The crucifix went in about three inches before stopping. Pablo clutched his neck, his eyes wide with shock and pain. He struggled for breath, making wet, choking sounds as he slowly died.

Father Alonzo stood over Pablo's body, his hands shaking. He was now in a bind. What should I do? he thought. Should I call the police? Should I dispose of the body? After contemplating the situation for a moment, he decided to call Frank.

Father Alonzo's voice was strained as he spoke to Frank on the phone, "I need your immediate help at the rectory; it's urgent." Frank heard the intense strain in the old priest's voice and said he would be right over.

When Frank arrived, his face grim, Father Alonzo summarized what had happened and expressed his fear that this entire mess of retaliation was about to escalate into an all-out war.

Frank stared at the dead Pablo, his mind racing through possible solutions. "I'm going to get Gino over here to help me remove the body," he said, his voice calm despite the gravity of the situation. "You say nothing about this to anyone. After tonight, this will be as if it never happened."

Gino arrived in the delivery van, his face covered in a grim mask. He and Frank worked quickly and efficiently, wrapping Pablo's body in a shower curtain and loading it into the van. They removed all his belongings—wallet, watch, rings, cell phone, etc.—and then drove to a secluded spot on Back River.

As they dumped the body into the murky water, the night was dark and still. It would float for a few days, then be carried by the current until an unsuspecting fisherman spotted it and reported it to the police.

The next day, Frank, Sal, and Gino met at Velleggia's after work, the restaurant's cozy atmosphere a stark contrast to the gravity of their conversation. Frank updated Sal on what had happened at the rectory. Sal listened intently, his face growing more concerned with each word.

After a few moments of heavy silence, Sal said, his voice low, "It's unfortunate Father Alonzo had to deal with this in his own home. My concern is, what does this mean going forward? Is the Mexican cartel targeting us now?"

Gino replied, leaning in closer, "I think that's exactly what it means. We've bought some time, but only if this Pablo guy didn't tell anyone else what he found. You might want to check his cell phone to see if he texted or emailed anyone."

Frank added, his brow furrowed in thought, "That's a good idea, Gino. But we have no way of knowing if he passed the information on to others in the cartel or if it died with him."

Sal chimed in, his voice tense, "We better keep our eyes and ears open. If the information reaches Mexico, we must be ready for a counterattack. If it didn't, then we have nothing to worry about, right?"

"Sounds about right to me, Sal," Gino responded, his eyes darting around the restaurant. "It's a waiting game, and we need to make sure we're ready when the stuff hits the fan."

As they finished their drinks, each man lost in his own thoughts; the weight of their actions and the uncertainty of their future hung heavy in the air. The calm before the storm was settling over Little Italy, but for how long, none of them could say.

Detective Matthew from Homicide investigated the floating body in the Back River. The coroner was able to lift his prints, but there were no hits in the police database.

A hotel manager reported to the police that they have not heard from a man who checked in several days ago. When they did a wellness check, he was not in the room and had not checked out. The manager wanted to know if it was okay to pack up the man's belongings and have the room cleaned. He was told that an officer would be over shortly to inventory the belongings, since this was a suspicious event that may simply be someone skipping out on their bill.

When the officer arrived at the hotel, he and the manager went to the room. As he started his inventory, he noticed a discarded boarding pass in the trash can. It showed the name, date, time, and original departure airport. Examining the remaining items, he noticed a stack of papers, crime scene photos, and numerous other details, all of which pointed to Detective Matthew. The officer called Detective Matthew and told him that based on what had been discovered, he should get to the hotel.

Detective Matthew arrived, looked over the documents and photos, and told the office he would take over the case. It appears this Pablo guy on the boarding pass may be the same guy they found floating in the river.

After contacting the FBI, Detective Matthew sent them the prints to see if they matched anything from their Mexican City files. Sure enough, they got a hit and now had an identification for the body in the morgue.

Further reading of the file left in the hotel room made Detective Matthew start to piece together parts of a larger puzzle. He now needed to speak with Father Alonzo and the *Baltimore Star* reporter, who was writing a story on drug crimes.

Over the next few days, Detective Matthew managed to get nowhere. Talks with Father Alonzo were of no use to him. The father was not giving up any information the police did not already have. Detective Matthew said, "Father, do you know a man named Pablo?"

"Of course, he lives down the street. I talked to him just yesterday. Why?"

"No Father. The Pablo I am speaking of was found dead floating in the river a few days ago."

"Oh dear. No I do not know who this man is you are speaking about."

"Do you know a reporter from the *Baltimore Star* named Marci?"

"Yes, I do. I met with her a week or so ago. She was telling a story about drug crime in the city. Despite the challenging task, she possessed a pleasant demeanor. Is she okay?"

"Yes. She is fine. It is just that the dead man named Pablo and your name came up in some papers we found in the hotel room of the deceased man."

"Well. I am sorry, Detective, that I cannot be of any help to you. I have told you all I know. Are we through?"

Detective Matthew left the rectory and headed to the *Baltimore Star*. The reporter at the paper said she was doing an investigative piece on drug crime, but her editor put a sudden end to the assignment, so she moved on to other things. However, when Detective Matthew pressed her on how her report and crime scene photos ended up in the hands of a man named Pablo, she had an answer.

"I had those files in the back seat of my car along with tons of other paperwork. I never knew they were missing until you called. I have no idea when or who may have taken them."

Detective Matthew was at a loss once again, deadended at every move he made. His frustration was short-lived, as he promptly received a call to investigate yet another homicide in Baltimore's troubled streets.

Chapter 18

Sal, Gino, and Frank gathered at Velleggia's after a long day of work. The aroma of garlic and tomato sauce filled the air as they settled into a corner booth, away from prying ears. Gino leaned in, his voice low. "So, Sal, were you able to dig up anything from Pablo's cell phone?" Sal nodded, his eyes darting around to ensure no one was listening. "I got a goldmine of info from the texts and emails," he began. "Here's the kicker: Pablo's last communication was when he landed at BWI. After that, radio silence. No contacts, nothing."

Frank's eyebrows shot up. "Nothing at all?"

"Well, almost nothing," Sal continued. "I checked the phone logs. His last call was from a local Maryland number. When I called it, it led to the editor's office of the *Baltimore Star*."

Gino leaned in closer. "Interesting. Any other leads?"

Sal lowered his voice even further. "There were six text messages from the same person in Mexico, all trying to reach Pablo. But here's the thing – Pablo never responded to any of them."

Frank listened intently, his mind working overtime. After a moment of contemplation, he spoke. "So, it sounds like Pablo never communicated what he discovered after arriving in Baltimore. My guess? He met up with some folks and then immediately went to see Father Alonzo. That's how I see it."

Sal nodded in agreement. "I think you're dead on, Frank. We can safely assume the cartel in Mexico is in the dark about the connection Pablo mentioned when he went to Father Alonzo."

Gino chimed in, his tone cautious. "That certainly sounds plausible. But let's not drop our guard just yet. We should stay alert, at least for a while longer."

The others murmured their agreement as the waiter approached to take their order. As they finished their meals, the weight of the day's events seemed to settle on their shoulders.

Frank pushed his plate away, stifling a yawn. "I'm beat. Think I'll head home and rest up."

"I'm with you," Gino added, signaling for the check.

As they left Velleggia's, the cool Baltimore night air carried a sense of unease. The city lights twinkled, oblivious to the dangerous undercurrents flowing beneath its surface.

Meanwhile, thousands of miles away in Guadalajara, a different kind of meeting was taking place. Juan, his face etched with worry, had requested an audience with the cartel lieutenants at their luxurious estate. Luis, the new leader, had reluctantly agreed.

As the sun dipped below the horizon, casting long shadows across the manicured lawns, the cartel members gathered in the opulent conference room. The tension was palpable as Juan cleared his throat.

"I called this meeting because I haven't heard from Pablo in almost a week," Juan began, his eyes scanning the faces around the table. "Has anyone been in contact with him?"

The lieutenants exchanged irritated glances, shaking their heads in unison.

Luis, his patience wearing thin, leaned forward. "Is this really why you called us here, Juan?"

Juan's voice quivered slightly. "Yes. I'm concerned something might be wrong. Aren't any of you worried?"

Luis's eyes narrowed as he looked around the table. "Do you see anyone here who looks concerned? Pablo could be gathering information, or he could be sleeping off a bender in some jail cell. We have no idea what he's up to, and frankly, it's not our primary concern."

Taking advantage of the gathered audience, Luis decided to change the subject. "While we're all here, let me update you on a few things. First, the hijacking of tractor-trailers has ceased. I don't know why, and I don't care. We're back to business as usual."

The lieutenants nodded; their interest piqued.

"Secondly," Luis continued, "our operation in Mexico City dealing with emeralds and precious stones has resumed. The profits are growing each month."

A murmur of approval rippled through the room.

"Lastly," Luis said, his voice filled with pride, "I'm making changes to our trucking company in Florida. The new company will drop off trailers to be modified at one of our chop shops. They'll then pick up the trailers after they're loaded with product and cash. This new arrangement will add three truck deliveries to our regular schedule."

Luis paused for effect, his eyes gleaming. "What this all means, gentlemen, is that our cartel is back. We're not just increasing our business; we're doing it ahead of schedule."

The room erupted in pleased murmurs and nods of approval. All except Juan, whose worry for his friend Pablo seemed to cast a shadow over the otherwise jubilant atmosphere.

As the meeting adjourned, Juan lingered behind, the weight of Pablo's disappearance heavy on his shoulders. The others filed out, already thinking about the promised expansion and increased profits. Juan couldn't shake the feeling that something was terribly wrong, and he was the only one who seemed to care.

Later that evening, Gino's phone rang. The caller ID displayed Fabio's name, causing Gino to furrow his brow. He answered, his voice cautious.

"Gino, my friend," Fabio's voice crackled through the line. "How are things going? Do you need anything?"

Gino hesitated for a moment before responding. "Things are... complicated, Fabio. We had an incident with a guy named Pablo and Father Alonzo."

"That's unfortunate," Fabio replied, his tone neutral. "I imagine Father Alonzo isn't taking it well. But it sounds like you and Frank handled the situation."

Gino nodded, forgetting for a moment that Fabio couldn't see him. "Yeah, we took care of it."

Fabio continued, his voice taking on a more businesslike tone. "We've halted our hijacking operations, so things should calm down. However, if your people encounter any more outsiders asking questions, let me know immediately. I can restart the hijackings within twenty-four hours. Otherwise, we're putting this whole mess to bed."

"I understand," Gino replied, relief evident in his voice. "We're laying low for now too. No sense in stirring the pot unless we're forced into action. I'll keep you posted if anything changes."

"Agreed, Gino. Let's all enjoy some peace and quiet for a change."

"Sounds good to me, Fabio. Ciao, my friend."

As Gino hung up the phone, he couldn't shake the feeling that this temporary peace was just the calm before the storm.

The following day, in a nondescript government building, the Director of the DEA called Agents Ming, Miller, and Santoni into his office. The three agents filed in, their faces a mix of curiosity and apprehension.

"I'm following up on our earlier meetings," the Director began, his piercing gaze moving from one agent to another. "What do you three have to report?"

Agent Ming spoke first, her voice steady. "We haven't received any more reports of truck hijackings since we last met, sir. It appears that those types of crimes have simply... stopped."

Miller nodded in agreement. "We never heard back from the anonymous caller after that first contact. Both Santoni and I concur with Ming's assessment. If this was some kind of retaliation or takeover attempt by a Mexican cartel, it seems the war is over."

The director leaned back in his chair, his fingers steepled beneath his chin. After a moment of contemplation, he spoke. "I hope you're all correct in your assumptions. What puzzles me is the intelligence from our people in Florida. They've informed me that there's a new person running the Mexican Sinaloa cartel, replacing Hector Torres. His name is Luis Cabrera, originally from Guadalajara."

The agents exchanged glances; their interest piqued.

"Our sources have been monitoring the situation," the Director continued. "They tell me Cabrera is running things quite differently from his predecessor. It's a situation we need to keep an eye on."

He paused again, his gaze sweeping across the room. "For now, let's put this on the back burner unless it rears its ugly head again. But stay alert. Sometimes, it's the quiet periods that precede the biggest storms."

The agents nodded their understanding, each lost in thought about the implications of this new information.

About two weeks after Pablo's body was discovered, Juan received a call from Pablo's sister, Teresa. Her voice was choked with sobs, barely able to form words through her grief.

"Pablo is dead, Juan," she managed to say. There was a heavy silence on the line, broken only by her muffled weeping. "Did you hear me? My brother is dead."

Juan's heart sank, a cold dread settling in his stomach. He had known Pablo for years, and the news hit him like a physical blow. Still, he fought to keep his voice steady, knowing Teresa needed support now more than ever.

"Yes, Teresa. I heard you. I'm so sorry," he said softly. After a moment to collect himself, he asked, "What happened?"

Teresa's words came in halting bursts between her tears. "I don't know for sure. The Mexico City police contacted me. They said... they said Pablo's body was found somewhere in Maryland. The Baltimore Police reached out to them, wanting to know if the body should be cremated or sent back to Mexico City." She paused, taking a shuddering breath. "I told them to send Pablo back to me. I'll pay for the arrangements. He's expected to be delivered in four days."

Juan felt a surge of anger rising within him, but he forced it down, focusing on comforting Teresa. After a few moments of offering what consolation he could, he said, "Give me the information, and I'll take care of having Pablo's body picked up and transported to a mortuary near your home. Have you told your mother yet?"

"Oh no," Teresa replied, her voice cracking. "I'm so upset right now, I can't bring myself to tell her the sad news. She'll be devastated, of course, and I'm worried about her health. She hasn't been well lately, and this news... it might kill her."

"I understand, Teresa," Juan said gently. "You know her best, so I'll leave that up to you. I'll take care of all the arrangements for Pablo."

After the call ended, Juan's carefully controlled emotions burst free. He was livid, his mind racing with questions and suspicions. One thing was certain: he was going to find out what happened to his friend, one way or another.

Pablo's mother was hospitalized after hearing the news, which postponed the funeral for a few days. Eventually, Pablo was laid to rest in the family plot just outside Mexico City, surrounded by grieving family and friends.

Juan, however, couldn't let the matter rest. Driven by a mix of grief and anger, he flew to Baltimore, staying at the same hotel Pablo had used during his last two visits. This information he knew from messages and conversations he'd had with Pablo after his first trip there.

Determined to retrace Pablo's steps, Juan began his investigation. It took a few days and a couple of thousand dollars paid to the right people, but he finally managed to locate the cab driver who had picked Pablo up and delivered him to a bar on the west side of the city.

With this lead, Juan took a cab to the bar Pablo had visited. Once again, he spread some cash around, showing the bartender a picture of Pablo on his cell phone. After some coaxing and more money changing hands, the bartender admitted that he recognized Juan's friend.

"Yeah, I remember him," the bartender said, pocketing the cash. "He was here a few times. Always met with the same guy, and on his last couple of visits, there was a lady with them too."

Juan leaned in; his interest piqued. "Can you tell me more about the man he met with?"

The bartender hesitated, then nodded. "I can get you in touch with him. He goes by the name Larry. Don't know much about the lady, though."

Juan paid the bartender handsomely to arrange a meeting with Larry. Several hours later, when Larry entered the bar, Juan invited him for a drink. As they sat down, Juan explained about Pablo's death and how his body had been shipped back to Mexico.

Larry's eyes widened in surprise. "I didn't know his name was Pablo," he said. "The man in the picture on your phone called himself Mr. Smith."

Sensing an opportunity, Juan offered Larry $5,000 for information about what Pablo had been working on. Larry hesitated, then began to share what he knew about the reporter's discoveries. However, he was quick to add a caveat.

"You see, Juan, "Larry said, leaning in close, "this is a very dangerous city. Your friend was throwing around a lot of cash. Hell, he could have been killed by any one of a dozen thugs in the area."

Juan nodded, his expression grim. "I understand. However, I only know why he was here. What I don't know is what he eventually discovered."

After hours of discussion and negotiation, Larry finally relented. "There's a reporter you should talk to. She had all the information and gave what she had to Mr. Smith—your friend Pablo. I never saw the contents of the package she gave him." Larry scribbled a name on a napkin. "You can reach her at the *Baltimore Star* news desk. That's all I can tell you. I hope you find what you're looking for."

The next day, Juan positioned himself outside the *Baltimore Star* headquarters. He called the news desk, asking for the reporter named Marci. When he got through, he explained who he was and what he wanted. Marci, immediately on guard, tried to cut Juan off, but he persisted, his tone growing more insistent.

Frightened by the intensity in Juan's voice, Marci abruptly hung up. As she left work that evening, her nerves frayed; she failed to notice Juan waiting in the parking area.

"Hello, Marci," he said to each woman who passed. When the real Marci instinctively responded, Juan approached her swiftly, producing a knife, which he held discreetly at her side.

"Don't say a word," he hissed. "Walk to your car. We're going to have a conversation. I'm not here to hurt you. I only want to know about the information you gave to my friend Pablo—or Mr. Smith, as you called him."

Trembling, Marci led Juan to her car, where they both got in. Once inside, Juan turned to her, his expression a mix of determination and barely contained anger.

"My friend is dead," he said, his voice low and intense. "And I believe it's because he was acting on information you supplied to him. I need to know what that information was. That's it. I'm not going to hurt you, but I need answers."

Marci, her heart pounding, looked into Juan's eyes. She saw grief alongside the anger, and something in her softened slightly. Taking a deep breath, she began to speak, unraveling the threads of the story that had led to this moment—and to Pablo's untimely death.

As Marci talked, Juan listened intently, piecing together the puzzle that had cost his friend his life. He knew that whatever he learned next would set him on a dangerous path, but he was determined to see it through, no matter the cost. For Pablo, for justice, and for the truth that someone had killed to keep hidden.

After Pablo's fateful visit to the rectory, Father Alonzo requested Frank and Gino's presence after confessions. The two men arrived at the rectory, curiosity and a touch of concern evident on their faces.

"Have a seat, boys," Father Alonzo said, gesturing to the worn couch in his office. "I have something to tell you, and I want you two to be the first to hear it."

Frank and Gino exchanged worried glances before settling onto the couch. Father Alonzo took a deep breath, his eyes filling with a mix of sadness and resolve.

"Boys, I've made a decision. I'm retiring," he announced, his voice barely above a whisper. "I'm moving back to Palermo, Sicily."

The shock on Frank and Gino's faces was palpable. Father Alonzo had been a constant in their lives for as long as they could remember. The priest continued, "I've notified the Archdiocese, and they have a replacement coming in a couple of weeks. He's a much younger man, Father Dominic Sulpizio."

Frank found his voice first. "What brought this on, Father?"

Father Alonzo's shoulders sagged slightly. "After the incident with Pablo, I... I haven't felt worthy of my position. I've wrestled with this decision, but I've finally concluded that it's best for me to retire and do some work with an orphanage in my hometown." His voice cracked slightly as he added, "This decision wasn't easy, but I can no longer function as a priest after taking a man's life."

Gino could see the internal struggle written across the priest's face. Father Alonzo had been the heart of their small Italian community for decades, and his departure would leave a void that would be hard to fill.

"I'll make the announcement to the parishioners on Sunday," Father Alonzo said, "but I wanted you two to be the first to hear it from me."

As Frank and Gino left the rectory, they walked slowly toward their homes, the weight of Father Alonzo's news heavy on their shoulders.

Gino broke the silence. "I'm really sorry Father Alonzo is leaving. He's been such a mainstay in our community for so many years."

Frank nodded solemnly. "I agree. If this kind of exodus continues, we may be the last two original members of the community left standing."

The two men continued their walk in contemplative silence, each lost in thoughts of change and the uncertain future that lay ahead.

As usual, Frank left the house at 4:45 a.m. to begin his shift at the bakery. As he passed by St. Leo's rectory, he noticed light coming from an open door. He thought it was strange that Father Alonzo would leave a door wide open, so he decided to investigate. As he was about to go up the steps, a man ran out of the rectory straight toward him. The man tried to run right over Frank but tripped and fell onto the sidewalk. Frank immediately jumped on the man and struck him in the face, shouting, "What are you doing in there?" The man was partially unconscious, so he was unable to respond.

Frank heard a man's voice crying for help from within the rectory. He recognized it as Father Alonzo's. Frank took off his belt, turned the man on the ground face-down, and secured his arms behind his back with the belt. He then struck him again, knocking him out cold. Frank rushed into the rectory, heading toward the cry for help. He pulled out his cell phone and called Gino.

As Frank approached Father Alonzo, he could see the priest lying on the floor by his desk, bleeding from his shoulder.

Gino answered the phone groggily and said, "What do you want?"

Frank replied, "This is an emergency. Get over to the rectory now. Get Sal, too. Father Alonzo has been attacked."

Frank applied direct pressure to Father Alonzo's shoulder. The priest was in a lot of pain, but the wound did not seem to be fatal. "What happened, Father?"

"A man was asking me questions about his friend Pablo, who was recently killed. When I told him I didn't know what he was talking about, he stabbed me in the shoulder and struck me several times."

"Father, I am going to call for an ambulance. I see there is a cash box on your desk. I'm going to take the money out of the box and hide it in the kitchen freezer. When you are asked about what happened, say, 'A man came in and robbed me. There was a struggle, and he stabbed me before running out of the rectory.' Do you understand?"

"Yes. Please help me up, Frank."

Gino arrived at the rectory, with Sal right behind him. "What the hell happened, Frank?"

"No time to explain. There's a guy outside on the sidewalk who tried to muscle Father Alonzo. You and Sal take that piece of crap to my basement and beat the information out of him. I'm calling 911 and will handle the police and ambulance. Go!"

Frank called 911, reporting a robbery and an injured priest. He then took the cash out of the box on the desk and placed it in the kitchen freezer. After returning to Father Alonzo, he continued to apply pressure to his wound. An ambulance and two police cars arrived. The EMTs came in to attend to Father Alonzo before loading him onto a gurney and whisking him away to Mercy Hospital.

Frank was now being questioned by two police officers. "What can you tell us about this attack?"

Frank explained, "I was on my way to work at the bakery, saw an open door and light coming from the rectory. This was not normal, so I walked over to the door and heard cries for help. I went inside and found Father Alonzo lying on the floor, bleeding. I then called 911 and waited."

"Did you see anyone leaving the rectory?"

"No, I saw no one. I just heard the cry for help."

One officer looked around and said to the other, "It appears that the cash box on the desk is empty. Probably a junkie pulling a robbery."

The other officer nodded. "Yep. Write it up and let's get forensics in here to check for prints and lock this place up so no one else comes in to steal anything."

The first officer said, "We'll take your name and number and call you if we have any more questions."

Frank replied, "Sure. I'm glad to help."

Frank went to the bakery and told Diego he would have to leave for an hour but would return as quickly as he could. Diego said, "No problem. We've got this, Frank. What was all the commotion down the street?"

"Someone tried to rob the rectory. Father Alonzo was hurt and taken to the hospital."

"Madonna, that is terrible."

Frank left the bakery and went home. He headed to the basement, where Sal and Gino had been working the man over. Sal was looking through his cell phone and said, "This guy's phone number is the one that was texting Pablo. His name is Juan, and apparently, he came up from Mexico to avenge the death of his friend."

Frank said, "Is that so, Juan? Well, you picked the wrong place to be. The priest is going to be okay, but you, my useless man, are going to suffer."

Gino said, "Hand me that portable drill off the bench. I'm going to drill some holes in his ankles and work my way up."

Frank handed Gino the drill with a small diameter bit attached. Juan's eyes widened in terror as Gino started the drill, positioning it an inch away from his left ankle.

"Please, no! No! Don't hurt me anymore."

Frank said, "Hold it, Gino. Let him talk."

"Yes, it is true. I came here because the reporter lady told me the priest had the answer as to who killed my friend Pablo."

Gino asked, "What is this reporter's name?"

"She calls herself Marci and works for the *Baltimore Star*. That's all I know about her."

Frank asked, "How did you get her information? Did Pablo send it to you?"

"No, Pablo never contacted me after he arrived here a few weeks ago. I found the reporter through a bartender where a man named Larry worked."

Gino asked, "What was the name of this bar?"

"Skullies."

Frank looked at Sal and asked, "Did you find anything more on that phone?"

Sal replied, "He's probably telling the truth. The phone log contains the same number I found on Pablo's phone for the *Baltimore Star*."

Gino looked at Frank and asked, "What do you think? Another river dump tonight?"

Frank looked at Sal, and they both nodded in agreement.

Gino picked up an ice pick off the workbench and drove it into Juan's brain through his ear.

The body of Juan was found floating in the Back River, and Detective Mathew, while reviewing the case, immediately noticed the similarities to Pablo's body. He retraced the steps and showed a picture of the deceased to the manager at a downtown hotel. The manager recognized him and led the detective to the room Juan had been assigned. The forensics team was called in, an inventory of his belongings was taken, and his prints were sent to the FBI.

Unlike the Pablo case, there was nothing in the room to indicate why Juan was there. The FBI identified the man as Juan from Mexico City and informed the local police they had a body. The Mexico City police, unable to identify any next of kin, instructed the Baltimore coroner to cremate the body and bury him in a potter's field.

Detective Mathew went to visit Father Alonzo in the hospital. He questioned him because the case was not just a robbery but also an attempted murder. However, the priest was of no help to Detective Mathew, who once again marked it as an unsolved cold case. Frustrated at the lack of information, he decided to follow up with Frank, the man who found Father Alonzo at the rectory. Again, nothing of substantive value was learned.

Gino, Frank, and Sal met at Velleggia's restaurant after work to discuss their next moves. Sal reported that he had an address for Skullies Bar on the West Side. He also mentioned that he continued to monitor the cell phones of Pablo and Juan but found no contact with either.

Gino finally said, "Well, do we clean up the remaining loose ends or let this end here and now?"

Frank thought for a few seconds and asked, "By loose ends, are you speaking about Marci the reporter and Larry at Skullies Bar?"

Sal added, "And the bartender at Skullies as well."

Gino said, "Exactly. Maybe there's nothing more we can do, but it still bothers me how those three individuals steered two Mexicans to Father Alonzo."

Frank nodded in agreement. "Gino, I agree. They are the ones pulling all the puppet strings. Who's to say they won't offer this information to another assassin?"

Sal, listening intently, finally broke in. "I say we take them all out. Let's put this thing to rest once and for all."

Gino said, "Hold on there, cowboy. There's a risk-and-reward thing here to consider. Are those three worth the chance of us getting caught?"

Frank replied, "I'm not so sure we need to include the reporter. That would probably bring a lot of heat on us. Larry, for sure, and the bartender as collateral damage, is my vote."

Sal agreed, "Okay by me. What do you say, Gino?"

"I think we have Sal do some recon on this bar. Then we need to get Larry into the bar, but we don't even know what he looks like. And shooting up the place... I don't know. The risk seems awfully high to me."

Frank said, "Let's gather the information about this bar first, then figure out the best way to identify this Larry guy. After that, we can make a final decision."

Father Alonzo was released from the hospital and returned to the rectory. He thawed out the money in the freezer and put it back in the cash box. A couple of nuns from the grade school would come by daily to change his bandages and make sure his meals were prepared.

Frank and Gino stopped by just as one of the nuns was leaving. Gino asked, "How is he doing?"

The nun replied, "He seems to be a bit depressed, but otherwise, he is doing well with his recovery."

Frank asked, "Do you think he is up to having visitors?"

"Oh yes. He has had many parishioners coming and going every day."

"Thank you, Sister."

Frank and Gino walked into the rectory and had a brief conversation with the priest. Frank said, "Father, I hear you are on the mend and doing well."

"Have a seat, boys. Yes, I am fine, thanks to your fast action, Frank. I must tell you, that man who attacked me scared the heck out of me. Anyway, he is gone, and the police have done their due diligence. I suspect that is the last we will hear about this going forward."

Gino said, "We are glad you are okay, Father. That kind of incident would scare anyone. However, like you said, it is probably something you no longer need to worry about."

Frank said, "Gino is right, Father. Best to move on and follow through on your retirement plans."

"That is exactly what I am doing, Frank. The sooner I get to Sicily, the better I will feel. Now, how about you boys take off so I can get in a short nap before those pesky nuns show up and make me eat some concoction they made in their kitchen."

Frank and Gino laughed and said, "We will let ourselves out. Take care, Padre."

At the bakery, the air was thick with the scent of fresh bread and the hum of machinery. Gina and Mikey were engrossed in their work, focused on automating the inventory and ordering processes. Frank entered the kitchen area, curiosity evident on his face.

"How's it going in here?" he asked, eyeing the computer screens and unfamiliar equipment.

Gina looked up, a proud smile on her face. "Those classes at the community college are really paying off, Frank. We've managed to create two systems and tie them into the computer on the mixer. Now, as ingredients are added to a mix, they're automatically deleted from the inventory."

Frank's eyebrows rose, impressed but slightly bewildered. "Sounds complicated to me. But as long as you two understand it, I guess we're okay."

Mikey, who had been quiet until now, spoke up. "Frank, if you have a few minutes, I'd like to speak to you and Diego."

Sensing the seriousness in Mikey's tone, Frank nodded. "Sure, come into the office. I'll get Diego."

Once the three men were settled in the office, Frank turned to Mikey. "What's on your mind, Mikey? You look troubled."

Mikey shook his head, a nervous smile playing on his lips. "No, no, I'm okay. I asked to see you two because... well, Frank, I wanted to thank you for giving me an opportunity to work here. It's definitely changed my life, and I'm grateful."

He turned to Diego. "And Diego, you taught me everything I know. I wanted to thank you for being such a good teacher and a patient man. I know I must have been a difficult student, but you managed to make me understand the right way to do things."

Frank and Diego exchanged surprised glances. Frank spoke first, his voice warm. "Mikey, I just gave you a chance. You're the one who took advantage of that chance and made it work for you. You've been a great employee and a good friend to all of us at the bakery."

Diego nodded in agreement. "Mikey, I can only tell you what I know. It was up to you to take that knowledge, understand it, and put it into practice. You're the one we should be praising. You've made this bakery what it is today. A success, as you and your future will be."

Mikey took a deep breath, his nervousness evident. "I have one more thing to ask of you two."

"Shoot," Frank said, leaning forward.

"I'm going to ask Gina to marry me," Mikey blurted out. "I haven't talked to her mother and grandmother yet, but I plan to do that tonight. If she says yes, I was wondering if you two would be the best men at my wedding?"

Diego's face broke into a wide grin. "Oh, I'm shocked. I didn't see that coming, did you, Frank?"

Frank chuckled, shaking his head. "Oh no, Diego. Hell, a blind man could see those two were meant for each other."

Diego stood up to hug Mikey. "Congratulations, young man. You're getting a wonderful girl in Gina. And smart too."

Frank joined in the embrace. "Diego's right. We wish you both much happiness and a long future together. Of course, we'll be honored to be the best men at your ceremony."

As the three men celebrated this moment of joy, the bakery seemed to glow with warmth and promise. Despite the challenges and changes facing their community, life was moving forward, bringing new beginnings and hope for the future.

Chapter 19

Sal met Frank and Gino at Velleggia's restaurant after work. The restaurant was lively, the scent of garlic and tomato sauce filling the air, and the chatter of patrons creating a comforting hum. Sal slid into the booth across from them, his expression serious. "I checked out Skullies bar," he began, his voice low enough to keep it between them. "It's a small place with a bar and about eight tables or booths lining the opposite wall. There's a front door that opens to a busy street and a back door leading to a narrow alley. Not exactly a good spot for a quick in-and-out. It'll be tricky."

Frank leaned back, considering. "Not great for us then," he muttered. "Too many chances for things to go sideways if we're not careful."

Gino thoughtfully tapped his fingers on the table. "Why not blow the place with a timed device? We don't need to be there to be effective. Set it and forget it."

Frank nodded slowly. "I like that idea, but we still have a problem. We need to identify this Larry guy and make sure he's inside when the place goes up. If we miss him, the whole thing's a bust."

Sal's eyes gleamed with an idea. "New plan. I go into the bar, tell the bartender I need to see Larry, and slip him some cash. Then, while I'm sitting at a table, I plant a remote-detonated explosive underneath. I give Larry a story about paying for information, leave the bar, and then Gino, who's outside in the car, detonates the explosive. We're gone before anyone knows what happened."

Frank glanced at Gino, who was grinning. "That sounds pretty good to me, Gino."

Gino chuckled, his grin widening. "I like it too. This calls for some thermite—a small, sticky charge that burns hot. It'll make sure there's nothing left but ashes."

Sal nodded, satisfied with the direction. "Okay, that covers the bar. But what do we do about the reporter?"

Frank rubbed his chin and furrowed his brow. "I've been thinking about that. After the bar is taken care of, I'll call this Marci woman using Juan's cell phone. I'll tell her if she passes any more information about anyone in Little Italy, she better be cautious when she starts her car."

Gino's smile faded slightly. "Do you think that's enough? Maybe we should throw in a mention of Juan and Pablo. Make it clear we're serious."

Frank considered this, then nodded. "Yeah, you're right. We need to make her understand that messing with us has real consequences. I'll work on the message and make sure it scares her out of the information-selling business for good."

The next several days were a blur of activity for Frank, Gino, and Sal. The bakery was bustling, with two new restaurants set to open soon and wanting the bakery to handle all their bread, rolls, cakes, and pastry orders. The news was good, but it meant more work for everyone.

Frank called Gina, Mikey, and Diego into the small office at the back of the bakery. The room was cramped, with the smell of yeast and sugar wafting through the open doorway. Frank got straight to the point.

"We've got two new restaurants coming on board, and they want us as their supplier," he began. Gina and Mikey smiled, but Diego looked concerned.

"How can we keep up with the staff we've got now, Frank?" Diego inquired, crossing his arms. "We're already stretched thin."

Frank nodded. "That's why I brought you all in here. I'm thinking we get rid of the old mixer or push it aside and order another of those fancy machines. It should help speed up production, right?"

Gina hesitated, then said, "Sure, but will it be enough?"

Mikey added, "I doubt it, Frank. We're going to need more hands for sure."

Gina leaned forward, a spark in her eyes. "I've got an idea. Why not call the culinary college on Baltimore Street? Ask them to send us some students. We bring them on as temps, see who's good, and maybe hire them full-time. They've got baking and pastry classes, everything we need."

Frank's eyes lit up. "Gina, that's a fantastic idea. Why don't you make the call? Diego, where do we need the most help?"

Diego thought for a moment. "If we get a new dough machine, that should take care of the pastry and bread dough. What we really need is a pastry chef or a cake decorator. That would help a lot."

Frank nodded. "Let's do both. Gina, tell the school we want a pastry chef and a cake decorator."

Gina smiled, clearly pleased. "I'm on it, boss." She laughed. "This is going to be fun and it'll give Diego a break."

Diego chuckled. "I'll believe it when I see it."

Meanwhile, over at DeLuca's, Mr. Perez had finished the remodeling of the bar and restaurant. The grand opening was set for next week, and the community buzzed with excitement. Jocy Jr. would be there to welcome his cousins, Paul and Sofi Esposito, who were taking over the place. They had decided to keep the name "DeLuca's" out of respect for their lost relatives, and everyone in the neighborhood was glad to see the place reopening.

The grand opening day arrived, and Father Alonzo came to bless the establishment. The whole neighborhood showed up to celebrate, turning the street outside into a lively festival. Food and drinks flowed freely, with tables set up inside and outside, laughter echoing down the block. The Espositos, a young couple with two kids, mingled easily with the crowd, their friendly smiles making a good impression.

Sal found Joey Jr. nearby, and they chatted about how much the neighborhood had changed. "None of the kids play hopscotch or stickball anymore," Joey lamented. "It's all about computer games and cell phones now."

Sal nodded. "I'm glad we grew up here when we did. It still breaks my heart to see Little Italy going through all these changes."

Joey sighed. "Change is inevitable, Sal. You either adapt or go extinct, like any other species."

Sal smiled, clapping Joey on the shoulder. "You're right, but some of us are just slower to adapt. Oh well, adapt or die."

The night of the plan, Sal dressed in a dark suit and carried a backpack into Skullies Bar. Gino and Frank waited outside in a delivery van, the engine idling softly. Sal walked to the bar, laid three one-hundred-dollar bills down, and told the bartender, "I need to see Larry right now. I'll be sitting at the table in the back."

While the bartender made a call, Sal discreetly opened his backpack and placed the remote-detonated device under the table. A few minutes later, the bartender returned with a draft beer, setting it down in front of Sal. "He'll be here shortly," he said.

Ten minutes passed before a man entered the bar, looking around. The bartender gave him a quick nod toward Sal. The man, Larry, approached, his expression guarded.

"I understand you wanted to see me?" he asked.

"If you're Larry, then yes," Sal replied calmly.

Larry sat down, curious but wary. "What can I do for you?"

Sal leaned in, lowering his voice. "I work for a man who's had two warehouses raided by the police in the past month. We understand you have connections to the cops, so this should be easy money. Find out who's tipping them off, call the number on this burner phone." He laid the phone on the table. "When you have the information, we meet here, and I give you $10,000. A picture will earn you another $2,000. Are we clear?"

Larry's eyes lit up at the prospect of easy money. "That's all you want? A name and an address?"

"That's right. And a picture, if possible," Sal confirmed.

Larry nodded eagerly. "You got it. I'll be in touch soon."

Sal stood up, smiling. "Good. Talk to you soon." He picked up his backpack and walked calmly out of the bar, heading down the block toward the waiting van. As he climbed in, Gino pressed the detonator. The thermite bomb ignited with a violent flash, taking out Skullies Bar and setting the two buildings on either side ablaze. The van sped away, leaving a trail of smoke and flames in its wake.

The next day, Frank called the *Baltimore Star* and asked for Marci. When she answered, he wasted no time. "Marci, I'm the one responsible for the deaths of Juan and Pablo, the men you supplied information to that pointed them to a priest in Little Italy. I'm also responsible for yesterday's removal of your friend Larry from Skullies Bar. Are you listening?"

Marci, her voice trembling, replied, "Yes, I'm listening."

"Good," Frank continued coldly. "If you want to live, stop feeding information about Little Italy to anyone. If you don't, you'd better have someone else start your car and consider increasing your security. Neither will help, of course. Do you understand?"

"Yes, I understand," Marci whispered, fear evident in her voice.

"Good." Frank hung up, satisfied. He could almost hear her shaking on the other end.

The following week, Sal, Gino, and Frank met at DeLuca's for a beer and dinner. The place was buzzing with life; the hum of conversations and the clinking of glasses filled the air. The renovations had done wonders; the new decor was tasteful yet still retained the old-world charm the neighborhood loved. The three men settled into a booth near the back, where they could talk quietly without interruption.

Gino took a deep breath, looking around with a small smile on his face. "It's good to be back here again," he said, his voice filled with nostalgia. "Feels like old times."

Frank nodded, taking a sip of his beer. "Yeah, a lot of memories in this place." He leaned in slightly, lowering his voice. "I spoke to Marci the other day."

Sal looked up, furrowing his brows. "What did she say?"

Frank's expression remained serious. "She was scared, that much was clear. I told her to stop spreading information about Little Italy, or things would get worse for her. She sounded like she got the message."

Sal leaned back in his chair, contemplating. "Do you think that's enough, or should we do more?"

Gino chimed in with a measured tone. "Let's wait and see. Give her a chance to back off. But if she doesn't get the message, we can always follow up. Make it clear we're not playing games."

Frank nodded, his face settling in agreement. "Yeah, that's probably the smartest move. No point in drawing more heat if we don't have to."

Their food arrived, interrupting their discussion. The dishes were set down in front of them with a flourish, and much to their surprise, the food was excellent. The flavors were rich and full; the pasta was cooked to perfection, and the bread was warm and fresh from the oven. Sal took a bite of his lasagna, and his eyes widened.

"Damn, this is good," Sal said with a grin, his fork already diving back in for more. "Better than I remember. Hey, Sofi, can I get another plate over here?"

Sofi, passing by with a tray of drinks, laughed and gave him a thumbs-up. "Coming right up, Sal. Don't worry, there's plenty for seconds."

Frank chuckled, enjoying the camaraderie. "Glad you like it, Sal. Anyway, I've decided to add more staff to the bakery. With the new restaurant orders coming in, we're going to need all the help we can get."

Sal groaned in mock frustration. "Great news, but that just means more work for me," he teased.

Frank laughed. "It's more work for everyone, not just you, Sal. Besides, you'll be too busy eating to notice."

Gino, who had been quietly enjoying his meal, spoke up. "You know, I've been thinking about getting my car out of mothballs. It's been sitting in the garage for years, gathering dust. It needs a lot of work, but I want to get it back on the road before I'm too old to drive."

Sal's interest peaked. "What kind of car is it again?"

"A 1972 Chevy Impala," Gino said, a touch of pride in his voice. "It's a beauty, but she's been neglected. Needs new tires, an engine check, probably a paint job, too."

Sal whistled. "Man, that's a classic. Sounds like a big project, though."

Gino nodded. "Yeah, but it's worth it. I miss driving her, feeling the engine roar. It's like... I don't know, freedom, I guess."

Sal turned to Frank, an idea forming in his mind. "What about your car, Frank? Are you going to get it back on the street?"

Frank shook his head slowly, a hint of nostalgia crossing his face. "Nah, those days are behind me. I'm done with all that. But if you want to buy it, Sal, I'll sell it to you."

Sal's eyes widened in surprise. "Are you serious?" he asked, almost not believing his ears.

Frank nodded, a small smile playing on his lips. "Sure, for $10. I've got no interest in keeping it anymore. It's just sitting there, taking up space."

Sal didn't waste a second. He reached into his pocket and pulled out a crumpled 10-dollar bill, slapping it down on the table with a grin. "Deal! I'll take it."

Frank laughed, a warm sound that seemed to lighten the mood. "All right, all right. Stop by the house later, and I'll sign over the title. It'll need a lot of work, but I hear Gino knows a good garage that can handle the job."

Gino chuckled. "You bet I do. We'll get both cars running like new. Maybe even take them out for a spin together, just like the old days."

Sal's grin grew wider. "I like the sound of that. Can't wait to see her on the road again."

The three of them laughed, the tension easing as they clinked their beer glasses together. For a moment, everything felt right again, like they were just three friends enjoying a meal with no worries or threats hanging over their heads. The laughter flowed easily, and the bond between them was as strong as ever, despite everything they'd been through.

Chapter 20

Several weeks had passed since Little Italy celebrated another successful festival. The community still buzzed with the warm memories of shared laughter, music, and the enticing aroma of homemade pasta and cannoli that had filled the air. Father Alonzo had safely returned to his hometown of Palermo, Sicily, where he was said to be enjoying his retirement, relishing the simple pleasures of his native land. Meanwhile, his replacement, Father Sulpizio, had been warmly welcomed by the parish. The new pastor had already presided over two baptisms and three weddings, bringing a fresh energy and vitality to the community.

Father Sulpizio's integration into the neighborhood extended far beyond his clerical duties. An avid bocce ball player, he quickly became a favorite at the local courts. With a mischievous twinkle in his eye, he promised to take it easy on the other players—provided they showed up for Sunday mass. This playful bargain endeared him further to his new flock, bridging the gap between spiritual leader and community member. The priest was already known for his engaging homilies, filled with humor and insight, which had begun drawing larger crowds each week. Little Italy seemed to be experiencing a quiet revival under his watchful, joyful eye.

Detective Matthew was mired in the complexities of the Skullies Bar homicides. His instincts told him these murders were connected to the killings of Pablo and Juan, but solid leads remained elusive. The cold case file documents discovered in Pablo's hotel room tantalized him with potential connections, yet the pieces refused to fall into place. Every time he felt close to a breakthrough, another dead end would emerge, frustrating his efforts to link the crimes definitively.

Convinced that *Baltimore Star* reporter Marci held crucial information, Matthew arranged a follow-up interview. He hoped to pry loose some detail that might illuminate the shadowy web surrounding these deaths. But his hopes were quickly dashed. Marci's reticence was palpable; fear seemed to choke her voice whenever the conversation veered toward the details she clearly knew but wouldn't divulge. It was a familiar feeling in Baltimore, where witnesses often shied away from involvement, fearing unseen repercussions in a city where crime and silence often walked hand in hand.

As the city's murder rate climbed past 300, with no sign of slowing, Matthew felt the weight of his badge more heavily than ever. Years of dedication and sleepless nights had taken their toll on his body and spirit. He began to consider retirement with a mix of dread and relief. The thought of leaving the force pained him deeply; being a cop had defined him for so long. Yet, the daily frustration of inconclusive investigations, the gnawing sense of futility, and the city's seemingly endless cycle of violence had finally worn him down. Matthew realized that for his own well-being, it might be time to step away from the relentless pursuit of justice in a city that seemed to generate more shadows than light.

In Guadalajara, Luis gathered his lieutenants for an all-hands meeting of the Sinaloa cartel. As he inquired about Juan's whereabouts, his absence hung heavily in the air, a noticeable gap in their usually tight circle. Silence followed, and the tension was almost palpable; no one had heard from him in weeks.

One member ventured, "Maybe he was upset about our handling of his friend Pablo's disappearance and decided to quit." Another, from Mexico City, reported a wellness check that had yielded nothing but concerned neighbors and an abandoned dog, further deepening the mystery.

Luis paused, his face unreadable. After a moment of contemplation, he dismissed the matter with unsettling casualness. "Oh well. If he eventually shows up, we can ask him where he's been. Let's move on to more pressing business." His indifferent tone seemed almost cruel, a reminder of the ruthless pragmatism that defined their world. The meeting continued, but the specter of Juan's disappearance lingered, a ghostly presence that none could ignore.

Fabio reached out to Gino, seeking reassurance about the situation in Little Italy. Gino informed him of the Skullies Bar case's closure and their strategic decision regarding the reporter. Fabio expressed relief over the silencing of the Skullies Bar connection and agreed with their cautious approach toward Marci.

"Taking out a reporter would cause a review of the stories she worked on," Fabio mused. "That could focus unwanted attention on Father Alonzo and create a domino effect. No, I think you were wise in making her think twice about providing such information to others, especially those from the cartel."

The conversation then turned to more practical matters. Gino mentioned the cache of cell phones and uncut cocaine still hidden in Frank's basement. Fabio proposed a solution: "Pack it all up in a plastic container. We'll arrange for it to be picked up in a couple of weeks. I'll give you advance notice of the day, time, and code word. My guys will collect the package from Frank's house, just like before."

Gino agreed, grateful for the assistance in clearing out the incriminating evidence. The two men exchanged well-wishes, their voices carrying the weight of shared history and mutual respect. In their world, trust was currency, and both understood its value all too well.

Frank's business judgment continued to serve him well. He had recently hired two promising graduates from the local culinary college to help meet the expanding demands of two new restaurants. The pastry chef and Diego were keeping pace with the increasing orders, with Diego assuming the role of mentor to the new chef, ensuring that the bakery's high standards were maintained.

The new cake decorator proved to be a valuable asset. Working alongside Diego's wife, she expanded the bakery's repertoire of designs, adding fresh and innovative options to their sample book. This collaboration not only improved their offerings but also injected new life into the bakery's creative process. Customers began to take notice, and orders started flowing in from beyond the immediate neighborhood, bringing a renewed sense of pride to everyone involved.

Meanwhile, Miguel and Gina's relationship blossomed. They had set a wedding date six months in the future, and their excitement was palpable to all who knew them. In a show of commitment to both their personal and professional lives, they purchased an apartment just down the street from the bakery. The couple hired Mr. Perez, a local contractor known for his meticulous work, to gut and remodel the space to their specifications—or more accurately, to Gina's exacting standards, as Miguel readily admitted his lack of expertise in interior design.

At the garage, a changing of the guard was underway. Pasquale, feeling the weight of his years and the ache in his bones, decided to retire and hand the reins over to his son, Mark. This transition necessitated hiring two new mechanics to fill the void left by the old man who had poured his heart and soul into building the business.

The technical trade school proved to be a valuable resource, providing two excellent hires. These young mechanics brought with them knowledge of the latest equipment and techniques, breathing new life into the garage. Their fresh perspectives even led to the establishment of sponsorships with parts companies, a move that promised to save the garage thousands of dollars annually through discounted prices.

Sal and Gino found comfort and excitement in their shared passion for vintage cars. After countless hours of work and a significant financial investment, they had both of their prized vehicles registered and roadworthy once more. The roar of engines and the gleam of polished chrome announced their presence whenever they took their beauties out for a spin.

When Sal completed the restoration of his car, he invited Frank for the inaugural ride. Frank eagerly accepted, sliding behind the wheel with Sal riding shotgun. In the early morning hours, they hit I-83, the purr of the engine a siren song of bygone days.

Sal, noting the wistful expression on Frank's face, grinned and said, "Go ahead. Punch it and let's see what this puppy can do." Frank needed no further encouragement. He pressed the accelerator to the floor, watching with boyish glee as the speedometer climbed past 110 and kept rising. For a few exhilarating moments, Frank felt transported back to a simpler time, when the open road held endless possibilities.

Their enthusiasm for their classic cars didn't go unnoticed. Sal and Gino began entering car shows throughout the tri-state area, their meticulously restored vehicles earning them numerous trophies and the admiration of fellow enthusiasts. Each show was an opportunity to connect with like-minded souls, swapping stories and tips, adding yet another layer to their friendship.

On a perfect sunny day, Gino and Frank found themselves sitting on a bench near the bocce courts, watching a lively game unfold before them. It had been a while since they'd taken the time to relax and share a moment together, and the rare break invited reflection.

Frank's eyes wandered over the familiar streets, noticing the subtle changes that had crept in over the years. "You know, Gino," he began thoughtfully, "I've been thinking. I see more young couples moving in, buying homes or renting apartments. The restaurants are busier, especially on weekends. But something feels different. That tight-knit community vibe just isn't quite the same anymore."

He chuckled, a blend of amusement and nostalgia softening his voice. "Hell, I remember when, if I did something wrong as a kid, my mother would've gotten three phone calls about it before I even made it to the front door. What I miss the most is how everyone knew everybody back then. Sure, we were all up in each other's business, but we also looked out for one another—for each other's homes, kids, everything."

Gino nodded, a gentle smile forming on his lips. "I know exactly what you mean, Frank," he replied. "For me, it's the physical changes that stand out. Tony's shoe repair shop? Gone. Nino's barbershop? Gone. And Mrs. Patrone's candy store—I still miss walking in there for a snowball or a scoop of gelato on a hot summer day." He sighed deeply, the years weighing on his voice. "I guess we're just two dinosaurs in a changing world."

Frank grinned, then teased, "Maybe so, Gino. But you know what happened to the dinosaurs, right?"

Gino chuckled, a hint of resignation in his laughter. "Yeah, I know, my friend. Our time will come soon enough. But for today, I'm content to just sit here and let time pass by. The neighborhood is still alive, even if it's changing. And I'm okay with that."

Frank nodded in agreement, echoing Gino's sentiment. "Me too. Alive, but changing."

As they sat together, watching the bocce players and observing the ebb and flow of life in Little Italy, a complex mix of emotions settled over them. There was a deep nostalgia for the close-knit community of their youth and an appreciation for the new energy and vibrancy brought by the younger residents. But there was also a bittersweet acceptance of the inevitable march of time.

Little Italy was evolving, as all neighborhoods do, but its heart—embodied in men like Frank and Gino—continued to beat strong, bridging the past with the future. And in that moment, as the sun warmed their faces and the laughter of the bocce players filled the air, they found comfort in knowing that while the details of the neighborhood might change, its spirit remained resilient and enduring.

Also by Dominic Fino

Paul Marco Thrillers
Lights Out
Nothing to lose
Death Hawaiian Style
Vendetta Vegas Style

Standalone
The Neighborhood

About the Author

Dominic Fino, who resides near his hometown of Baltimore, Maryland, is retired from the computer technology sector. For Dominic, writing is not just a task but a cathartic release, offering him a platform to channel his frustrations and construct a world where clarity reigns. As a Vietnam War veteran, a graduate of Johns Hopkins University, and a seasoned professional in corporate America, Dominic brings a depth of experience and authority to his storytelling.

www.ingramcontent.com/pod-product-compliance
Lightning Source LLC
Chambersburg PA
CBHW061437150726
47987CB00001B/248